Cancer

Other Books of Related Interest

Opposing Viewpoints Series
Addiction
AIDS
Biomedical Ethics
Death & Dying
Epidemics
Euthanasia
Genetic Engineering
Health Care
Health and Fitness
Suicide
Tobacco and Smoking

Current Controversies Series
Alcoholism
Assisted Suicide
The Disabled
Medical Ethics
Reproductive Technologies
Smoking

At Issue Series
Cloning
The Ethics of Euthanasia
Physician-Assisted Suicide
Sexually Transmitted Diseases
Smoking
The Spread of AIDS

Cancer

Lisa Yount, *Book Editor*

David L. Bender, *Publisher*
Bruno Leone, *Executive Editor*
Bonnie Szumski, *Editorial Director*
David M. Haugen, *Managing Editor*
Brenda Stalcup, *Series Editor*

Contemporary Issues
Companion

Greenhaven Press, Inc., San Diego, CA

Every effort has been made to trace the owners of copyrighted material. The articles in this volume may have been edited for content, length, and/or reading level. The titles have been changed to enhance the editorial purpose. Those interested in locating the original source will find the complete citation on the first page of each article.

No part of this book may be reproduced or used in any form or by any means, electrical, mechanical, or otherwise, including, but not limited to, photocopy, recording, or any information storage and retrieval system, without prior written permission from the publisher.

Library of Congress Cataloging-in-Publication Data

Cancer / Lisa Yount, book editor.
    p.   cm. — (Contemporary issues companion)
  Includes bibliographical references and index.
   ISBN 0-7377-0160-9 (pbk. : alk. paper). —
ISBN 0-7377-0161-7 (lib. : alk. paper)
  1. Cancer. I. Yount, Lisa. II. Series.
RC254.C33 2000
616.99'4—dc21   99-11431
                                                                                CIP

©2000 by Greenhaven Press, Inc.
P.O. Box 289009, San Diego, CA 92198-9009

Printed in the U.S.A.

Contents

Foreword 7

Introduction 9

Chapter 1: The Nature of Cancer

1. Defining Cancer 13
   Robert Buckman
2. A Renegade Cell: How Cancer Starts 17
   Robert A. Weinberg
3. A Series of Genetic Changes Leads to Cancer 20
   Michael Waldholz
4. Deadly Evolution 28
   George Klein

Chapter 2: Triggers of Cancer

1. Tobacco Threatens Women's Health 36
   Jane E. Brody
2. Secondhand Smoke Raises Cancer Risk 40
   Philip J. Hilts
3. Environmental Carcinogens Cause Cancer 45
   Mike Weilbacher
4. Hormone-Disrupting Chemicals May Be Linked to Breast Cancer 53
   Orli Belman
5. Reducing Environmental Cancer Risk 57
   Sandra Steingraber, interviewed by Multinational Monitor
6. Animal Tests Exaggerate Risks from Chemicals 65
   Elizabeth M. Whelan
7. A New Way to Evaluate Environmental Cancer Risks 72
   Mark Caldwell

Chapter 3: Preventing and Treating Cancer

1. Changing the Focus of Research to Prevention 80
   Robert N. Proctor
2. Lifestyle Changes That Prevent Cancer 88
   R. Grant Steen
3. The Debate over Screening for Breast Cancer 94
   Delia Marshall
4. Genetic Tests: The Dangers of Knowing Too Much 99
   The Associated Press

5. Providing Emotional Support   102
   Robert Buckman
6. Informed Decisions: Taking Charge of a Treatment Program   111
   Leslie Laurence
7. The Chief Methods of Treating Cancer   117
   Gerald P. Murphy, Lois B. Morris, and Dianne Lange
8. New Acceptance of Alternative Cancer Treatments   124
   Doug Podolsky
9. How to Evaluate Alternative Treatments   127
   Barrie R. Cassileth

Chapter 4: Coping with Cancer: Personal Views
1. Sharing Cancer Information on the Internet   135
   Glenn Fleishman
2. An Opportunity for Growth and Learning   140
   Georgia Brown
3. When Treatments Fail   143
   Stewart Massad

Chapter 5: The Outlook for Cancer
1. Managed Care, Cost Cutting, and Cancer   150
   Susan Brink
2. Arsenal of Hope: New Approaches to Cancer Treatment   153
   Robert Langreth
3. The Ordeal of Testing a New Treatment   162
   Terence Monmaney
4. A Turnaround in Cancer Statistics   169
   Sheryl Gay Stolberg

Glossary   174

Organizations to Contact   176

Bibliography   180

Index   182

Foreword

In the news, on the streets, and in neighborhoods, individuals are confronted with a variety of social problems. Such problems may affect people directly: A young woman may struggle with depression, suspect a friend of having bulimia, or watch a loved one battle cancer. And even the issues that do not directly affect her private life—such as religious cults, domestic violence, or legalized gambling—still impact the larger society in which she lives. Discovering and analyzing the complexities of issues that encompass communal and societal realms as well as the world of personal experience is a valuable educational goal in the modern world.

Effectively addressing social problems requires familiarity with a constantly changing stream of data. Becoming well informed about today's controversies is an intricate process that often involves reading myriad primary and secondary sources, analyzing political debates, weighing various experts' opinions—even listening to firsthand accounts of those directly affected by the issue. For students and general observers, this can be a daunting task because of the sheer volume of information available in books, periodicals, on the evening news, and on the Internet. Researching the consequences of legalized gambling, for example, might entail sifting through congressional testimony on gambling's societal effects, examining private studies on Indian gaming, perusing numerous websites devoted to Internet betting, and reading essays written by lottery winners as well as interviews with recovering compulsive gamblers. Obtaining valuable information can be time-consuming—since it often requires researchers to pore over numerous documents and commentaries before discovering a source relevant to their particular investigation.

Greenhaven's Contemporary Issues Companion series seeks to assist this process of research by providing readers with useful and pertinent information about today's complex issues. Each volume in this anthology series focuses on a topic of current interest, presenting informative and thought-provoking selections written from a wide variety of viewpoints. The readings selected by the editors include such diverse sources as personal accounts and case studies, pertinent factual and statistical articles, and relevant commentaries and overviews. This diversity of sources and views, found in every Contemporary Issues Companion, offers readers a broad perspective in one convenient volume.

In addition, each title in the Contemporary Issues Companion series is designed especially for young adults. The selections included in every volume are chosen for their accessibility and are expertly edited in consideration of both the reading and comprehension levels of the audience. The structure of the anthologies also enhances accessibility. An introductory essay places each issue in context and provides helpful facts such as historical background or current statistics and legislation that pertain to the topic. The chapters that follow organize the material and focus on specific aspects of the book's topic. Every essay is introduced by a brief summary of its main points and biographical information about the author. These summaries aid in comprehension and can also serve to direct readers to material of immediate interest and need. Finally, a comprehensive index allows readers to efficiently scan and locate content.

The Contemporary Issues Companion series is an ideal launching point for research on a particular topic. Each anthology in the series is composed of readings taken from an extensive gamut of resources, including periodicals, newspapers, books, government documents, the publications of private and public organizations, and Internet websites. In these volumes, readers will find factual support suitable for use in reports, debates, speeches, and research papers. The anthologies also facilitate further research, featuring a book and periodical bibliography and a list of organizations to contact for additional information.

A perfect resource for both students and the general reader, Greenhaven's Contemporary Issues Companion series is sure to be a valued source of current, readable information on social problems that interest young adults. It is the editors' hope that readers will find the Contemporary Issues Companion series useful as a starting point to formulate their own opinions about and answers to the complex issues of the present day.

Introduction

Cancer is one of the most feared diseases, particularly in the industrialized world, where it is a major cause of death. As of 1998, cancer killed more people than any other illness in the United States except heart disease, and many experts believe it will move into first place around the beginning of the twenty-first century.

Cancer has existed throughout human history; it is mentioned in medical writings from as early as 1500 B.C. However, little was understood about the disease until the twentieth century, when advances in medical technology enabled physicians and researchers to diagnose and study different types of cancer more accurately. This improvement in research was spurred partly by a steep increase in the rates of cancer incidence and death during the twentieth century. In the 1950s, for example, cancer struck one American out of every four and killed one out of five, but by 1998 these numbers had risen to one out of three contracting cancer and one out of four dying from the disease. Part of this apparent increase was no doubt due to improvements in diagnosis and the lengthening of life expectancy, since cancer is a disease primarily of the old (two-thirds of the people who die of cancer are over sixty-five years of age). But when statistics are corrected for these factors, the increase remains visible, so most researchers believe that the overall incidence of cancer is indeed escalating.

With the rise in cancer has come an equally steep growth in research worldwide. Hoping to find ways to either cure or prevent cancer, researchers have focused on identifying the cause or causes of the disease. There are two primary approaches to cancer research. Some scientists look outward, searching for lifestyle or environmental factors that trigger cancer. Others turn their gaze inward, studying genetics and the chemistry of individual cells to learn how cancerous cells differ from normal ones.

Because the incidence of particular types of cancer varies considerably with geographical location, culture, occupation, and social status, many researchers believe that external variables can act as catalysts for cancer. For instance, women in Japan have one-fourth as high a chance of dying from breast cancer as do women in the United States, yet the granddaughters of Japanese immigrants to America are just as likely to die of the disease as are Americans of other ethnic backgrounds. This finding suggests that the difference between the breast cancer rates of Japanese and American women is caused by environmental rather than genetic factors. In another example, a study of high rates of lung cancer among shipbuilders in Norfolk, Virginia, led to the discovery that the asbestos used in shipbuilding was a potent carcinogen.

Some cancer researchers place most of the blame for the disease on lifestyle choices. Chief among these choices is cigarette smoking, which a 1996 report from the Harvard School of Public Health held responsible for approximately 30 percent of cancer cases in the United States. The Harvard report also cited obesity and diets high in fat and low in fruits, vegetables, and fiber for another 30 percent of U.S. cases. Other lifestyle factors, such as alcohol use and sun exposure, have been credited with triggering certain types of cancer.

Other researchers and activists maintain that environmental pollution plays a large role in the recent increase in cancer rates. They stress that many pesticides, food additives, industrial waste products, and other chemicals have been linked to cancer. Rachel Carson sounded an early warning about the uncontrolled use of pesticides in her 1962 book *Silent Spring*, writing that "in terms of evidence gained from animal experiments . . . five or possibly six . . . pesticides must definitely be rated as carcinogens." In recent years, environmental cancer researchers have publicized findings that certain chemicals such as dioxin may cause cancer by mimicking or disrupting the action of human hormones. Joe Thornton of the environmental activist group Greenpeace argues, "We have a cancer epidemic on our hands, and evidence links it to chemicals and pollution in the ecosystem."

The second approach to cancer research focuses on the internal workings of the body, especially concentrating on cells, genes, and molecules. This type of research has led to a complete revolution in the understanding of the physiological process of cancer, including the discovery of oncogenes (normal genes that cause cancer when mutated into a more active form) and tumor suppressor genes (which allow cancer to develop if mutated in a way that makes them inactive). As of the late 1990s, scientists have identified thirty-six genes that play a role in the development of cancer.

Scientists have also answered the question of why cancer usually takes decades to develop. Beginning in the late 1980s, Bert Vogelstein of Johns Hopkins University Medical School in Baltimore and other researchers discovered that changes in several different genes, which may occur years apart, are usually required for a malignant tumor to reach its full growth potential. At least four changes are required to produce colon cancer, for instance. Moreover, scientists have made great strides in identifying inherited genetic problems that can predispose a person to developing cancer.

These two approaches to cancer research often reflect differences in researchers' aims and attitudes toward the disease. Those who concentrate on internal factors tend to direct their work toward the goal of finding new treatments or potential cures, such as drugs that block biochemical processes that lead to cancer or medical techniques to replace defective genes. Such research has produced a number of promising treatments that are currently in testing stages, as well as several drugs now in general use that have improved survival rates for patients with certain types of cancer. "Early in the next millennium, we will significantly extend the life expectancy of cancer patients. I have no doubt about that," asserts cancer researcher Joseph Schlessinger of New York University.

On the other hand, the epidemiologists who focus on external factors tend to emphasize the importance of preventing cancer from ever developing. They maintain that efforts to prevent cancer by removing environmental and lifestyle triggers would be effective in reducing the number of cancer cases. John Bailar, chairman of health studies at the University of Chicago, states, "We are not questioning the value of [cancer] treatment; treatments are curing half of all patients. This is not a dispute over whether the glass is half full or half empty. The problem is that it is the same half full now as it was several decades ago. . . . I'm convinced that a major emphasis in cancer research should be shifted from cancer treatment to cancer prevention."

The two different approaches to cancer research and treatment may seem to be mutually exclusive, but research using both approaches is essential to understanding the disease. Most scientists agree that only 5 to 10 percent of cancer cases are caused solely by inherited genetic defects. The rest arise, at least in part, from genetic mutations that are triggered by environmental or lifestyle factors. Similarly, both prevention and improved treatment are likely to be needed in order to reduce cancer mortality substantially. According to J. Michael Bishop of the University of California at San Francisco, who won a Nobel Prize for his research on oncogenes, "Application of . . . our newfound knowledge of the genetic maladies that appear to underlie all cancers . . . will bring the once disparate disciplines of epidemiology and molecular biology into a fecund mating. The offspring should be a new era."

The progress made by scientists employing both the internal and external approaches to cancer research is just one of the subjects addressed in *Cancer: Contemporary Issues Companion*. This anthology also presents information on standard and experimental methods of detecting and treating cancer and provides personal accounts of dealing with a diagnosis of the disease. Finally, it offers different perspectives on the future outlook for cancer research and treatment—an outlook that is still grim but, many experts believe, offers increasing possibilities for hope.

Chapter 1

The Nature of Cancer

Contemporary Issues Companion

Defining Cancer

Robert Buckman

Physician and cancer specialist Robert Buckman examines several misconceptions about cancer that make people more afraid of it than they need to be. For instance, people usually think of cancer as a single disease, whereas in fact, as Buckman explains, "cancer" actually describes a group of many different diseases that are more accurately known as "the cancers." Moreover, some of these cancers are easily treatable and almost never fatal, he notes. In exploding false beliefs, Buckman sheds light on the true nature of cancer. He emphasizes that understanding cancer can help people deal with it in themselves or their loved ones. Buckman has written several books about medical topics, including *What You Really Need to Know About Cancer: A Comprehensive Guide for Patients and Their Families*, from which the following excerpt is taken.

We are all afraid of cancer. In fact we usually feel more frightened of cancer than of any other equally serious (or equally curable) medical condition. Often a diagnosis of cancer seems to produce in our minds a particular and deep feeling of helplessness, sometimes verging on terror or paralysis. It is as if those mental strategies that we could use coping with a diagnosis of, say, a heart attack or multiple sclerosis disappear and are no use to us when the diagnosis is a cancer. . . .

I think it is worth spending a moment or two looking at our attitudes to cancer, to try and find out why we are *so* afraid of it—so much more afraid of it than we are of other medical diseases, even ones that have just the same potential for harm and the same chance of treatment or cure. There seem to be four major elements to our fears of cancer.

Cancer Is Not a Single Disease

The first component of our fear is that we tend to think of cancer as a single disease. . . . In fact, *cancer is not a disease at all but a process* that happens to be shared by more than two hundred different diseases (the cancers) which have some other features in common. . . .

Reprinted from Robert Buckman, *What You Really Need to Know About Cancer: A Comprehensive Guide for Patients and Their Families*, pp. 1–3, ©1995, 1997 Robert Buckman, by permission of The Johns Hopkins University Press.

Cancer is what happens when a group of cells grows and multiplies in a disorderly and uncontrollable way and some of those cells are then able to invade into neighboring tissues. But apart from that process which they have in common—uncontrolled growth and then invasion—cancers vary enormously in their potential for causing harm or threatening life. Some cancers, for example, in addition to growing and invading, also have a high tendency to spread to distant parts of the body, and it is this that makes them dangerous and potentially lethal. Other cancers—in fact many of them—have a *low* tendency to do that and are much more likely to be cured at the first surgical operation. Some cancers (such as the two commonest types of skin cancer) almost never spread to distant areas of the body and are therefore never life threatening.

So the cancers are not one disease but a group of more than two hundred different diseases, each of which has its own behavior pattern and therefore its own chance of spreading to distant parts of the body and therefore threatening health and life. To lump them all together and think of them as one disease called "cancer" is not only inaccurate but is also very frightening because it makes this supposed single disease "cancer" appear to be infinitely variable and therefore entirely unpredictable and lethal. Here's a useful comparison. Suppose we had only one word to describe these infectious illnesses: *the common cold, flu, tuberculosis, measles, hepatitis, AIDS.* Suppose we had just the one word, *infection,* to describe all of those different illnesses. Wouldn't that *infection* be a frightening illness? You would probably think of it as an illness that might give you a runny nose for a few days or might cause a red rash or might give you weakness and nausea for a few weeks—or might kill you in a few years. If you thought that all of those different infectious illnesses were actually different manifestations of a single "infection" disease, then the word *infection* would appear to you as a very frightening, unpredictable, and always dangerous disease. If you had a friend with a cold or flu, you would wonder—as would they—whether the "infection" illness might suddenly and unpredictably turn into the deadly kind of infection and cause rapid deterioration. The diagnosis of *infection* would be very likely to cause deep and widespread feelings of terror and helplessness.

And that is what has happened to our understanding of *cancer.* Because we say *cancer* instead of *the cancers,* it appears to us that we are dealing with a single dangerous, unpredictable disease that at any moment might suddenly change its track and threaten our life. Whereas once we understand the facts—that the cancers are a group of some two hundred diseases, some of which are potentially very serious, some of which are never life threatening, and most of which are in between—the whole picture becomes more intelligible and less frightening.

Cancer Is Not an Alien Invasion

Another important component of our fear is the feeling that somehow cancer is a condition that has its own intelligence, almost like an invasion from outer space. This fear is probably a basic and primeval fear built into the human species. Some centuries ago, the kinds of medical conditions that caused something to grow inside and burst out were usually infectious abscesses (for example, in the chest, abdomen, or skin). Nowadays, with antibiotic treatment, abscesses are very rare, and this basic fear of something growing inside fits our perceived image of the cancers. So a diagnosis of cancer "buys into" a basic human fear. In fact, of course, cancer cells are normal cells that have gone slightly wrong in their behavior—they are not alien at all (unlike, for example, viruses, which some scientists believe *might* have originated on other planets!). Yet even though the cancer process is caused by our own cells escaping growth control mechanisms, that image of an alien, animal-like intelligence lurking inside, growing, and doing damage is a powerful one and an important and deep-seated component of our feelings about cancer.

Cancer Is Not Inevitably Mysterious

Another feature that seems to make cancer unusual among other chronic or potentially serious diseases is that it seems to have acquired a label of inevitable mystery. As in "they'll never really understand cancer." Of course, there are millions of questions that we cannot answer about the cancer process, but the same is true of almost every other condition you can think of. We don't understand why some people get multiple sclerosis and others don't, what causes ALS (Lou Gehrig's disease), what triggers ulcerative colitis, and so on. Yet somehow as a society we accept these areas of mystery relatively calmly, and we believe (I'm sure correctly) that some of the important questions about these conditions will be answered in the future. Yet with cancer there is a public perception that the major mysteries will *never* be unraveled and *can* never be. Of course, that too is true. Still, we are beginning to learn a great deal about the pathways that lead to the cancer process . . . and some of the methods by which cancers keep themselves growing. . . . Yet the aura of "inevitable mystery" seems to cling to cancer, perhaps partly because there have been so many stories of major breakthroughs in the press and on TV—when these seem to have failed to produce eradication of cancer, the myth of inevitable mystery gets another boost. So this, too, adds to the fear of cancer as an unknown and unknowable condition.

Cancer Is Not Caused by Mental Problems

Of all the reactions that cancer patients and their families experience, perhaps the most damaging and crushing is the idea that somehow the cancer patient might have brought the condition on himself or herself by having the wrong attitudes, thoughts, or personality. . . . Humankind has always had a tendency to blame the patient for the disease, and there has been a recent upsurge of this in cancer. There are very many carefully conducted studies that show that attitudes, personality, life events, grief, and depression do not cause cancer at all (as opposed to behavior patterns such as smoking, which does cause cancer). Furthermore, there are also important studies that show that changing your attitude and your thinking undoubtedly has a positive effect on your quality of life but does not change the behavior of cancer. Even so, the belief that somehow a diagnosis of cancer is a metaphor for some undefined "wrongness" of the person is a very subtle and powerful part of many people's reactions.

So, for all those reasons, the word *cancer* produces particular and deep-seated feelings of fear and dread. That is why [it is important] to explain and demystify cancer and its treatment and so reduce as far as possible those feelings of fear and helplessness. As has often been said, "understanding what's going on always makes things better," and that's especially true of cancer. A clear understanding will always help you feel more in control of your own situation, and by doing that it will really help you cope.

A Renegade Cell: How Cancer Starts

Robert A. Weinberg

> Robert A. Weinberg is an award-winning cancer researcher, a founding member of the Whitehead Institute for Biomedical Research in Cambridge, Massachusetts, and a professor of biology at the Massachusetts Institute of Technology (MIT), also in Cambridge. In the following excerpt from *Racing to the Beginning of the Road: The Search for the Origin of Cancer*, his book about his laboratory's groundbreaking investigations into the root cause of cancer, Weinberg explains how cancer starts from a single cell that refuses to follow the rules that control the growth and development of other cells in the body. According to Weinberg, this one cell generates a host of other "selfish cells" that crowd out neighboring cells and then invade distant parts of the body.

The human body is assembled from more than 30 trillion cells, each a semiautonomous living being that requires nourishment, reproduces, excretes wastes, and, in its time, dies. The lineage of all the cells in a human body can be traced back to a single common ancestor, the fertilized egg. Following fertilization, an egg cell divides into two cells, and these in turn divide, yielding four, the process continuing through endless rounds of growth and division that generate thousands, millions, ultimately trillions of descendants. . . .

Early in embryo development, only a few cell generations removed from the fertilized egg, the cells in an embryo appear identical to one another, but soon each begins to choose its own very distinct path. One cell takes on the role of a nerve, yet another assumes the function of muscle, a third commits itself to becoming blood. Once each of those cells has chosen a fate, its descendants follow suit. Soon specialized cells aggregate with one another to form specialized tissues, and those in turn begin to collaborate with one another, forming a complex, interdependent, mutually supporting community, a functional organism.

From *Racing to the Beginning of the Road: The Search for the Origin of Cancer*, by Robert A. Weinberg. Copyright ©1996 by Robert A. Weinberg. Reprinted by permission of Harmony Books, a division of Crown Publishers, Inc.

Selfish Cells

A cancerous growth—a tumor—represents a violation of this grand scheme. It very much resembles a specialized tissue, like the brain, pancreas, or liver. But this mass has not been specified in the master blueprint, the genetic plan that lays out the architecture of the normal human body.

Those of us who worked on cancer knew that all of the billions of cells in a human tumor descended from a single progenitor. Like . . . the recently fertilized egg, an ancestral cancer cell was able to generate an enormous number of descendants through repeated rounds of growth and division.

At least one distinctive hallmark, however, sets cancer cells apart from their normal counterparts. Normal cells are programmed to collaborate with one another to create an interdependent community—a functional tissue. Cancer cells, in stark contrast, seem to act selfishly, each being concerned only with its own possibilities of growth rather than with the needs of the community of cells around it. The fact that the descendants of a single ancestral cancer cell stay together to form a tumor mass is only an accident of their common history, really a temporary marriage of convenience. Given the slightest opportunity, each of the cells in a tumor would go off and live on its own.

The cells in our normal tissues are bathed constantly in a sea of nutrients that far exceeds their needs. Still, the ample food supply is not enough to encourage their growth. They hold back, waiting for other kinds of cues before they commit themselves to programs of growth and division. We imagined that those cues came from yet other cells around them. The resulting cross-talk between neighboring cells would inform each of the needs of the others around it. Such cues would override any impulse an individual cell might have to take advantage of the unlimited nutrients around it and begin to grow.

Cancer cells seem to abandon themselves to the primitive impulse to grow and divide, doing so without deferring to the needs of their neighbors. Once cancer cells begin following their growth agenda, the ample nutrients brought to them by the blood from elsewhere in the body will stoke their expansion for years. But eventually the food supply available in one or another corner of the body reaches its limit. Only then do the cells in a tumor colony come into direct competition with one another, first elbowing each other for the available space and food supply, then pushing the nearby normal tissue aside. Seen through the microscope, they form a chaotic jumble rather than the finely crafted architecture of normal, functional tissue.

Striking Out on Their Own

Some of the more entrepreneurial cells in the tumor may break off, float away, and seed new colonies at distant sites in the body. Such metastases soon wreak additional havoc, compounding the damage inflicted by the mother colony. More and more normal tissues become compromised, shoved aside, out-competed. Sooner or later the whole house of cards that is the human body collapses as its vital props are knocked from under it, one after another.

So the problem of cancer, we agreed, needed to be understood in terms of the cells that invent their own, self-directed manifesto of growth and destruction. In fact, the problem could be reduced even further. The ultimate answer to the cancer problem would come from looking at the single ancestral cell that founds the colony of cancer cells by transforming itself from a normal, well-behaved member of a community into a renegade.

A Series of Genetic Changes Leads to Cancer

Michael Waldholz

In the following selection, Michael Waldholz describes how Bert Vogelstein, a cancer researcher at Johns Hopkins University Medical Center in Baltimore, Maryland, discovered that changes in several different genes usually must occur in order for a life-threatening cancer to develop. Vogelstein focused his studies on colon cancer, Waldholz explains, because his laboratory was able to obtain tissue samples from colon tumors at many stages of development. Furthermore, he writes, a new laboratory technique using genetic markers called RFLPs allowed Vogelstein and his coworkers to pinpoint the location of genetic mutations that occurred as tumors progressed. According to Waldholz, Vogelstein's discovery reveals why most cancers take years or even decades to develop. Waldholz is a Pulitzer Prize–winning reporter for the *Wall Street Journal* and is the author of *Curing Cancer: The Story of the Men and Women Unlocking the Secrets of Our Deadliest Illness*, from which the following selection is taken.

Focus!
   The word is scribbled in crayon, graffiti-style in foot-high letters, on the white wall of a laboratory practically hidden behind locked doors in a renovated brick supermarket on the fringes of Johns Hopkins University medical center in Baltimore, Maryland. The laboratory, just a maze of tiny rooms and offices, and hallways that tumble into one another, is where a small troupe of gene scientists led by Bert Vogelstein changed forever the direction of cancer research.
   Beginning with a quiet trickle of reports in 1985, and then bursting in a cascade of findings from 1989 to 1994, the laboratory was by the reckoning of many one of the most prolific and, perhaps, the most influential of any in the cancer gene field. In 1993, and then again in 1994, *Science Watch,* a newsletter that tracks trends in basic research, anointed Bert Vogelstein the world's "hottest scientist" of the year. Second in the newsletter's ranking in 1993, just behind Vogelstein,

was the lab's codirector, and Vogelstein's protégé, Kenneth Kinzler.

By 1994, the 46-year-old Vogelstein was widely regarded as a leading candidate for a Nobel prize.

A Single-Minded Scientist

More than 300 graduate students apply for the three to five research slots open every year at the lab. "This is one of the most exciting and extraordinary places to conduct research," says lab member Todd Waldman. "There may be no place in molecular biology like it."

Much credit for the lab's success is due to the word that Vogelstein one day hastily scrawled in an arc around the room's thermostat, an unwitting metaphorical gesture, to be sure, for the intense scientific heat that it was meant to convey as well as generate. "I don't care what kind of crazy idea you want to pursue," Vogelstein tells new recruits. "But whatever you choose, make certain that's what you focus on. There's a million things that can distract you, there are probably ten, twenty, thirty ways to ask a question. Pick one, focus on it. Ignore everything else."

Vogelstein's own single-minded, fifteen-year focus on understanding the step-by-step genesis of cancer was impressive even among scientists absorbed by the cancer gene hunt. If indeed Vogelstein does win a Nobel prize, fellow researchers say he likely will be cited for a simple but persuasive notion about cancer progression that he relentlessly pushed his lab to uncover and then to extend in dozens of impressive, and often, groundbreaking experiments.

These experiments showed, beyond doubt, that cancer first arises in a single cell and then expands into its deadliest manifestations only after the cell and its progeny acquire and accumulate defects to a set of critical genes that govern the cell's life cycle. This is the cornerstone research underlying the "tumor suppressor" theory of cancer. And it came first from the labs of Bert Vogelstein. "Bert is the single most important basic researcher in cancer genetics," says cancer researcher Francis Collins. "Nobody else comes close."

By the early 1990s Vogelstein's multistep model of cancer genesis, so rational, elegant and provable, was embraced by nearly every major basic cancer research lab in the United States and abroad. It soon became the foundation for the most innovative research into the biological causes of cancer of the lung, breast, prostate, pancreas, and colon, the major cancer killers in the United States and elsewhere. . . .

The Start of a Research Career

Vogelstein went to college at the University of Pennsylvania in Philadelphia, returned home to Baltimore for his medical degree, internship, and residency in pediatrics at Johns Hopkins, and then in 1976, he went just forty miles down the highway to Bethesda, Maryland, for postdoctoral training in molecular biology at the National Cancer

Institute. By then, the young Vogelstein had settled on a career choice: while treating young cancer victims at Hopkins he decided he could have the greatest impact by studying the underlying cause of the disease.

"I could have become a pediatrician; it would have been satisfying at the time," Vogelstein says. "But I felt, through basic research, I'd touch a lot more kids." Moreover, at the time cancer research was hot. Only a few years earlier, in 1971, the federal government had undertaken its famous "war on cancer," pumping unprecedented funding into basic research, much of which was gobbled up by new molecular biology labs springing up in academic institutions all across the country. In addition, "the cancer cell was a black box," Vogelstein says. "Nobody knew what was going on inside there. There was some evidence it was a result of genetic mutations. But that was a hypothesis. The proof didn't exist. Back then I can't say I knew how to get at the evidence. But I did know it was an area where it was possible to have an impact."

Vogelstein had begun to reason his way into a career-long strategy for shining a light into the mysterious darkness surrounding the cancer cell. In 1971, Vogelstein had married Ilene Cardin, whose family was deeply involved in Baltimore's business, philanthropic, and political scene. So in 1978, seeking a chance to combine his new research interest and stay close to his family, Vogelstein applied for a junior position in a new cancer research program being set up with federal seed money at Johns Hopkins School of Medicine. "Baltimore is my home," he says. "I wanted to be here."

Rejecting Prevailing Theories

It wasn't long after Vogelstein joined the cancer center labs that "he started coming up with whole new ways of doing things," says Donald Coffey, a researcher who was Vogelstein's supervisor. By then, Vogelstein had rejected two of the three prevailing theories about what caused cancer. Some scientists believed then that cancer was caused by a breakdown in the body's immune system, its natural disease-fighting mechanism. Under this notion, scientists argued, a glitch in the immune system might allow errant cells to escape detection from "sentinel" cells in the bloodstream that seek and destroy unwanted germs and other foreign invaders. A healthy immune system, scientists believed, would perceive a growing cancer cell as abnormal and cast it out as if it were an unwelcome virus or bacterium. A defective immune system would be blind to the cancer growth.

A second idea then current among basic scientists was that most cancers were caused by mysterious viruses that somehow integrated themselves into a cell's nucleus. Once there, the theory went, the viruses wrench control of the cell, forcing it to replicate uninhibited into a tumor mass.

Neither of these explanations, even if true, described to the satisfaction of Vogelstein and others what happens to the cell's genes to cause unwanted cell replication. Even if a virus drives cell growth into high gear, or even if the immune system can't identify or deactivate such accelerating cell division, something unknown inside the cell's nucleus, which holds the DNA, is at the root of both problems. "By 1980 or so, I was pretty convinced the key to figuring out cancer was at the genetic level," Vogelstein says.

There was some evidence for this line of thinking. Researchers found that survivors of the atomic bombing in World War II who developed cancer late in life had contracted strange rearrangements of their DNA. In addition, there was a growing certainty that radiation caused cancer by damaging DNA. Some of the first medical technicians working with x-ray materials—who touched radiated particles with their hands—developed skin cancers; and women with tuberculosis administered high doses of radiation later developed breast cancer at a higher than expected rate.

"I thought these were all clues that the problem in cells was in genes," Vogelstein says. "But I could only prove that by actually finding the genes that were affected and showing that, in cancer, they were mutated."

A "Two-Hit" Theory of Cancer

One other idea was swirling about. Why, many wondered, did cancer usually take so long to emerge? Even people exposed to radiation didn't develop disease for a decade or more. And most cancers don't arise until late in life. Vogelstein suspected that was because a cancer cell had to collect several mutations. A defect to one gene might be dangerous, but not until the same cell sustained damage to other genes was it likely to spin out of control, he theorized.

Indeed, the suggestion that cancer involved several genetic steps had been put forward, but with only scant attention, by an obscure researcher in Texas. In the early 1970s, Alfred Knudsen, then at M.D. Anderson Cancer Center in Houston, suggested that a rare childhood eye cancer, retinoblastoma, was caused when the cells in the retina sustained two "hits" to a specific gene within the cells. He speculated that if a child was born with one of two copies of the defective gene (either the one inherited from the mother or the one inherited from the father), the child was at risk of disease. But if during early childhood, when the retina cells are dividing rapidly, a random error occurs in the production of the otherwise healthy copy of the gene, the double damage to the genes allows the cell to become cancerous.

This "two-hit" idea obsessed Knudsen. In 1976, he and others showed that children with the eye cancer had a loss of bits of their DNA on chromosome 13, suggesting that loss of a particular gene or its function was at the heart of the disease. Then in 1983, while

Vogelstein was searching for a way to study genetic machinery of a cancer cell, scientists elsewhere produced a landmark finding that dazzled the fledgling field of molecular genetics. Researchers working with Ray White in Utah, using his new RFLP genetic markers, showed that a specific area of chromosome 13—likely a gene—was missing in children with the eye cancer. The scientists discovered this by showing that in these children an RFLP marker in the chromosome 13 region that should have been present was consistently absent from tumor tissue, suggesting that the marker resided in a part of the DNA that was deleted.

"It suggested that the gene in that site somehow was critical to sustaining a healthy cell, and when it was gone, the cell became cancerous," Vogelstein says. "Now that was the kind of proof I wanted to find in my cancers, too." The RFLP marker "was the critical" tool to finding "missing genes" in other cancers, Vogelstein says.

Focusing on Colon Cancer

By 1983, Vogelstein had decided that if cancer was as Knudsen described, a multiple-step disease involving the progressive loss or damage to certain genes, then he needed to study human cells as they incurred these various genetic changes. At about the same time, an elderly physician at Johns Hopkins named Ben Baker had convinced a group of young researchers to tackle colon cancer. Baker gathered around him a team that called itself the Hopkins Bowel Tumor Working Group, and "he gave us some of the resources as well as the encouragement to take on colon cancer," Vogelstein recalls.

Back then "Bert didn't know a colon from a kidney," says one of the group's members, a young pathologist named Stanley Hamilton. "But he had this idea of looking for genes in various stages of cancer progression, and we told Bert that colon cancer might be the best disease available to undertake that kind of research." Indeed, within a few short weeks of becoming part of the working group, "I was convinced colon cancer held the key," Vogelstein says.

Vogelstein was attracted to colon cancer for several reasons. First off, "I soon learned from Ben that it was a major public health problem," he says, noting that about 130,000 Americans developed the disease each year. About 45,000 people in the United States annually succumb to the disease, often because the cancer isn't discovered until it reaches an advanced stage and has spread elsewhere in the body. From a research perspective, colon cancer was important because its stages of development were identifiable and, perhaps as important, accessible to researchers.

Snaring Tissue Samples

The first sign of a colon cancer is blood in the stool. Tipped off early enough to the presence of a problem, doctors can insert a catheter into the colon to see and then remove the disease's first precancerous stage, when it is merely a polyp. This mushroom-shaped tiny growth over the years is fertile ground for other molecular changes that can force the polyp to grow progressively more dangerous, eventually exploding into a fast-dividing carcinoma, which is the first sign of a tumor. Vogelstein figured that, as with the eye cancer, damage to genes might be what allows normal cells to expand into a polyp, and that an accumulation of additional genetic losses might transform a benign polyp into a cancerous form.

But studying the colon cells as they went through such changes "was something nobody else had even thought about doing," says Hamilton. "I don't think Bert was prepared for what we had to do next."

In order to make headway against colon cancer, Vogelstein needed samples of tissues removed from patients. Nobody had ever tried to analyze genetic alterations in human cancer cells directly removed from tumors. Previously, researchers had studied animal cells, or human cells cultured painstakingly over the years in test tubes. But Vogelstein was convinced that looking at genetic changes within human tissue was essential. He enlisted Hamilton, whose pathology lab regularly received and analyzed cell abnormalities in biopsies of tissue suspected of being cancerous.

"Whenever we heard that someone was being operated on for colon cancer, Bert and I rushed over to surgery and stationed ourselves directly outside the surgical suite," Hamilton says. The two men then took tissue samples and began immediately sifting through each one to find those cells that were cancerous. In order to do this Vogelstein's team had to invent a technique for "purifying" the tumor tissue.

Telltale Differences

Back at the labs, Vogelstein and Eric Fearon, a postdoctoral researcher, set to work looking for RFLP marker deletions in DNA extracted from the purified colon cancer cells. "What we were looking for was differences between healthy colon cells removed from the patients and cells removed from their tumors," Vogelstein says. But looking for marker changes throughout the genome was an impossible task. Scouring the medical literature, they soon found a clue that they hoped would shorten the hunt. Scientists in France looking at colon cancer tissue under microscopes had found large sections of chromosomes 17 and 18 missing. So, one by one, Vogelstein and Fearon tested RFLPs up and down chromosome 17.

Finally, in 1987, they made an electrifying discovery. In 22 of 30 tumor samples they studied, markers in one particular spot in chromosome 17 were consistently missing. When they went back and studied polyps from the same patients, they found no such chromosome 17 abnormalities. To the scientists this meant they were on the track of a gene that, when damaged or missing, transformed a polyp growth into a cancer. In a research paper published that October, the scientists said that "on the basis of the data presented here and elsewhere, one can begin to formulate a hypothesis for the development of colorectal [cancer]." The formal language of scientific research papers doesn't allow a scientist to communicate emotions. But for Vogelstein's lab "the chromosome 17 discovery was a watershed," recalls Fearon. "It seems like everything came like a rush after that."

An Assembly-Line Gene Hunt

By 1988, Vogelstein's lab was running much like an assembly line. Vogelstein had as many as a dozen postdocs, graduate students, and technicians whizzing about the labs or poring over experiments at their lab benches. Every day, the scientists would examine another bit of chromosomes 17 and 18 and 11 and 5—all spots where DNA losses in colon cancer tissue had been identified—trying to determine if, as they now fully expected, specific genes were involved in tumor growth. Standing over test tubes, the scientists examined bits of tumor samples still flowing from Hamilton's pathology department. They then digested the samples with special enzymes and extracted DNA. Then, once more using special molecular biology techniques, they fished out of the DNA those segments of the four chromosomes under study and examined the RFLP markers mixed in with the DNA.

By this time, "we were pretty convinced we were on the track of a tumor suppressor, a gene that kept a cell from becoming a tumor when it wasn't defective or damaged," says Ken Kinzler, who had joined the lab.

A Series of Changes

By the middle of 1988, Vogelstein's clutch of researchers had produced evidence that they were tracking specific genetic changes that occurred at identifiable stages as the cancer progressed from an adenoma, or benign polyp, until it reached a full-blown tumor. By examining 172 samples with dozens of RFLP markers, the lab found missing bits, or mutations, in chromosome 5 in about one-third of noncancerous adenomas, and they found mutations in a gene on chromosome 11 in about half the carcinomas. The labs found no evidence of deleted or missing DNA in chromosome 17 or 18 until they peered at samples removed from end-stage, lethal tumors. In those deadly forms of disease, the lab consistently found that bits of DNA were absent in these chromosomes.

To Vogelstein the data were clear. Certain specific and identifiable genetic changes sent normal colon cells spiraling, first, into a benign growth, and then, as the genetic changes mounted within a cell, into an out-of-control tumor. "Our results support a model in which accumulated alterations affecting at least one dominant-acting [gene] and several tumor-suppressor genes are responsible for the development of colorectal tumors," Vogelstein and his team announced to the world in a study published in September of 1988 with much fanfare in the prestigious *New England Journal of Medicine*. In an essay solicited by the *Journal* for commentary on the implications of the new insight produced by the Vogelstein team, Peter Nowell, a cancer researcher in Philadelphia, wrote the following: "At the molecular level, an outline is beginning to emerge of the series of genetic events involved in a fully developed human cancer and of the underlying mechanisms."

Of the report, Nowell says, "I had only heard vaguely of Bert before seeing his study. It certainly put him and his lab on the map. It seems like, after that, we heard something new from Bert almost every other month or so." Indeed, in his commentary Nowell wrote that it seemed clear from the Vogelstein research that some of the genes identified were part of a new class of tumor suppressors. . . .

Confirmation of a Theory

Vogelstein felt with the release of the *Journal* data that he finally had confirmed his original idea: cancer was inspired by a specific set of genetic alterations. The lab had collared a rogues' gallery whose actions had turned a well-mannered human tissue into cancerous outlaws. Moreover, he had uncovered a novel scenario for human cancer development that, in the words of [cancer research pioneer] Robert A. Weinberg, "seemed to resemble the process of Darwinian evolution." Each gene mutation seemed to free the cell from one of its normal growth controls, giving it a growth advantage over its neighbors, to replicate and divide more often than cells without the mutations. As the cell split itself over and over, it created frequent opportunities for additional mistakes, or mutations, to emerge during the production of new DNA required for each new cell offspring. With each new mutation, the cell lost another growth regulator and became more likely to outpace the growth of normal cells nearby, robbing them of circulating nutrients to feed its own tumor-massing needs. Thus, the cells with the most mutations overtook a neighborhood, by turns becoming a cancerous tumor mass. Because these replicating mistakes, or mutations, were rare events, Vogelstein proposed that it might take a cell years to accumulate the precise genetic miscreants that drove it to misbehave.

Deadly Evolution

George Klein

In the following selection, George Klein relates how the development of cancer is similar to the development of a new type of organism (species) as set forth in Charles Darwin's theory of evolution. In both cases, Klein writes, accidental changes in DNA (the complex chemical that carries genetic information from parents to offspring) produce characteristics that give the organism an advantage over others that lack those characteristics. As a result, he states, the organism can multiply more successfully than its neighbors. Klein also describes the three types of cancer-causing genes and tells why research into the genetics of cancer may someday lead to a cure for this often-deadly disease. Klein is the head of the department of tumor biology at the Karolinska Institute in Stockholm, Sweden.

By now most people are familiar with philosopher Daniel Dennett's characterization of natural selection as "Darwin's dangerous idea"—dangerous because it acted as a "corrosive acid" capable of dissolving the established structures of human society. That acid can be just as corrosive of scientific structures, which one might have thought more impervious to the damage. Thus a Darwinian idea has eaten away at some of the foundations of my own field of research for the past half-century, tumor biology, and forced cancer researchers to reexamine some cherished notions about the origins of cancer that were current during the first half of the century. Today, with the discovery of new genes that contribute to the development of cancerous cells, we are keenly aware that cancer is, above all, a disease of DNA. But more important, we know that this disease does not occur in a preprogrammed manner. Only through the gradual emancipation of a cell from the controls that govern its normal process of division does a cell turn cancerous. And that emancipation, it turns out, proceeds by the mechanics of Darwinian evolution.

In hindsight, perhaps, that is not surprising. Since Darwin's day we have known of the power of natural selection to shape the organisms of the world. And over the past 50 years biologists have come to under-

Excerpted from George Klein, "Malign Evolution," *Discover*, August 1997. Reprinted by permission of *Discover* magazine, ©1997.

stand how mutations in DNA provide the array of genetic variation through which natural selection operates. Yet the importance of evolution has only slowly crept into the field of cancer research. To be sure, the process by which cells of the body turn malignant is a very limited one compared with the evolution of a species. But just as we have come to understand that microorganisms evolve resistance to drugs, we now know that cancerous cells evolve to become unresponsive to the growth-controlling forces of the body. How those genetic changes occur is based on Darwinian principles of variation and selection.

That insight changes our understanding of cancer. It lays to rest the hopes of finding a single key change or infectious agent that can explain all forms of the disease. . . .

The ever-recurring theme in science is that what appears to be most important can turn out to be trivial, and vice versa: a seemingly unimportant discovery may later acquire paramount significance. In this process, theories are like the scaffolding around a building that's under construction: it exists only to be removed as the building grows.

Cancer-Causing Viruses

The experimental results of Peyton Rous in 1911, for example, provided unexpected insights into tumor growth. Rous, a young researcher at the Rockefeller Institute in New York, suspected that cancer was caused by a virus—at the time a rather new and poorly understood entity. He soon had the opportunity to test his idea when a Long Island farmer sought his help in treating a prize hen with a tumor. In an attempt to isolate the cancer-causing pathogen, Rous removed the tumor, ground it up, filtered out the cells, and then injected the remaining cell-free material into a young chicken. The result: A cancerous growth. Rous concluded that the cells from the tumor produced an infectious agent that could transmit cancer.

Over the next four decades, many researchers tried to repeat Rous's experiments in mice and rats, without success. However, in the 1950s that changed. Ludwik Gross, a Jewish refugee from Poland working at a Veterans' Administration (VA) hospital in the Bronx, successfully isolated a virus that caused leukemia in mice. Soon after his discovery, other researchers began isolating viruses that, when injected into different types of experimental animals, could cause tumors. Some of these viruses could also turn normal cells in culture into cancer cells. By the 1960s and 1970s, the theory that cancer had a viral cause had developed a strong following.

These studies eventually identified two families of tumor viruses—DNA viruses and RNA viruses—with different modi operandi [ways of working]. When a DNA tumor virus inserts its genes among the genes of the host cell, it can disrupt the regulation of cell division, causing tumor growth. (Fortunately, the immune system usually recognizes—and eliminates—these altered cells.) More puzzling were the insidious reproductive habits of RNA tumor viruses. It turned out that these viruses copy their own genetic material, which exists as RNA, into double-stranded DNA. They then splice this DNA into the host cell's DNA. In the cell's DNA the virus can lie low and hide from the immune system. Because the researchers were ignorant of these things, they did not yet realize that the cancer-inducing effect of these viruses was merely a side effect of their lifestyle.

Stolen Genes

RNA viruses are effective but sloppy reproducers. Unlike the host cell, the virus doesn't have any mechanism for proofreading what it copies into DNA. It can afford to produce a vast number of incorrect copies, including some that have accidentally picked up genes from the host DNA. Usually when this pickup occurs, other viral genetic information is lost. The resulting virus particles are so defective and disadvantaged that they could not survive in nature. But the tumor virologist, motivated by the desire to show that viruses can cause tumors, may save some of them from extinction.

Consider what Peyton Rous did back in 1911. He ground up the hen's tumor, passed the material through a very fine filter that would not allow cells through, and injected the filtered material into newly hatched chicks. Then he looked for tumor development. What Rous could not have realized is that he was selecting virus particles that had accidentally picked up a host gene that promotes cell growth. He had selected the viruses that were capable not only of infecting new cells in the recipient chick but of prompting them to divide incessantly.

The key to unlimited growth was the stolen cellular gene, switched on by the virus, that forced the cells to divide without having been instructed by the normal signals of the organism. Not until some 60 years after Rous's experiment did researchers realize that the cancer-inducing gene from Rous's virus was in fact derived from a normal chicken cell. Later, other RNA tumor viruses picked up from chicken, mouse, rat, or monkey tumors were found to harbor similar growth-promoting cellular genes. These genes were also found to play important roles in the spontaneous development of human tumors.

Stages of Cancer Growth

The hunt for *virally* encoded genetic information that could turn normal cells cancerous had instead led to the discovery that viruses could hijack and alter growth-regulating cellular genes. That finding highlighted the importance of DNA in tumor development, and later studies showed that mutations could "turn on" these genes in normal cells and promote cancer even without any viral intervention. Recognizing the role of mutations in the cellular DNA helped make sense of the emerging picture of steplike cancer development. Studies of the natural history of human cancers strongly hinted that they proceeded through a number of distinct stages, which emerged through a series of multiple changes that occurred at unpredictable intervals. In fact, back in the 1930s, Peyton Rous had begun documenting the changes in the tissue as cancer developed. He coined the term *tumor progression* to describe the process whereby tumors went "from bad to worse."

Some 20 years later, Leslie Foulds, an experimental pathologist at the Chester Beatty Research Institute in London, formulated a set of "rules" to describe this process. He stressed the importance of distinguishing each of the traits that characterize the cells as they progress, step-by-step, toward cancer. Foulds's work was critical for our later understanding of the role mutations play in the disease—one may, in fact, refer to the stepwise evolution of malignant tumors by sequential changes as Foulds's dangerous idea. Foulds spoke about traits such as growth rate, hormone dependence, and the ability to invade surrounding tissues or to spread by metastasis. Moreover, he pointed out that these properties could change independently of each other as the tumor "progresses." In other words, there didn't appear to be one straight line a cell had to take to become cancerous.

A Disease of DNA

Over the last four decades, research has fully vindicated Foulds's ideas, with one important exception. Foulds believed that the changes were not caused by mutations. Instead, he hypothesized that the genes of a cancerous cell were normal; only their expression was disturbed. Thought of in this way, cancer was a disease of abnormal development, in which the wrong genes were being turned on and off. In this respect, Foulds was clearly wrong. Today we know that cancer is not only a disease of abnormal gene regulation but a disease of the DNA itself.

To Foulds, it seemed highly unlikely that mutations could be responsible for the steps of tumor development and progression. Each cell carries two copies of every gene, one from each parent. The two genes sit on two different chromosomes, and if one gene loses its function by mutation, its normal counterpart on the other chromosome can usually do the job. Random mutations were expected to affect only one of the two copies—mutations of both genes seemed highly improbable.

We have learned, however, that it is easy to lose a second copy of a gene during cell division if the first copy is already impaired. Often the whole chromosome on which the second gene sits is lost. It turns out that cancer cells tolerate such losses very well because, unlike normal cells, they do not need to perform any specialized function. All they have to do is reproduce themselves.

In other words, the rules of their game have changed. Ordinary cells in multicellular organisms abide by rules that regulate their growth and ensure that they perform particular metabolic tasks. But as mutations accumulate, a cell stops being a team player and plays instead by the rules of natural selection. And those rules favor the fastest-growing cells. Many mutations may crop up during the evolution of a tumor, but it is the cell that has acquired the most growth-promoting mutations that will thrive and spread.

Deadly Genes

The genes involved in this gradual evolution fall into three somewhat overlapping categories. The first group are the oncogenes, the cancer-causing mutated genes that virologists first stumbled upon in the 1970s. All oncogenes urge cells to divide, and they can do so with a change in only one of the two gene copies.

The second group of genes are the so-called tumor suppressor genes. The first sign that normal cells may contain genes that can inhibit cancerous growth came from experiments performed nearly three decades ago by Henry Harris in Oxford in collaboration with our group, at the Karolinska Institute in Stockholm. When we fused normal and malignant cells, the resulting hybrid cell—and its progeny—were nonmalignant. But when some chromosomes from the normal parent cell were lost in the course of cell division in culture, the cells become malignant again. This indicated that tumor cells have suffered a genetic loss, and that normal genes can compensate for the loss.

Other researchers later identified the individual tumor suppressor genes. Eventually it became clear that suppressor genes make proteins that prevent inappropriate cell division. One of the best-known examples is the gene that produces the protein p53. Normal cells make very little p53. But whenever DNA is damaged—either by radiation, chemicals, or lack of oxygen—p53 levels rise dramatically. The p53 binds to DNA and prevents the cell from dividing—and thereby makes time for the DNA repair enzymes to perform their task. After the DNA has been repaired, p53 levels decline and cell division can go on. But if the damage has been too extensive, the cell undergoes programmed cell death, called apoptosis.

More than half of all human tumors contain mutated p53 that cannot bind to DNA and cannot, therefore, arrest the growth of cells with damaged DNA. The mutation does more than just impair the cell-death program. In cells where both copies of p53 are lost or mutated, damaged DNA doesn't elicit the signals that halt growth long enough for it to be repaired. These cells nevertheless survive and are therefore prone to other mutations, including mutations in oncogenes and suppressor genes. This is why an inherited p53 mutation can lead to Li-Fraumeni syndrome, a condition in which patients often develop multiple tumors, arising in different tissues.

The third group of cancer-causing genes are the DNA repair genes themselves—the genes that ensure each strand of genetic information is correctly copied during cell division. Mutations in these genes predispose humans to hereditary nonpolyposis colon cancer syndrome.

Families with this syndrome tend to be at risk for cancer in the colon, the rest of the gastrointestinal tract, the ovaries, the uterus, the urinary epithelium, and the skin. Mutations in at least five other DNA repair genes have now been discovered as well, and they are associated with other cancer syndromes.

Cancer Gains an Advantage

The destabilizing effects of this set of mutations were first identified in organisms like bacteria and yeast. Because mutations in DNA repair genes increase the frequency of other mutations, they may enhance these single-celled creatures' ability to survive in a stressful environment. But the same phenomenon in multicellular creatures like ourselves may result in cancer. The more cancer cells break away from the rules that ensure cooperation among the many cells of the body, the more they resemble populations of microorganisms. Among free-living bacteria, yeasts, and amoebas, for example, natural selection favors variants that can use nutrients and other resources more effectively. Among cancer cells, natural selection favors cells that are less and less responsive to the growth-controlling forces of the organism. And much as natural selection favors bacteria that can adapt to a new environment, so too does it favor cancer cells with mutations that help them survive in the low-oxygen environment of a growing tumor. . . .

Fortunately, it takes more than one genetic change to emancipate an ordinary cell from growth control. No single mutation is in and of itself cancer-causing. As Foulds suspected nearly four decades ago, cancer progression does not unfold in a rigid, predetermined manner. It unfolds slowly through a string of mutations, changes that provide a series of green lights to cellular growth.

Hope for a Cure

How complete is our present picture of the three "gene worlds" that may influence cancer development? Are there others? Yes, certainly, but their study is at an earlier stage. Some genes influence the ability of the fledgling tumor cell to attract the blood vessels that bring it nutrients, a precondition for tumor growth. Others interfere with the process of normal cellular aging, helping to make the precancerous cell "immortal." Still others help disguise the cancerous cell from the surveillance of the immune system.

What does our new understanding of tumor evolution hold for the future? Some of our clinical colleagues and most of the lay public have long awaited a "cancer cure." Some say the investment in cancer research has been a waste, or in its nasty version, that cancer supports more people than it kills.

For the cancer biologists who have followed in Darwin's and Foulds's footsteps, there is no return. We must not only live with this new complexity but embrace it. Even though tumor development represents an evolutionary process on a very small scale, it is nonetheless an evolutionary process, with many subtle, seemingly unconnected steps, and with almost infinite variability. This does not mean that we have to know all the steps in minute detail before we can control the cancer cell. The new cancer biology may also provide methods to stop a multiply changed tumor cell in a single step.

Gene therapy may halt the growth of cancerous cells by introducing a powerful suppressor gene or a gene that promotes cell death. Still other approaches include cutting off a tumor's blood supply—the source of its nutrients. If the capillary blood supply of the tumor is cut off, it will die. Yet another approach is to construct "immune missiles" composed of a toxin or a radioactive tag along with a specific antibody. Although the origins of cancer are far more tangled than Rous ever imagined, the light of Darwin may yet let us find our way through the thicket.

CHAPTER 2

TRIGGERS OF CANCER

Contemporary Issues
Companion

Tobacco Threatens Women's Health

Jane E. Brody

A link between substances in cigarette smoke and lung cancer is almost universally accepted. What is less well known, says *New York Times* health writer Jane E. Brody, is the special risk that smoking presents to women. Brody attributes the recent rise in lung cancer deaths among women to the increase in the number of women who smoke. She points out that smoking also increases women's risk of developing other cancers, as well as illnesses such as heart disease. Research suggests that women may be more vulnerable genetically to the effects of tobacco than are men with similar smoking habits, Brody writes.

An epidemic is raging in this country, and no one seems to be paying much attention to it. It is an epidemic of lung cancer in women.

When I started writing about medicine in the early 1960s, lung cancer in women was a rarity. It was considered a man's disease. In 1964, when the Surgeon General's first report on smoking was issued, men were six times as likely as women to die of lung cancer. But to paraphrase a popular ad campaign aimed at female smokers, "You've come a long way, baby"—toward a shorter life.

An Understudied Epidemic

The American Cancer Society estimates that lung cancer will be diagnosed in 1998 in 80,100 women—just 11,300 fewer women than men. And in 1998 67,000 women will die of lung cancer, only 26,100 fewer than the number of men who will die of the disease, and 23,500 more women than will succumb to breast cancer. Every year for the last 11 years, lung cancer deaths in women have exceeded breast cancer deaths, and the gap continues to widen. Furthermore, only 14 percent of women who get lung cancer are alive 5 years later, but 67 percent of women with breast cancer survive at least 10 years.

Yet, in 1996, the Federal Government invested $600 million in breast cancer research, but allocated only $100 million for lung cancer studies.

Reprinted from Jane E. Brody, "A Fatal Shift in Cancer's Gender Gap," *The New York Times*, Personal Health, May 12, 1998, by permission. Copyright ©1998 by The New York Times.

Where are the advocacy groups fighting for greater awareness of the lung cancer risk to women and pleading for more money for research into this major killer? Are women with the disease too embarrassed, knowing that as many as 90 percent of them got sick because they smoked cigarettes? Are they so wedded to tobacco that they are willing to pay for it with their health and lives?

Although the incidence of lung cancer peaks between ages 60 and 70, many women in their 50s succumb as well. Two women I know who are that age are battling incurable lung cancer. Both were once chain smokers. One quit smoking seven years before her cancer was detected; the other puffed away until the day of diagnosis. Both are intelligent, well-educated, accomplished women. Both knew all too well the risks associated with smoking, yet they couldn't—or wouldn't—stop until it was too late. Lung cells that had been damaged by decades of exposure to inhaled carcinogens could no longer recover and progressed into a full-blown metastatic cancer.

Frightening Trends

These women are two decades shy of the life expectancy of American women. They would like to see their children marry and have children of their own. But it may not be possible. Were the years of puffing away worth it?

In April 1998, in the inaugural issue of the medical journal *Women's Health in Primary Care*, Dr. Carolyn M. Dresler, a thoracic surgeon at Fox Chase Cancer Center in Philadelphia, pointed out that if current trends continue, more women than men will be smoking cigarettes by the year 2000. Now, teen-age girls are taking up smoking at higher rates than boys, and women who smoke have a much harder time quitting than men do. So while the number of men who smoke has dropped significantly since its peak in the early 60s, the decline in the number of women who smoke has been far smaller, such that smoking rates in both sexes are now about equal.

Furthermore, women who smoke today smoke more heavily than in decades past, coating their respiratory tracts from mouth to lungs with carcinogens 20 or more times a day. So Dr. Dresler was not surprised to find that the incidence of lung cancer is rising nine times faster in women than in men—an increase of 4.6 percent for women compared with 0.5 percent for men each year between 1973 and 1991. Death rate figures are similar. Dr. Dresler predicted that within a decade the number of lung cancer cases in women and men will be roughly equal.

Of course, lung cancer is not the only risk incurred by smoking, nor are women the only victims of their tobacco addiction. Smoking also increases a woman's risk of developing cancers of the cervix, larynx, esophagus, bladder, pancreas, kidney and stomach and it accounts for nearly 100,000 deaths a year from cardiovascular disease. A woman's

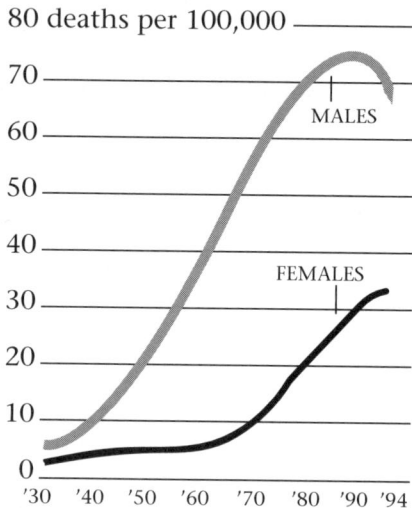

Lung Cancer Death Toll

The yearly lung cancer death rate in the United States among males is declining, while the rate among females continues to rise significantly.

Source: American Cancer Society, Facts and Figures, 1998.

risk of suffering a heart attack or dying of heart disease is increased even if she smokes only one to four cigarettes a day. Smoking also causes strokes, emphysema, premature wrinkling and early menopause and it increases a woman's risk of developing ulcers and osteoporosis.

Then there are the hazards to their children. In addition to such pregnancy complications as miscarriage, stillbirth, premature delivery and impaired fetal growth, smoking by a baby's mother increases the risk of sudden infant death by two to four times and increases the baby's risk of developing respiratory and ear infections, asthma and pneumonia.

Women Are at Greater Risk

Perhaps the most frightening fact from Dr. Dresler is this: Lung cancer is up to three times more likely to develop in women who smoke than in men with comparable smoking habits. While the reasons for this susceptibility have not been fully identified, Dr. Dresler said that women seem to be genetically more vulnerable to the effects of tobacco. For one thing, she said, women who smoke experience a much greater decline in pulmonary function than men do. . . .

Dr. Dresler said that among the patients she has operated on for lung cancer, men got the disease after a smoking history averaging 77 pack-years, whereas it occurred in women after an average of 54 pack-years. The number of pack-years is calculated by multiplying the amount smoked each day by the number of years a person smoked. Thus, someone who smoked 1½ packs a day for 40 years would have a 60 pack-year history.

Furthermore, even after a woman quits smoking, the risk of developing lung cancer does not disappear. Dr. Dresler said that 50 percent of her patients were former smokers when their cancer was diagnosed.

"Unfortunately, with lung cancer, the risk never goes back to zero," she said, although the risk of smoking-related heart disease eventually approaches that faced by people who never smoked.

Secondhand Smoke Raises Cancer Risk

Philip J. Hilts

Philip J. Hilts asserts that breathing secondhand smoke from others' cigarettes has been proven to significantly increase nonsmokers' risk of developing lung cancer and other illnesses. Secondhand smoke exposes nonsmokers' lungs to several potent carcinogens, he maintains. Slow acceptance of research showing the dangers of secondhand smoke, combined with millions of dollars' worth of counterpropaganda by the tobacco industry, has resulted in inappropriately weak legislation against smoking in public places, Hilts believes. He recommends that people support stronger antismoking legislation and avoid exposure to secondhand smoke whenever possible. Hilts reports on health and science policy for the *New York Times*. He has also written *Smokescreen: The Truth Behind the Tobacco Industry Cover-Up*.

Imagine that the President calls a press conference to announce that a toxic substance is being pumped into the air. In just one year, it will kill at least 50,000 people and send four million children to their doctors. The substance contains the most potent poisons known, including 43 different carcinogens and thousands of other chemicals, such as cyanide, carbon monoxide, and strychnine.

It would be an environmental crisis: the American Medical Association, the National Academy of Sciences, and the Environmental Protection Agency (EPA) would all urge immediate action. Congress would quickly respond.

A Protected Poison

In fact, such a substance *is* being pumped into our air, and medical and scientific organizations have called for action to stop the hazard. Almost 90 percent of Americans regularly inhale the toxic mix and carry traces of it in their blood. It can even be detected in fetuses still in the womb.

However, Congress has not responded. The substance in question is the smoke from cigarettes—and it is the only highly toxic substance

Reprinted from Philip J. Hilts, "Secondhand Smoke: The Real Risk for You and Your Family," *Good Housekeeping*, November 1996, by permission of the author.

in this country that is explicitly exempted from consumer protection regulations and hazardous substance laws. And despite increasing evidence of the harm secondhand smoke can cause, it's unlikely that Congress will take action to change the situation anytime soon.

"It's extraordinary," says Douglas Dockery of the Harvard School of Public Health. "It makes no sense that we'd accept higher levels of pollution indoors than outdoors."

Unexpected Harm

How did we come to this? It began with the simple assumption, even by scientists, that secondhand smoke might be irritating, but not harmful because it's so diluted by the air.

During the 1970s and 1980s, scientific data began to disprove that. When the actual amounts of smoke in the environment were measured, it was discovered that the amount taken into the lungs by those who don't smoke was far higher than expected. Then researchers found that ounce for ounce, secondhand smoke is more hazardous than the kind inhaled directly by smokers. That's because the smoke that comes off the end of a smoldering cigarette is created by lower-temperature burning than that inhaled by a smoker; this temperature difference creates a unique set of chemical reactions, leading to a compound that contains more carcinogens. In addition, a nonsmoker does not have the advantage of inhaling through a filter.

It took time for medical and scientific groups to establish the facts, and it was only in 1986 that the surgeon general cited secondhand smoke as a cause of lung cancer. Then in 1993, the EPA issued its definitive report, declaring secondhand smoke (also called environmental tobacco smoke) a Class A carcinogen—the most dangerous type.

To put this in perspective, the EPA commonly calls for regulations on a chemical when its risk of causing death exceeds one person in a million. With passive smoke, a person's lifetime risk of lung cancer alone is one in 500. For someone exposed to unusually high amounts of smoke—for instance, a waiter in a smoky restaurant—the risk rises to one in 50. The risk of getting heart disease because of secondhand smoke is even higher: one in 50 for a person with average exposure; as much as one in five for a person with the heaviest exposures over a lifetime.

A Multimillion-Dollar Smoke Screen

Yet since the EPA's 1993 report was issued, the tobacco industry has mounted a multimillion-dollar campaign to convince people that the hazards of secondhand smoke are far less than scientists and doctors think. And with a variety of misleading ads, they have largely succeeded.

In one ad, for example, R.J. Reynolds claimed that a nonsmoker working with smoking colleagues would inhale the equivalent of only one and a quarter cigarettes per month. That's true, but only in terms of the nicotine that worker would inhale—one of the least hazardous compounds in cigarettes. One estimate of the actual hazard for that same office worker shows that he or she would take in per month as much benzene as someone who smoked six cigarettes, as much of the carcinogen 4ABP [4-aminobenzpyrene] as in 17 cigarettes, and as much of the carcinogen NDMA [N-nitrosodimethylamine] as in 75 cigarettes.

Over the past ten years, tobacco companies have given an average of $21,000 to each of the members of the House of Representatives who serve on health committees and are in key leadership positions. And that figure does not include trips, parties, and other perks.

The money has clearly had an effect. There hasn't been a major tobacco control bill passed since 1990, when smoking was banned on domestic airline flights. A bill to curb smoking in child-care centers on federal property was passed in 1993, but its reach is limited, because most child-care facilities are not located in federal buildings.

"There are some poisons that are more deadly than secondhand smoke, but nothing with the kind of wide exposure in the population," says Jim Repace, an environmental scientist who is an expert on secondhand smoke. The only way to change things? "In the election booth," says Repace. "This is a democracy, and if tobacco becomes an issue that drives votes, maybe politicians will begin to listen."

How Secondhand Smoke Kills

When secondhand smoke enters the air and you inhale its dirty cloud, the same thing happens in your body that happens in the body of a smoker: Nicotine and cancer-causing tars are deposited in your mouth, throat, and lungs. Your blood picks up the poisons from your lungs and transports them throughout your body.

The Environmental Protection Agency estimates that secondhand smoke causes about 3,000 deaths per year from lung cancer alone. That's far higher than the number of deaths caused by almost any other kind of exposure to toxic substances—more, for example, than the number of cancers caused by intense chemical exposure found among workers in chemical plants who are exposed to those toxins every day.

The more smoke you are regularly exposed to over the years, the greater your risk. For example, being married to a two-pack-a-day smoker for 20 years increases your risk of getting lung cancer by about 35 percent. Exposure for 40 years makes the risk 80 percent higher than for those who live with nonsmokers. For those exposed as children, then later as adults, the risk doubles—to 160 percent.

So why don't nonsmokers get sick as often as smokers? To some degree, nonsmokers are protected by the air, which dilutes the smoke, and by the surfaces around them—furniture, clothing, drapes, and windows—on which the most hazardous substances settle. In addition, smokers suffer from the effects of both the filtered smoke they

Secondhand Smoke Levels

If You're in This Location . . .	For This Long . . .	It's as if You've Smoked This Many Cigarettes . . .
Smoky bar	2 hours	4
Restaurant (typical nonsmoking section)	2 hours	1½
Office	8 hours	6
Pack-a-day smoker's home	24 hours	3
Fenway Park, Boston (sitting behind someone who is smoking)	3 hours	⅔
Car (when someone's smoking and the windows are closed)	1 hour	3

Good Housekeeping, November 1996.

breathe in *and* the secondhand smoke that surrounds them.

But nonsmokers are still clearly at risk. "You needn't even be in the same room with a smoker to inhale substantial amounts of tobacco smoke," says Michael Siegel, M.D., an expert on secondhand smoke at the Boston University School of Public Health. It takes from several hours to a full day to clear the air of chemicals in a room in which someone has smoked. And rooms that have been repeatedly exposed to smoke can have deposits of the tarry substances from cigarettes on the furniture, drapes, and walls, which can continue to give off small amounts of toxic substances for days or weeks. Researchers generally consider these odors to be unpleasant rather than dangerous; however, they are strong enough for those with sensitive noses to instantly tell a "smoking" from a "nonsmoking" hotel room.

Many Health Risks

To date, there are several hundred studies of the effects of secondhand smoke, and they demonstrate a variety of health risks—not only for lung cancer, but also for cancers of the urinary system, colon, kidneys, pancreas, and ovaries. Among the other risks to nonsmokers who inhale substantial amounts of smoke at home, work, or regular social situations:

More than 50,000 deaths per year from heart and artery disease are brought on by exposure to secondhand smoke. It also causes other heart and blood-system problems in other ways, since blood cells will carry the carbon monoxide from the smoke to all the cells in the body, significantly reducing amounts of oxygen flow to the brain and other organs.

Scientists believe that many of the other illnesses that smokers get from cigarette smoke will probably also show up in nonsmokers exposed to substantial amounts of secondhand smoke. Researchers have already demonstrated that the risk of developing respiratory ailments such as bronchitis and pneumonia is particularly high. "We're not near a full list of what the problems are," says Jonathan Samet, M.D., professor and chairman of the department of epidemiology at the Johns Hopkins University School of Public Health. "The science continues to evolve."

Environmental Carcinogens Cause Cancer

Mike Weilbacher

In the following selection, Mike Weilbacher presents the view that pesticides and other human-made chemicals in the environment trigger many cases of human cancer. He quotes authorities who claim that American researchers are losing their "war on cancer" because they pay too little attention to these environmental carcinogens. After describing the two primary techniques by which the danger from these carcinogens is evaluated, Weilbacher explains that researchers disagree over the reliability of both methods. He concludes with a call for further research and political action aimed at preventing cancer by identifying carcinogens and removing them from the environment. Weilbacher is a writer and educator who formerly hosted a Philadelphia radio program about the environment.

Frank Wiewel lives the Joni Mitchell song: He's looked at clouds from both sides now. At home in the heartland of Ohto, Iowa, where corn is king, he once saw clouds simply as harbingers of rain. Not anymore. Now he sees them as floating concentrations of toxic waste. As president of People Against Cancer, a grassroots group dedicated to cancer prevention and promotion of alternative therapies, Wiewel was shocked to learn from an article in *The Des Moines Register* that the soil of America's bread basket is so saturated with chemicals that "our clouds are laced with pesticides like atrazine that have actually evaporated out of the ground along with the water, and rain down on us from out of the sky."

And when Wiewel sees clouds, he thinks numbers. "Eight million Americans have cancer right now, with 1.2 million diagnosed just last year," he says. Your odds of contracting cancer are currently one in three and climbing, and cancer now kills one in four in this country. The federally funded National Cancer Institute (NCI) reports that 526,000 Americans died from cancer in 1993.

Wiewel's organization is just one foot soldier in the 24-year War on Cancer, but his own decade of cancer research has led to a stark con-

Excerpted from Mike Weilbacher, "Toxic Shock: The Environment-Cancer Connection," *E/The Environmental Magazine*, June 1995. Reprinted with permission from *E/The Environmental Magazine*, subscription department: PO Box 2047, Marion, OH 43306; telephone: (815) 734-1242. Subscriptions are $20 per year.

viction: "We have permeated our food, our air, our water, and our living environment with poisons and we have little—if any—evidence of their safety."

Dangers Everywhere

No matter how well you've lived over the years, whether you're vegetarian or beef-eater, city-dweller or Eskimo, you live on a polluted planet. Measurable quantities of chloroform, freon and carbon tetrachloride flow from your lungs when you breathe, and your fatty tissue and blood carry trace amounts of the infamous DDT [a pesticide that was banned in the United States in the 1970s] and its breakdown partner DDE. Every man's semen swims with 35 different kinds of PCBs, plus ethers and phenols, and every woman's breast milk boasts a Frankensteinian brew of the pesticides chlordane, dieldrin, lindane and mirex, mixed with some 65 isomers of PCBs and dioxins.

Greenpeace reports that, through activities as diverse as incinerating trash, spraying crops, chlorinating drinking water and bleaching paper, your body is burdened with some 177 different kinds of organochlorines, reactive compounds with carbon-chlorine bonds that include pesticides, dioxins, PCBs, solvents, acids and more. The Environmental Protection Agency's (EPA) reassessment of the dangers of dioxin, the chemical that shuttered Times Beach, Missouri, in 1982 and earlier rained over Vietnam in the defoliant called Agent Orange, calculates that the average American carries some 40 to 60 parts per trillion of dioxin compounds in our tissues, a level of exposure that, while minute, is "very near the levels expected to cause adverse health effects."

Toss into your tissues the heavy metals lead (in food and air), mercury (mostly in fish), cadmium (in food and cigarette smoke), chromium (a by-product of steel production) and arsenic (from pesticides and burning coal). Throw a pinch of radioactive strontium 90 (from nuclear testing) in your bones and iodine 131 (concentrated in milk since Chernobyl) in your thyroid. Shake vigorously . . . and the cancer war has just begun. For while industry has introduced anywhere from 50,000 to 70,000 synthetic chemicals into the environment, the National Research Council has substantive toxicity data available on a meager two percent of the chemicals used in commerce. While some 1,500 new chemicals—plastics, solvents, cleaning agents and reformulated fuels—enter the marketplace annually, underfunded government watchdogs check the toxicity of only about a dozen, or maybe 20. That's it.

We know that 750 million pounds of some 20,000 different pesticidal potions are poured over the American landscape annually, and regulations legally allow for 40 pesticides in carrots, 67 in strawberries and 82 in grapes. A 1992 Food and Drug Agency (FDA) study concluded that the average American shopping trip is laden with some 60 to

80 pesticides, herbicides, rodenticides and fungicides—several of them considered carcinogenic—though, of course, all at "acceptable levels."

A Hidden Health Problem?

John O'Connor, who ran the now-defunct National Toxics Campaign, calls "uncontrolled toxic chemicals and waste perhaps our nation's number one hidden health problem." Jay Feldman, director of the Washington, D.C.–based National Coalition Against the Misuse of Pesticides (NCAMP), has "declared war against environmental contaminants and the legislators who allow the pollution of our bodies to continue." And many environmentalists are demanding that chemicals be considered guilty until proven innocent, not vice versa. In response, a nervous Chemical Manufacturers Association has flooded TV, newspapers and magazines—even environmental ones—with ads touting their stewardship of natural resources and concern for environmental responsibility.

Caught in the crossfire are you and your cells. Is cancer killing us softly with environmental toxics? Or are we, as insists "father of the green revolution" Norman Borlaug, the 1970 Nobel Peace Prize winner and chemical fertilizer proponent, in the "grip of a virulent strain of chemical-phobia" induced by the "pseudo-scientific promoters of toxic terror"?

Losing the War

In a White House ceremony that echoed both John F. Kennedy's space race and Lyndon Johnson's "War on Poverty," Richard Nixon gave Americans a Christmas present in 1971 by signing the National Cancer Act to unleash the "War on Cancer," a crash program to cure cancer by the Bicentennial five years later. The National Cancer Institute, which as of 1995 has missed the deadline by 19 years and counting, has funneled $25 billion into this war—and requested from Congress another $3.6 billion for fiscal year 1995, a whopping 80 percent increase over 1994. What has been the bang for our tax buck?

Dr. Samuel Epstein, a professor of occupational and environmental medicine at the University of Illinois School of Public Health, says, "Cancer rates are escalating to epidemic proportions." The "Big C" grows bigger: It's the number two killer, trailing only heart disease. Epstein's numbers show that since 1950 overall cancer incidence has increased by 44 percent, breast cancer and male colon cancer by 60 percent, and prostate and kidney cancers by 100 percent. Testicular cancer has tripled since 1938, and melanoma, prostate cancer, non-Hodgkin's lymphoma, multiple myeloma and cancers of the brain and liver are all climbing.

Dr. John C. Bailar III of McGill University in Montreal, Canada, has told the President's Cancer Panel (a "joint chiefs" of the Cancer War) that cancer death rates have climbed seven percent between 1975 and

1990—even with breakthroughs in chemotherapy and new imaging techniques that allow us to spot cancerous growths sooner (though a sizeable portion of the increase is attributable to lung cancer mortality from cigarette smokers). He concluded his testimony glumly: "Our decades of war against cancer have been a qualified failure."

The numbers for African-Americans are especially grim: Although the incidence of cancer in blacks is only eight percent higher than in whites, African-Americans die from cancer 35 percent more frequently than do whites. And for children, though survival rates have climbed, the NCI reports that so have childhood cancer rates from acute lymphocytic leukemia and cancers of the brain and nervous system. More than 6,000 children younger than 14 will be diagnosed with cancer in 1995—and the disease is a leading cause of death in kids, second only to accidents.

Epstein estimates that Americans spend "about $110 billion annually on cancer treatment, nearly two percent of our GNP [Gross National Product]." And 10 percent of our total health care bill. The American Hospital Association predicts that, by the year 2000, cancer will replace heart disease as the nation's leading killer.

Lifestyle—or Chemicals?

Popular discussion of cancer lurches from one headline to the next. Last week, it was trans-fatty acids in margarine; this week, the heterocyclic amines produced when we grill chicken and beef on backyard barbecues. At cocktail parties nationwide, we shrug off the latest bad news with a blithe, "Oh, everything causes cancer," and everyone smirks knowingly.

But in cancer circles, there's a stunning dismissal of the impact of chemicals on rising cancer rates. Dr. Clark Heath, the American Cancer Society's chief epidemiologist, speaks for his profession when he characterizes your risk from low-dose chemical exposures as "minuscule. That's not denying," he says, "that trace chemicals do carry a risk, but the popular, lay perception of the risk is greatly exaggerated."

Any epidemiologist will tell you that the horsemen of cancer's apocalypse are smoking and diet, which cause perhaps two-thirds of all cancers. The rest can be blamed on a host of factors: excessive sunbathing promoting skin cancer; occupational exposure, especially among asbestos workers; genetic proclivity to cancer; excessive drinking; and infectious diseases like AIDS.

Environmental toxins are the Rodney Dangerfield of cancer research—they get no respect, and that makes Epstein fume. "The National Cancer Institute is totally silent on the role of toxic chemicals in cancer causation, and the American Cancer Society also trivializes the risks from chemicals."

That's because of the way science conducts its cancer work. The research cathedral rests squarely on twin towers: toxicology tests and epidemiological studies. In a process worked out through decades of convention, a substance undergoes rigorous testing on a variety of animal species to search for carcinogens and toxic levels of exposure.

Next come epidemiological studies. Since science doesn't test carcinogens on unsuspecting human guinea pigs, epidemiologists study large groups of people who have been exposed to measurable concentrations of substances for known periods of time (often workers who've received occupational doses of a substance) and their results confirm, contradict, or lead to the oft-written "more research is needed at this time."

Epidemiological studies present Olympian hurdles, most notably the pulling of single threads from the rich tapestry of lives. The search for cancer pockets around Superfund sites [extremely polluted places marked for government cleanup] and petrochemical factories, for example, has often been inconclusive. A factory neighborhood with a blue-collar or minority population presents a variety of possible cancer-causing factors, like high smoking rates, preference for high-fat, low-fiber diets, and high incidence of drinking. "We saw an association between lung cancers and truck drivers," explains Aaron Blair, chief of NCI's Occupational Studies Section, "and assumed it was from breathing diesel fume exhaust. But sometimes you see an association between A and B because C is lurking in the background. Later, we discovered that most truck drivers smoke; that was the lung cancer risk."

And animal tests carry legendary problems since they are always performed at high doses. "What regulatory agencies are concerned about," says F. Jay Murray, who performed ground-breaking studies on dioxin 20 years ago, "is very low risk, the theoretical one in a million. But if we try to figure what dose causes one cancer in a million individuals, you'd need more than a million rats in a test, and no one can do that. So we test on 50 or 100 rats, use much higher doses, then assume we can draw a straight line down what happens at low doses," what science calls a dose-response curve. "But it's just not that simple."

How Valid Are Laboratory Tests?

Consider three widely repeated criticisms:

One, Elizabeth Whelan, president of the industry-funded American Council on Science and Health, decries the mouse test as "essential to those who seek to terrify us about food additives, pesticides and other trace-element chemicals. The time has come for us to recognize that mouse terrorism poses a serious problem in terms of both maintaining our high standard of living and our good health."

Two, from University of California–Berkeley microbiologist Bruce Ames: "High doses kill cells, causing neighboring cells to divide to help healing. But chronic cell division is a strong risk factor for cancer. The high dose itself causes cancer, and most chemicals pose no risk—zero risk—at low doses. At high dose, fully one half of the natural chemicals we test are carcinogens."

Three, from toxicologist M. Alice Ottoboni, writing in the now-defunct *Garbage* magazine: "Every chemical has some set of exposure conditions under which it is toxic, and conversely, every chemical has some set of exposure conditions in which it is not toxic." She then cites a maxim of toxicology: "The dose makes the poison."

These criticisms infuriate Samuel Epstein. "There is overwhelming agreement by most qualified scientists that if a chemical causes cancer in well-diagnosed animal tests, there is a strong likelihood that it will also cause cancer in exposed humans. Usually, the animal studies are ahead of the human studies." Is there a safe threshold level for a substance? "Nonsense," he insists. "The overwhelming evidence from every single expert is we have no way to set a threshold. One part per billion (ppb) represents quadrillions of trillions of molecules." Since just one molecule of a carcinogenic substance may unlock a cell's DNA and promote the growth of a tumor, the notion of a threshold (i.e. "harmless") level—like the 40 ppb of dioxin residing in your tissues—quickly unravels.

A "Smoking Gun"

What are not compatible are cancer researchers. What was once a war on cancer has degenerated into a war among researchers, vying for headlines, funding, and access to popular opinion. The trial of chemical carcinogens by a jury of doctors, media, industry and environmental groups remains hung until a smoking gun is discovered.

Mary Wolff might have found one.

In a widely discussed, widely embraced and widely derided study, Mary Wolff of the Mount Sinai School of Medicine in New York concluded that women with high blood serum levels of DDE, a metabolic breakdown product of DDT, showed a quadrupled rate of breast cancer. She fears that DDT's molecular structure mimics the hormone estrogen, and elevated estrogen levels may lead to breast cancer. "The data suggest," she explains, "that estrogens exert a cancer-promoting effect and that a diet rich in animal products and fat may increase a woman's risk of breast cancer. Our data suggest that organochlorine residues, and in particular DDE, are strongly associated with breast cancer risk. These observations are important in light of the fact that DDE is a widespread contaminant of animal food products, and that human absorption is related to the ingestion of animal fat."

Though fatty diet has long been known as a leading factor in cancer's climb, science is less certain why. Are fats carcinogenic? Or does a fatty diet rob people of the cancer-killing chemicals of fruits and vegetables? Wolff's study suggests a third, more sinister, possibility: Fat-soluble organochlorines, like DDT, PCBs and dioxin that are transferred from fatty foods to body fat, are a hidden risk factor.

But when a California study failed to replicate Wolff's results, industry press releases—which many newspapers dutifully printed—chirped, "No link between cancer, DDT seen." Not quite true, for the study did discern a weakly positive correlation between breast cancer and DDE levels in African-American and white women. Oddly, a third group, Asian-Americans, showed the reverse: high DDE, low breast cancer. Lump all three together, no correlation. Experts like the American Cancer Society's Clark Heath all too quickly hailed this study as definitive "proof" that Wolff was wrong.

Support for a Pollution Link

Truth is, Wolff's already got a second opinion. In 1994, the New York State Department of Health found that almost 15 percent of the women studied on Long Island who were victims of breast cancer after menopause had lived within one kilometer of a chemical, rubber or plastics plant. Their conclusion: Proximity to such places elevated breast cancer risk by 62 percent. State health commissioner Mark Chassin noted that "if this association proves real, it will be the first time that an environmental risk factor that is avoidable has been identified."

A second smoking gun points at farmers, normally a healthy group with a lower overall cancer risk, perhaps because farmers tend to smoke less and exercise more. But the NCI has uncovered a fatal trend in farmers: Cancers of the lip, skin, prostate and brain, as well as multiple myeloma and non-Hodgkin's lymphoma, are higher than normal. "The very tumors that are excessive in farmers are now increasing and appear to be drifting into the general population," says NCI's Blair, "and we ought to be worried about this."

Devra Lee Davis, a senior advisor within the Department of Health and Human Services, co-authored a study which concluded, "In all age groups, cancer incidence is increasing in the United States." Contrasting current adults with those of a century ago, she found that a white male in his 40s has twice the risk of developing cancer that his grandfather did; a white female has a 50 percent greater probability of all cancers than women of that era, as well as a doubled risk from breast cancer specifically. She thinks that "changes in carcinogenic hazards, in addition to smoking, are likely to have occurred," and recommends environmental toxics as a likely place to start the search. Joe Thornton, who directs Greenpeace USA's anti-toxics campaign, says the "Davis study provides very strongly argued scientific support for what many people have intuitively understood all along—we have a cancer epidemic on our hands, and evidence links it to chemicals and pollution in the ecosystem.". . .

A Call for Research—and Action

For the National Cancer Institute, activists demand wholesale changes. "They put virtually no effort whatsoever into reducing avoidable exposures to carcinogenic chemicals in air, water and food," Epstein avers. Perhaps even the NCI, with its well-established bias for funding diagnosis and treatment—not prevention—is evolving as well. Dr. Kenneth Olden, director of the National Institute of Environmental Health Sciences, a sister agency of the NCI, notes that his agency is co-sponsoring a major study "with the NCI and EPA, a large epidemiological project in Iowa and North Carolina, on the health effects of agricultural chemicals on farm workers, pesticide applicators, and their families." His policy recommendation is elegant, but impossible: "We need to identify agents that cause cancer or any health problem, and get them out of the environment."

Sure, but we've produced 70,000 different chemicals, and understand only a fraction of them. Even dioxin, the most studied chemical in history, and an accidental byproduct of several industrial processes, produces no consensus on either its health effects or removal options. And that's why Greenpeace is demanding removal of all chlorinated hydrocarbons—since we can't afford to study them painstakingly one by one, they argue, we should remove the entire family of 11,000 substances from the environment.

Which brings us back to Frank Wiewel, staring at a pesticide-strewn cloud floating over Iowa's landscape. "We still don't know what acceptable limits are, and we've never studied them in combination," which is how they end up in your tissue, phenol next to ether, DDE floating alongside dieldrin. "If we wait for the proof, we're all dead."

HORMONE-DISRUPTING CHEMICALS MAY BE LINKED TO BREAST CANCER

Orli Belman

Orli Belman, a writer for the television news program *Frontline*, examines the debate about whether exposure to environmental contaminants that mimic or disrupt the action of hormones increases women's risk of breast cancer. Breast cancer is linked to high levels of the female hormone estrogen, Belman explains, so increased exposure to chemicals that act like estrogen might encourage such cancer to grow. Belman describes a study suggesting that exposure to pesticides such as DDT, which can mimic estrogen, may be involved in the unusually high number of breast cancer cases in New York's Long Island. However, Belman also cites unanswered questions about the role of hormone disrupters in breast cancer. Experts agree that the question of these factors' relationship to cancer is far from settled, Belman states.

More women in the United States are diagnosed with breast cancer than any other type of cancer. In 1998 alone, the National Cancer Institute estimates that there will be close to 180,000 new cases and over 40,000 deaths from the disease. And while simply growing older and having a family history of breast cancer are considered major risk factors, these factors only account for about a quarter of breast cancer cases, according to the American Cancer Society. In other words, for about seventy-five percent of all breast cancer cases, there are other forces at work. Some scientists and many in the general public feel that those risk factors could include endocrine disrupters: environmental contaminants that act like hormones.

The hypothesis that certain chemicals have the ability to mimic or block hormones like estrogen and disrupt the body's own hormonal balance has particular resonance for some seeking to explain the high rates of breast cancer. This is because breast cancer, like prostate cancer, is a hormone dependent cancer. Women who start their periods early in life, end them later, have fewer children or have their children later increase their lifetime exposure to the female hormone

From Orli Belman, "Hormones and Breast Cancer." This viewpoint was adapted from an article originally published by *Frontline Online* (www.pbs.org/frontline) and is reprinted with permission.

estrogen. Researchers believe this increased estrogen exposure may put some women at greater risk for developing breast cancer.

Whether or not man-made chemicals that the body thinks are estrogen actually play a role in the incidence of breast cancer remains an unanswered scientific question. But what cannot be disputed is the role that this notion has played in bringing government attention and dollars to the issue of endocrine disruption. Possible links to breast cancer is one reason the Clinton administration has made researching the hypothesis a top environmental priority.

High Risk on Long Island

In the early 1990s, it became apparent that women on Long Island faced a higher risk of breast cancer than women in other parts of New York. According to the New York State Department of Health, from 1980 through 1988 there were 116.14 cases of breast cancer for every 100,000 women in Nassau County. The numbers from Suffolk County were slightly lower at 112.54. These numbers contrasted with 96.3 cases of breast cancer per every 100,000 women statewide. Studies looking into why the rates were higher in Nassau and Suffolk counties found that many women there had some known risk factors for the disease. These included being affluent, Jewish, postponing childbirth until later in life, and the absence of breastfeeding. Women on Long Island were outraged that no one was looking into environmental causes of their disease.

Out of their anger, they formed the group "One-in-Nine: The Long Island Breast Cancer Action Coalition" in 1990. The group took its name from what the American Cancer Society says are a woman's chances of contracting the disease if she lives to be 85 years old. Just a few weeks later the National Breast Cancer Coalition was formed and women with breast cancer became a political force. Members of One-in-Nine met with and persuaded Senator Alfonse D'Amato (R-NY) to help them secure more funding for disease research. Their efforts paid off. In 1993, D'Amato, with the help of Senator Tom Harkin (D-IA), was able to multiply a $25 million line in the Department of Defense budget to $210 million for breast cancer research.

That same year, Congress directed the National Cancer Institute to begin a study looking at environmental factors and breast cancer in Long Island and two other counties in the Northeast. Known as the Long Island Breast Cancer Study Project, it is actually a collection of over ten different studies being conducted at research institutions throughout the Northeast. The project's major study is being headed by Marilie Gammon at Columbia University. Gammon and her colleagues are trying to determine if the pesticide DDT contributes to breast cancer. Results from this as well as the other studies are expected in the next few years. All told, the National Cancer Institute estimates that it is spending at least $20 million on the research.

Also in 1993, Mary Wolff, an associate professor at Mount Sinai Medical Center in New York, authored a paper indicating that exposure to certain chemicals may indeed play a role in the disease. Wolff's study, published in the *Journal of the National Cancer Institute*, found that women who had high blood levels of DDE, a DDT breakdown product, had a much greater risk of developing breast cancer—four times higher than women with low levels of DDE. DDT, an insecticide banned in the US in the 1970s, can mimic the hormone estrogen and is a known endocrine disrupter. It was used heavily on Long Island earlier in the twentieth century.

Wolff looked at blood samples from 58 women in New York who developed breast cancer and compared them with 171 women who didn't have cancer. In addition to DDT, Wolff looked at another hormone disrupting contaminant: a class of banned chemicals known as PCBs, which were used to insulate electrical transformers. While the PCB levels were slightly higher in women with breast cancer, the elevated levels were determined to be statistically insignificant. Wolff's 1993 study was small, but it got a huge response from activists, the media, and politicians. For the women in Long Island, it was new evidence that the environment may have played a role in their cancers.

Before it became a suburban mecca, Long Island was farmland. In the 1940s it was the nation's largest potato growing region and home to a US Department of Agriculture (USDA) sponsored program to quarantine a pesky potato-eating worm called the golden nematode. Millions of gallons of pesticides, including DDT, were poured into area fields.

After Wolff's study came out, Long Island's newspaper *Newsday* ran a series of stories on breast cancer and the island. The paper looked into the history of chemical use in the area—pesticides like aldicarb, chlordane, types of dichloroprane and others. The paper reported that many of these chemicals had not been tested for their abilities to mimic hormones, and that the government did not require this sort of screening.

Within days of the *Newsday* stories about Long Island, politicians in Washington were calling for change. In the House of Representatives, Henry Waxman (D-CA), then the head of the subcommittee on Health and the Environment, announced he would work to pass legislation requiring that all pesticides be screened for their ability to mimic estrogen. Senator D'Amato vowed to do the same. In 1996 President Bill Clinton signed the Food Quality Protection Act, which included their requirement that the Environmental Protection Agency (EPA) develop a way to screen chemicals for estrogenicity by the end of 1998.

Unanswered Questions

Since Mary Wolff's 1993 study, more papers have come out on the subject. Ironically, a study co-authored by Wolff herself downplayed

DDT's and PCBs' connections to breast cancer. The study, published in the *New England Journal of Medicine* in October of 1997, analyzed frozen blood samples taken from nurses in 1989 and 1990. Blood samples from 240 nurses who subsequently developed cancer were compared with control samples from nurses without cancer. The results showed that the women with cancer did not have higher levels of DDT breakdown products or PCBs in their blood.

To confuse matters more, other scientists have come forward to say that certain PCBs, breakdown products of DDT, and other known toxins like dioxin might actually prevent breast cancer. These chemicals can act as anti-estrogens, which have the ability to protect against the disease. Dr. Steve Safe of Texas A&M asserted this in an editorial published in the same issue of the *New England Journal of Medicine* as Wolff's more recent study.

But some researchers say there are questions about whether the current studies have focused on the correct timing of a woman's exposure to environmental estrogens. Many activists and researchers, including Wolff herself, have noted that it may not be the amount of chemicals present in a woman's body at the time she gets cancer that is important, but rather her levels of exposure when her breasts are just developing at puberty. Others suggest it may even be fetal exposure in the womb that is important. In addition, there are countless chemicals in addition to DDT and PCBs that have not yet been tested for their links to breast cancer.

Experts agree that the issue is far from resolved, nor should it be. A spokeswoman from the American Cancer Society said that even though there isn't yet any significant evidence to indicate that estrogenic chemicals are causing breast cancer, the matter needs to be studied further. Because breast cancer is clearly a disease based on estrogen exposure, she stressed that all types of potential exposure—natural and man-made—should be studied.

REDUCING ENVIRONMENTAL CANCER RISK

Sandra Steingraber, interviewed by *Multinational Monitor*

The following selection consists of an interview that the magazine *Multinational Monitor* conducted with Sandra Steingraber, a scientist and the author of *Living Downstream: An Ecologist Looks at Cancer and the Environment.* Steingraber presents evidence that exposure to toxic chemicals in the environment leads to cancer. She also relates her personal experience with bladder cancer, which she believes may have been caused by high levels of a carcinogenic dry-cleaning chemical in the drinking water of her hometown. Finally, Steingraber offers suggestions for reducing the risk of cancer triggered by chemical carcinogens, including the substitution of nontoxic alternatives in industry and agriculture. *Multinational Monitor* is a monthly periodical that tracks corporate activities, including the export of hazardous substances and environmental degradation.

Multinational Monitor: *What made you decide to write* Living Downstream?

Sandra Steingraber: I was searching around for a book like this and couldn't find it. The closest to it is a book that Dr. Samuel Epstein wrote in the mid-1970s, *The Politics of Cancer.* And even that wasn't exactly what I was looking for. I was looking for a close examination of all of the lines of evidence linking cancer and the environment. I wanted to look at all of the evidence and ask, "How strong is all of the evidence? Where are the data gaps? Do we have enough information now to act on what we already know?" Instead, the kind of commentary I got back from cancer researchers was, "The evidence is preliminary, it is a possibility, but nobody really knows." With these answers, I became more and more frustrated. We didn't know and we couldn't act because nobody had pulled all the data together in one place so we could sit back and just look at it. When I realized that there was no such book out there, I decided to write it myself.

Reprinted from "Living Downstream," an interview with Sandra Steingraber, *Multinational Monitor*, March 1998, with permission of *Multinational Monitor*.

Strong Evidence for Environmental Triggers

And what did you find?

The evidence we have is very strong. The environment is playing a significant role in our current burden of cancer. There is no one study that I could hold up and say, "Here is the absolute proof of a profound link between rising rates of toxics and rising rates of cancer." But there are many studies from various disciplines that make the point. There are studies of wildlife showing that wildlife get cancer in very contaminated areas of the United States. There are studies from the cancer registries showing rising rates of cancer in all age groups—childhood cancers, testicular cancers. We can't explain these cancers by the aging of the population. We can't explain the cancers' increase by better detection methods. I looked at the molecular biological data, which provides the smoking gun evidence. Molecular biologists have gotten better at determining which carcinogens cause which cancers. You can actually go into somebody's cells and determine which carcinogen the person has been exposed to.

They can look at the cancer cells of a human being and determine which carcinogen caused the cancer?

Not for every chemical and not for every cancer, but certainly for some. When you combine this evidence with the molecular animal data and with the data from cancer registries, you end up with a strong link between these toxics and the increase in cancer.

We'll never have what my detractors might call absolute proof. First, absolute proof in science is very rare. Second, it would require controlled human studies. That is, having two populations and exposing one human group to known amounts of certain chemicals and then watching the results. We will never do that. So, we will always have to infer from humans that have been inadvertently exposed to unknown amounts of chemicals for unknown amounts of time, from lab animal studies, from wildlife studies and from cells growing in a petri dish. We will have to do the best we can and use our judgment.

I argue in *Living Downstream* that more and better data should never be a substitute for good judgment. At some point, there is enough information to act in a precautionary manner to protect human health.

A Personal Motivation

You have cancer, is that right?

Yes. I had bladder cancer.

How old were you when you learned of this?

I was 20. I'm now 38.

How are you doing?

I never know how to answer that. I've had good news over the years, I've had bad news over the years. Bladder cancer, like so many other cancers, is the kind of cancer that can come back years or even decades later. I have never declared myself cured. On the other hand, I don't live my life waiting for the other shoe to drop. Like so many cancer patients, I feel it is not only behind me, but perhaps in front of me. I see it all around me, in good friends who have had recurrences years later.

Do you believe the environment caused your cancer?

As a biologist, I can't answer that. There is no way you can look at one individual and assign a cause. We know that cancer is a multi-causal disease. I've had a microscope since I was nine years old. I've been a biologist for a long time. When I learned that I had this unusual cancer, I went to the biological literature to find out who gets this cancer and what we know about its causes.

It turns out that bladder cancer is the classic environmental cancer. The evidence on bladder cancer and its relationship to environmental contaminants is stronger than most diseases. Exposure to contaminants in tap water is a pattern I found over and over again in human studies that looked at whole populations.

That gave me grounds years later to go back to my hometown—Pekin, Illinois—and become a kind of environmental detective there. Pekin is just downstream from Peoria.

Tracing the Cause

You mentioned that molecular biologists now can go and look at a person's cancer and determine what carcinogen caused it. Did they do that for you?

No. You can't walk into a doctor's office and ask for these tests. They are part of research protocols. Between doctor and patient, the issue of causality is almost never discussed.

Why is there this lack of curiosity on the part of the medical community about the causes of cancer? Part of the answer to that is simply that doctors don't need to know the cause of the disease in order to treat it. You can have your tumor successfully treated by a whole variety of methods without the doctor knowing anything about what might have triggered it. On the other hand, I do believe the medical community has a responsibility to get curious about these things and ask these questions. If they don't, they may be returning their patients to a very toxic environment where they may be exposed to some of the very same carcinogens that caused the cancers in the first place—whether it's a workplace or home environment.

What are your suspicions as to the causes of your cancer?

The first half of *Living Downstream* is my best attempt as a biologist to outline all the lines of evidence linking cancer to the environment. The second half of the book, which is interwoven in and out of the first science-based part of the book, is my own story about growing up in Pekin, my cancer and the cancer in my family. My family is an adopted family, so we don't share chromosomes in common, but we do share an environment. It also tells the story of my return to my hometown and my use of the right-to-know laws that give us access to information about what toxic emissions industry is putting into our environment, air, water and soil. I also filed some Freedom of Information Act requests and uncovered the presence of dry cleaning fluids in my hometown drinking water wells.

A Human Rights Issue

Dry cleaning fluids are chemicals with suspected links to bladder cancer. Do I think that's what caused my cancer? I don't know. It is like asking which straw broke the camel's back. We know that you need about eight to 10 mutations to a single cell before that cell is placed definitively on the pathway to tumor formation. One of the straws in that heap on your back might be from the environment, another might be from genes that you inherited, another might be from a lifestyle choice like smoking.

But it seems to me that no matter how large or small the burden is from the environment, it is a human rights issue. Unlike lifestyle choices, those are risks that we have not consented to. Unlike hereditary contributing factors, we can do many things about toxics in the environment. There is nothing we can do about our ancestors. Cancer genes play a role in maybe 5 to at most 10 percent of all cancers. That 5 or 10 percent of the puzzle we can do nothing about.

All of that logically argues for looking at the environment as a place to begin a meaningful program of cancer prevention.

How do we know that cancer genes only cause 10 percent of the problem?

My citations for this are from the cancer geneticists who are doing the research. When they isolate and identify one of these cancer genes, the most famous being the breast cancer gene (BRCA-1), there is a way that they can trace the gene back in certain families. They can look at how the pattern of inheritance flows through families. And then they can do some random testing to see what percent of the general population might carry this gene. In the case of BRCA-1, maybe 2 to 5 percent of breast cancers might be attributable to that cancer gene. There are other genes that seem to play a role in things like colon cancer. When you add it all together, it appears that at most 10 percent of all cancers are attributable to cancer genes.

Lifestyle Choices or Environmental Poisons?

Does that mean that 90 percent of cancers are caused by lifestyle and toxics in the environment?

Yes, but distinguishing between the two is where the real argument begins.

We know for a fact that 90 to 95 percent of those of us who contract cancer are born with a perfectly healthy set of genes to which something bad happens during our lifetimes. Any one cancer might be caused both by mutations from lifestyle and by mutations from the environment. And you cannot always untwist these two variables from each other—they are not independent of each other.

Consider high-fat diet, which has been implicated as a classic lifestyle risk factor in several big-ticket malignancies. Why is high-fat diet associated with several cancers? Of all the foodstuffs, animal fat is the substance in our diet that is the most heavily contaminated with dioxins as well as very persistent pesticides that bioaccumulate as you move up the food chain. The fatty portion of the meat, milk or eggs is what is carrying the huge load.

So, on the one hand, fat is a lifestyle choice, but on the other hand, it is also a vehicle for carrying fat-soluble carcinogens into our bodies.

If we weaned U.S. agriculture from its dependency on pesticides and stopped incinerating plastic waste, which is a major source of dioxin production, we could get these chemicals out of animal fat and people could choose to eat what they want to eat. Perhaps a high-fat diet would not carry such a cancer risk.

Geographical Patterns

How geographically concentrated is cancer in the United States?

It depends on what cancer you are looking at. I spend one chapter looking at cancer maps. For cancers like bladder, colon and breast cancer, on a map, you would light up in red an area from Maine down to Washington, D.C. and then you would also light up in red the area all along the Great Lakes Basin. Those of course are the two areas of the United States that are the most heavily industrialized.

But there are other cancers that show very different patterns. One of them is non-Hodgkins lymphoma. It is one of the more swiftly rising cancers right now. It has tripled in incidence rate over the past 50 years. It has no known lifestyle risk factors. It has no known hereditary risk factors. And it is rising the fastest. It is the cancer that killed Jackie Kennedy Onassis, so it is getting more attention now.

If you looked at the mortality map of non-Hodgkins lymphoma, you would light up in red the central part of the United States—the Midwest and Great Plains area. That is the part of the country where we use pesticides in agriculture most intensively. That correlation does not necessarily indicate cause, but it certainly does give us grounds for further inquiry.

When you look more closely at the possibility that pesticides are playing a role in non-Hodgkins lymphoma, you find some interesting studies. For example, dogs whose owners regularly use certain kinds of weed killers have twice the rate of canine non-Hodgkins lymphoma than dogs whose owners don't use these lawn chemicals. If you look by occupation at who gets non-Hodgkins, you find that farmers, golf course supervisors and Vietnam Vets exposed to Agent Orange have higher rates of non-Hodgkins than folks in the general population. Those are all occupations that have exposure to pesticides.

In the molecular biological literature, there are studies by Dr. Vincent Garry at the University of Minnesota about what kinds of mutations pesticide exposure causes. He looked at a population of pesticide applicators and found they had a very unusual mutation in one of the middle chromosomes. The chromosome actually breaks off, flips upside down and reattaches itself. It is called a chromosome inversion. The only other population besides pesticide applicators where he has seen that kind of mutation in high frequency are non-Hodgkin lymphoma patients.

All of the evidence—the occupational literature, the cancer maps, the cancer registry data, animal studies, and studies from inside humans themselves—is pointing to certain pesticides playing some kind of role in the increase of certain cancers.

But the idea that genes cause cancer is grabbing more of the media spotlight.

It has been. But I believe we are in the middle of a sea change. When you read the media reports on the inheritance of cancer genes, you eventually come to a paragraph explaining that this applies only to a tiny minority of cancers. Certainly, the identification of heritable cancer genes does not offer hope for prevention. Other than the remote possibility of gene therapy, the most that the discovery of these so-called cancer genes offers us is the possibility for marketing and commodifying a test that would allow you to know whether you carry one of the genes that would make you susceptible. That has raised the question of what value is that knowledge if there is nothing you can do about it. The promise and excitement of that has waned a bit, as it should.

Now we have two powerful databases: the Toxic Release Inventory [which includes extensive information data on industry pollution emissions] and the cancer registries, which measure the incidence of cancer in every county of every state. Together, they give us the ability to ask questions and get some answers as to whether or not there are relationships between toxic emissions and cancer rates. So, we are seeing a shift in focus in the medical research community. Perhaps the media will be the last to come on board. But I've seen a shift in reporting in the last year or two, with more emphasis on the environment.

Criticism and Response

What were the reviews like for Living Downstream?

Other than the *New England Journal of Medicine*, they have all been very positive. I was very gratified. The *Chicago Tribune*, *Washington Post*, Portland *Oregonian* and others—they all gave it great reviews. I was disappointed that the *New York Times* did not review the book.

Who reviewed the book for the New England Journal of Medicine?

Dr. Jerry Berke. His review ran on November 20, 1997.

What did he say?

It was a scathing review. It accused me of emotionalism, bias and exaggeration. He said I was speaking as a victim. He launched a broadside against environmentalists in general. He talked about the work product of environmentalists being controversy. He said environmentalists scare people in order to raise money for their organizations.

What was your response to the review?

Sometime in November, I was in Austin, Texas, and heard that the *New England Journal* had reviewed my book and it was not favorable. Somebody read it to me over the phone and I felt terribly sad and depressed. But I thought there was nothing I could do except shrug it off and go on. I flew from Austin to Vermont. I was giving a lecture at the University of Vermont hospital when someone asked me my response to the *New England Journal* review. And I assumed they meant the content of the review. And they asked if I knew about the controversy that had been generated by the review. They told me that in fact the reviewer was a senior official at the W.R. Grace chemical company. I remember just stopping in my tracks and my mouth just fell open for a moment. I think of the *New England Journal* as a cut above the other journals.

Berke signed his name to the review with a home address and didn't reveal that he was with Grace.

Right. That is very unusual in the *New England Journal*. You usually provide an institutional affiliation. In fact, he is director of toxicology at W.R. Grace.

Approaches to Prevention

What are the implications of focusing on prevention of environmental causes of cancer? Does it mean shutting down the petrochemical industry?

It means moving toward non-toxic alternatives for chemical carcinogens. At the end of the book, I stake out a philosophical argument about the use of chemical carcinogens and our dependence on them in our economy. I make comparisons with slavery. At one point our economy was dependent on slave labor, and at some point, we had to abolish the institution completely—not reform it, not regulate it, but simply abolish it.

So, are you saying abolish the petrochemical industry?

No. We need to eliminate chemicals that have been linked to cancer and immediately move to find non-toxic substitutes.

What would be an example?

The dry cleaning industry. I feel particularly passionate about this one, since I grew up drinking dry cleaning fluids myself. I feel as if I have an intimate relationship with this particular solvent—perchloroethylene (perc).

Perc is classified as a probable human carcinogen. Eighty percent of the production of perc in the United States is used for dry cleaning clothes. Perc is found in drinking water of communities around the country, it is in the bodies of fresh water fish, it is in ambient air. We are contaminating the world with a chemical that has been strongly linked to human cancer in order to clean our clothes.

I spend most of my time in Boston, where we have a wet cleaner, which relies on soap and water to wash wools and silks. But they have re-engineered washing machines that have computerized controls to control humidity and agitation. It's not like you or I throwing our clothes in the washing machine. And all of my clothes come back looking great. And I know that no one is going to get cancer from cleaning my clothes.

Are you convinced that we can determine which synthetic chemicals are carcinogenic and which are not?

Sure. Science is a powerful tool. There are many chemicals on the market now that have never been tested. That overwhelms us. We should reverse the burden of proof. Industry must be required to demonstrate to us that the chemicals are safe before they are allowed onto the market. Now, the public has to prove that we are being harmed by the chemical.

We don't know what impact reversing the burden of proof will have on the petrochemical industry. Does it eliminate all plastics? Does it shut down the industry?

We can't continue in the direction we are going. It is essentially premeditated murder. We don't know who the victims are, but we know that when you release certain chemicals into the environment, a certain number of people are going to get cancer and die because of that. That is just wrong. When we decided to eliminate slavery, we didn't know the implications to society and to the economy.

Animal Tests Exaggerate Risks from Chemicals

Elizabeth M. Whelan

> To determine whether an environmental factor is a carcinogen, scientists usually expose laboratory animals such as mice or rats to it and wait to see whether the animals develop cancer. In the following selection, Elizabeth M. Whelan, president of New York's Council on Science and Health, argues that these animal tests are frequently inaccurate. For instance, she says, the animals are often given such large doses of test substances that they may develop cancer because of the toxic effects of the sheer quantity of material fed to them. Whelan decries environmental groups' publicizing of animal test results to obtain the restriction or banning of pesticides and other useful chemicals, a tactic she calls "mouse terrorism." Whelan, who has a doctorate in public health, is the author of *Toxic Terror* and *Panic in the Pantry*.

Most Americans do not realize the extent to which rodents negatively influence our priorities when it comes to public-health expenditures. Spending on environmental regulations is affected along with the cost of goods and services, insurance premiums, employment opportunities and federal taxes. Mice and rats are interfering with our nation's pursuit of an improved standard of living and longer, healthier lives.

"Mouse Terrorism"

If prodded, you might recall something about the Food and Drug Administration (FDA) wanting to ban the sweeteners cyclamate and saccharin because they caused cancer in rodents. Or you may remember the 1989 Natural Resources Defense Council/*60 Minutes* debacle which caused parents around the nation to discard apple products to avoid Alar, a chemical purported to cause cancer.

But the phenomenon I call "mouse terrorism"—defined as a knee-jerk extrapolation from a high-dose animal study to a declaration of human cancer risk no matter how low human exposure—influences a vast array of federal and local regulations.

Abridged from Elizabeth M. Whelan, "Stop Banning Products at the Drop of a Rat," *Insight*, December 12, 1994. Reprinted with permission from *Insight* magazine. Copyright 1998 News World Communications, Inc. All rights reserved.

Using mouse terrorism, self-appointed "environmentalists" and their allies in regulatory agencies can ban a product or technology no matter what the cost involved and no matter how beneficial the technology compared to the minuscule risk. Their campaigns have been successful in dramatically inflating local, state and federal budgets to underwrite what is, in effect, a far-reaching, taxpayer-supported, chemical witch hunt.

Reconsidering Animal Tests

Because of the enormous costs engendered by mouse terrorism and the clear implications for our country's economic future and health, the time is long overdue to consider the origins and major premises of the mouse-to-man extrapolation. The time has come for us to consider that mouse terrorism and policies that require chemicals to be banned literally "at the drop of a rat" pose a serious problem. Could we, for example, by elevating rodent testing to its current unchallengeable level, be reducing our food supply (by banning pesticides), raising taxes (to pay for the crusade against trace levels of chemicals) and siphoning money from more worthwhile avenues of medical research?

Animals have long been used as surrogates for humans in evaluating safety issues. But it was not until the late 1950s that researchers began to examine the possibility that cancer had its origins in environmental—or external—factors, rather than in differences in genetic susceptibility. It seemed a promising assumption that if carcinogens could be identified and human exposure limited, the cancer toll could be reduced.

Some scientists and policymakers during the 1950s and 1960s limited their definition of "environment" almost exclusively to "chemicals." Overwhelmingly, scientists today define "environmental causes of cancer" not as trace chemical exposures but as lifestyle factors such as smoking. Back then, however, those who accepted the assumptions that carcinogens were only of synthetic origin and that dose was not a relevant factor set out to test a variety of industrial chemicals for animal carcinogenicity.

Rats Instead of People

Intuition would dictate that if you want to know whether something causes cancer in humans, you should study people, not rats. And through epidemiology, human disease patterns are studied to detect factors that affect cancer risk. However, epidemiology suffers from several inherent limitations: First, it is difficult to observe small effects with statistical confidence by epidemiological means. Second, it frequently is difficult to find groups of people who have never been exposed to a factor under study (the so-called zero-exposure control group).

Thus, a traditional alternative (or supplement) to epidemiology is the animal test. Rats and mice generally are used because they are less expensive to maintain than other mammals. A standard test has been developed in which animals are exposed to a test substance at a very high dose to maximize the chance of detecting cancers during the animal's relatively short life span. The whole procedure for testing and evaluation of one chemical takes three or more years to complete—at about $1,500 per animal or $1 million for a typical test.

Limitations of Animal Tests

Large doses of the test chemical are used to detect the effects of even a weak carcinogen. The maximum-tolerated dose, or MTD, is the largest estimated dose that animals can tolerate without experiencing considerable (10 percent) weight loss compared to controls. These MTDs usually are orders of magnitude—thousands or millions of times—above the dose humans encounter.

While using the MTD is standard practice, this procedure is much in question. The central issue is whether dose levels that are nearly toxic in and of themselves can predispose an animal to develop cancer. It is very possible that physiological events occur in such stressed animals that would not occur at the much lower doses typical of human exposure. Thus, the lack of recognition of the sound toxicological principle "the dose makes the poison" seriously jeopardizes the scientific validity of animal cancer testing.

But there are still more limitations. In designing animal carcinogen studies, scientists often maximize the chance of "positive" results by choosing species or strains of animals most likely to respond to the chemicals being studied. Furthermore, we now know that animal carcinogens are numerous rather than few. We also know that many naturally occurring substances cause cancers in laboratory animals, and with more natural products tested, it becomes increasingly apparent that Mother Nature's own foods are full of animal carcinogens. For example, chemicals in edible mushrooms (hydrazines), spices (safrole), parsley (psoralens) and bread (ethyl carbamate) have produced cancers in laboratory animals. Bruce Ames, a leading biochemist from the University of California at Berkeley, asserts that so many plant toxins are carcinogenic that synthetic chemical carcinogens virtually can be ignored as a source of human carcinogenic exposure.

Regulatory Overreaction

Even more important than these scientific limitations and inconsistencies is the unscientific and unreasonable manner in which the tests are applied in the regulatory arena. The first major regulatory application of the mouse-to-man premise came in 1958 with passage of the Delaney Clause, which banned the use of any food chemicals that when ingested caused cancer, no matter what the dose. [This law was repealed in the 1990s.]

The first public impact of the Delaney Clause—indeed what might be considered the debut of mouse terrorism—occurred in November 1959. Just 15 days before Thanksgiving, the Secretary of Health, Education and Welfare announced that the nation's cranberry crop was contaminated by trace levels of a weed killer which, at high doses, caused cancer in laboratory rats. Panic ensued, and hundreds of millions of dollars worth of wholesome cranberry products were destroyed. Most Americans had Thanksgiving dinner without the sauce!

The Dose Makes the Poison

Comparing Animal and Human Doses of Selected Chemicals

Chemical	Experimental Daily Dose (percentage of dietary intake)	Equivalent Human Intake
Cyclamates	5%	**240 times** or 522 12 oz. bottles of soda *daily*
Saccharin	7.5%	**500 times** the typical *daily* consumption of sweeteners
DES	1 treatment*	5 million pounds of treated beef liver eaten over 50 years
Safrole	0.5%	613 12 oz. bottles of root beer *daily* over a lifetime
Alar (d)	1%	28,000 pounds of apples *daily* for 10 years

*The experimental dose in this case refers to the clinical DES dose given to women, not an animal dose.

Source: The American Council on Science and Health.

The great cranberry scare was the first of a series of incidents triggered by anxiety about the effects of chemicals which at megadoses caused cancer in rodents. In subsequent years, the artificial sweeteners cyclamate and saccharin, Red Dye No. 2, nitrites and the grain fumigant EDB all were labeled carcinogens on the basis of animal studies. In the spring of 1989, Americans developed cancer phobia when actress-turned-toxicologist Meryl Streep told the nation that the chemical Alar, a growth regulator used on apples, "causes cancer." The evidence, again, was from one rodent test. . . .

Does Animal Cancer Equal Human Cancer?

The essence of mouse terrorism is the assumption that one study that identifies a chemical as carcinogenic in one species at only the highest dose is sufficient to justify the total elimination of that chemical from the human environment—no matter what the cost, no matter what the lost benefit to society, no matter whether lower toxicity substitutes exist or what potential new health risk might be introduced instead.

However, there are many reasons to be skeptical about extrapolating from experiments performed under extreme conditions on animals to humans. This is not to say that animal testing is not useful or necessary. Testing is necessary, but we must reject the doomsayer's simplification that "a mouse is a little man" and critically assess the results of animal experiments.

To date, all but one of the chemicals that causes cancer in humans also causes cancer in animals. The exception is arsenic. Such good agreement between human carcinogenicity and animal test results suggests that the reverse correlation should be equally predictive. However, this assertion does not appear to be correct.

True, seven chemicals (including aflatoxin, mustard gas and vinyl chloride) first found to be animal carcinogens in one or more species later were discovered to be human carcinogens. But there are hundreds of chemicals classified as carcinogens in at least one animal test for which it has not been possible to establish that the substance also causes human cancer. These include DDT and saccharin, just to name two. Often epidemiological studies show that populations exposed to these chemicals have much less cancer than would be expected if the animal studies were correct. For example, studies of diabetics who have an unusually high lifetime intake of saccharin show no cancer increase that could be linked with the sweetener.

Insufficient evidence exists to argue persuasively that animal cancer tests as conducted and evaluated confidently can predict whether a given substance will cause human cancer. This situation is unfortunate because regulatory officials suggest that they are left with little choice but to resolve uncertainties by assuming the worst. Four extreme assumptions arising from this orientation include: using the MTD so as not to miss "weak" carcinogens; using the most susceptible species of rodent as the basis for inferring human risk even when negative results in other-test animals abound; ignoring decades of safe human use or other negative evidence; and ignoring the level of human exposure which is generally hundreds to thousands of times less than that of animals in laboratory studies. The compounded impact of these choices biases the analysis of animal tests.

Degrees of Hazard

If animal tests across several species produce similar results, then one reasonably could argue that the substance under study is affecting a basic aspect of metabolism; hence, the substance is likely to pose a human hazard as well—if the dose is high enough. Some carcinogens do, in fact, show such behavior. Asbestos causes cancer in mice, rats, hamsters and rabbits, and DES [diethylstilbesterol, a synthetic hormone] is carcinogenic in mice, rats, hamsters, frogs and squirrel monkeys. It is no surprise that these substances also are human carcinogens.

While aflatoxin, a naturally occurring fungal metabolite, is a carcinogen in mice, rats, fish, donkeys, turkeys, marmosets, tree shrews and monkeys, many chemicals test as carcinogens in one species but not in others. For example, saccharin was designated as a carcinogen although it caused tumors only in one species of several tested, in one sex at exaggerated doses in an unusual study design—and the tumors produced were detectable only under the microscope after the animals had died of other causes. Clearly there is a world of difference between the degree of hazard of these two substances. For aflatoxin, traditional animal cancer tests produce clear evidence of carcinogenicity, whereas only exaggerations in the test protocol produced a carcinogenic response for saccharin after many negative animal studies.

Animal tests can be valuable in assessing possible human cancer risk when interpreted with intelligence and discrimination. The main problem in current animal cancer-test interpretation is the policy that obscures the very large differences in the degree of risk that animal tests demonstrate.

Revising Regulatory Policy

The wide range of potential hazard means that under conditions where most animal studies show no ill effects, one study shouldn't necessitate drastic regulatory action. Under conditions where most of the animal data indicates a carcinogenic effect, animal test data alone should constitute a sound basis for setting conservative limits on human exposure or in rare circumstances banning a substance. A chemical should be regulated more conservatively if the material causes cancer in two or more animal species; if it causes highly lethal tumors or types of tumors that do not occur spontaneously in that animal species; if the tumors appear after a short latency period; and if the substance causes cancer at doses similar to or lower than the expected levels of human exposure. Then the chemical should be viewed with great concern, and human exposure should be avoided or reduced to the lowest practical level.

Based on such criteria, aflatoxin certainly should be regulated much more strictly than saccharin, but in fact just the opposite is the case! Current food-safety policy regulates substances not on the degree of risk they pose, but according to how and why they are present in food. Because aflatoxin is a naturally occurring substance, the FDA sets acceptable tolerance levels for it. But because saccharin is a man-made food additive, the Delaney Clause required that it not be added to the nation's food supply. Only a special act of Congress in response to overwhelming public demand has, for the time being, delayed the saccharin ban.

When properly understood and applied, animal cancer studies can be useful for evaluating human cancer risk. But the current policy fails to distinguish real risks from trivial ones. It leads to lumping major human health hazards with minute, hypothetical ones. This results in the inability of regulatory agencies to set sensible priorities and formulate wise policies to protect the nation's health.

A New Way to Evaluate Environmental Cancer Risks

Mark Caldwell

Mark Caldwell describes a new form of epidemiology (the study of how a disease spreads through human communities) that may identify cancer-causing factors in the environment more accurately than the animal tests currently used. This new method of study, Caldwell explains, is called molecular epidemiology because it identifies changes that occur in DNA and other molecules in human cells after those cells are exposed to carcinogens. Caldwell writes that cancer risk from exposure to particular carcinogens differs among ethnic groups and even among individuals, and he predicts that molecular epidemiology will eventually help doctors calculate that risk. Caldwell is a professor of English at Fordham University in the Bronx, New York, and the author of *The Last Crusade: The War on Consumption 1862–1954*.

Cancer is terrible enough—still resisting cure 25 years after President Richard Nixon declared war on it, often intractably painful, and lamentably frequent. In 1994 the United States recorded 538,000 deaths from cancer, more than a fifth of the nation's total. Yet bad as it is clinically, the fear it inspires magnifies its agony. We can't trace cancer to any single agent or fateful event. It claws its way into existence out of the billions of complex interactions that make up our cellular biochemistry; its causes, as a decades-old drumbeat of research demonstrates, are myriad. Some are inherited—like the gene called BRCA-1, whose malfunction appears to be a component in many cases of breast cancer. But many are environmental and hence presumably avoidable: asbestos, infamously; tobacco; air pollution; a diet low in vegetables and fruits; alcohol; the ultraviolet radiation in sunlight.

If we could count out the dangers on the fingers of one or two or even a dozen hands, we might consider ourselves forearmed. But as researchers screen more and more substances, a dizzying number emerge from the lab festooned with skull and crossbones. Peanut butter, mustard, mushrooms, all-natural root beer—they've all been found to contain at least trace amounts of known carcinogens. So

Reprinted from Mark Caldwell, "Beyond the Lab Rat," *Discover*, May 1996, by permission of *Discover* magazine, ©1996.

long has the list of possible carcinogens become that a certain cynicism has set in. Are you really courting malignancy every time you crunch a slice of bacon or take in a deep draft of your mobile home's formaldehyde-laden air? Is life itself the ur [original]-carcinogen?

Evaluating Carcinogens

On the face of it, there's no good reason to flout the warnings. The animal experiments traditionally used to measure toxicity are eminently sensible. Researchers dose a population of laboratory-bred rats or mice with a suspect substance for an extended period of time, then measure the number of tumors that appear against a control population of genetically similar rodents that haven't been given the test chemical. If the exposed animals show a significant rise in malignancies, the implication seems clear: you've found a carcinogen.

Much of the virtue of this system lies in its simplicity. Lab animals are bred for genetic uniformity. Unlike people, they live uncomplicated lives. They haven't eaten thousands of foods, come into contact with hundreds of chemicals, breathed dozens of atmospheres. You can subject them to carefully designed and tightly controlled experiments, dosing them with a suspected carcinogen while shielding them from exposure to other substances that might confuse your results. If they develop a telltale symptom in response to your experiment, you can be reasonably confident that it's not the result of some long-ago exposure you can't recover or even imagine. Trying to monitor disease in large human populations, by contrast, is far messier. Suppose a thousand people contract cancer in a city blanketed by carcinogen-laden smog. You might plausibly infer that their illnesses originated in the air—but you can never be absolutely sure. Ten, 100, or 950 of the cases might have come from some hidden cause you've overlooked: a quirk of local diet or a forgotten lump of plutonium in the bus station basement.

Flaws in Animal Tests

Nevertheless, when it comes to assessing cancer risk, some scientists aren't happy relying exclusively on rodents. First of all, rats and mice, while they share with us humans our mammaldom, are far away from us genetically. Some of the strains often used in experiments are naturally more prone to tumors than people, and the malignancies they get are different from those that typically afflict us. Biochemist Bruce Ames, of the University of California at Berkeley, has long cited these differences in criticizing the way we use animal models to determine cancer risk. In one test, Ames and his colleagues surveyed 226 known carcinogens: 96, it turned out, caused cancer in mice but not in rats; 56 were carcinogenic in rats but harmless in mice. What, Ames asks, are you to expect when you make the Grand Canyon–size leap from rodents to humans?

The root of the problem, really, is that cancer is such a complex disease, ever ramifying as you burrow into the microscopic processes that cause it. A carcinogen may work by causing a mutation in an oncogene—a gene that, if it malfunctions, lays the groundwork for the uncontrolled proliferation of the cell where it resides. But a slew of other factors can come into play as well. For example, says Ames, whenever you poison healthy cells you increase the likelihood of tumors arising, because any kind of cell injury stimulates cell division. The more cells you poison, the more cell division you cause, and the higher the probability that a spontaneous cancerous mutation will occur.

This, as Ames has pointed out, raises a considerable difficulty for animal testing, which often subjects experimental animals to megahits of suspected carcinogens. The aim of those high doses is to smoke out even low-level carcinogens. But if you flood an animal with high levels of the test substance, it may produce cancer by poisoning great numbers of healthy cells, even though it's incapable by itself of triggering a cancerous mutation. Of course, that makes it a carcinogen for the mouse or rat inundated with it. But what if it's a substance no human would ever be exposed to in quantities sufficient to kill healthy cells?

A New Approach to Testing

Small wonder, then, that researchers have been casting about for a surer link between the microscopic realm of carcinogenesis and the sometimes expensive and disruptive practical decisions individuals and governments have to make about the threat of cancer. What's safe to eat; what poses a real cancer risk? What substances can we allow in water and air; what's dangerous and should—whatever the cost—be eliminated?

There's a developing scientific field designed to address such difficult questions with a new degree of confidence and accuracy. It's called molecular epidemiology: "molecular" because it enlists techniques pioneered in the 1970s and 1980s to peer into the submicroscopic arena where cells interact with (and occasionally battle) foreign chemicals; "epidemiology" because it's concerned with how a disease spreads through the human community and how it can be controlled.

The field may ultimately offer definitive answers as to whether a suspect chemical is really a human carcinogen and not just a rodent one. More important, once something has indeed been identified as a carcinogen, molecular epidemiology may be able to distinguish between an insignificant dose of the substance and a potentially harmful one. It may even be able to establish the different risks a single dose of a substance poses to different individuals. And ultimately, it may produce a simple blood test that shows whether you're harboring a clinically dangerous amount of a cancer-causing substance.

Marks of Danger

Molecular epidemiology won't do away with lab rats. As Frederica Perera, of Columbia University, one of the field's pioneers, notes, "Animal experiments have held up pretty well in their ability to predict." Molecular epidemiology, though, aims to achieve a greater accuracy and reliability by spying on the biochemical interplay between a suspected substance and human cells, in the hope of either catching a potential carcinogen red-handed as it inaugurates the cancer process or absolving it of suspicion. Then, with their submicroscopic evidence in hand, molecular epidemiologists want to make clear the connections between their microbiological data and human disease, for both individuals and society.

Perera and her colleagues in the field begin their work not with rodents but with humans. They amass tissue and body fluid samples from human volunteers who either have cancer or have been exposed to suspect chemicals. They then comb through these tissues for telltale "biomarkers"—chemical products that reveal interaction between a suspected carcinogen and human cells.

Molecular epidemiologists pursue a wide range of such biomarkers, since they want to monitor every aspect of cancer's progression, from the first infiltration of troublemaking chemicals to the subsequent complex array of bodily responses that end in a full-scale malignancy. Often the smoking gun they're hunting for—an activated oncogene, for example—indicates that your body has reacted to a carcinogen with a fateful cellular move. But other biomarkers can reveal an earlier stage—the first arrival, say, of a potential cancer-causing substance in your system. In this case investigators most often hunt for an "adduct"—a suspicious chemical bond between the substance and human DNA.

DNA-carcinogen adducts can be the first stage in a process that disrupts DNA replication during cell division. That can cause mutations. So when an adduct happens to form along an oncogene, the machinery of cellular replication can run haywire, setting the stage for malignancy. Over the last decade and a half, researchers have devised several highly sensitive assays for adducts between human DNA and various carcinogens. Finding a high level of them is a danger signal, suggesting that some of the conditions for cancer have been met.

Linking Markers to Risk

Eventually, Perera thinks, molecular epidemiologists may establish a link between the quantity of adducts and other biomarkers in somebody's tissue and that person's likelihood of developing cancer. Ideally, you would be able to calculate your personal risk exactly by means of a simple blood test. Should it turn out to be high, you could take precautions. "Adducts aren't disease," Perera notes, "but if somebody had a high level of them, we might reduce or eliminate his exposure, or give him supplements of certain micronutrients—antioxidant agents like vitamins A, C, or E, and carotenoids. They all inhibit the formation of adducts."

As yet, such a linkage between biomarkers and risk is not practical. Any realistic assessment of individual risk will have to wait for the completion of extensive studies. According to Perera, the method most likely to yield a useful payoff is the prospective study. In it, you assemble a group of volunteers, collect and store blood and tissue samples, and then monitor their health over the long term. Whenever a member of the group contracts cancer, you can perform what's known as a nested case control study by going back and looking at the history of the patient's fluctuations in whatever biomarker you're trying to evaluate. You can then find controls from the same group—people who match the sick volunteer in every respect (age, sex, smoking history, ethnic group, and history of exposure to a suspected carcinogen) except that they haven't gotten sick. If there's a significant and consistent difference in levels of DNA-carcinogen adducts between the people who get sick and those who don't, you're on the road to a potentially revealing test.

Amass enough data of this sort and it should be possible to set parameters—to decide what level of a given DNA-carcinogen adduct in your blood establishes that you've been exposed to a serious danger. It may also be possible to calculate whether a given ethnic group is unusually susceptible to a given kind of cancer. If researchers can assemble a sufficiently large library of adducts and other biomarkers, each peaking at a different twist in the long path that leads from initial exposure to tumor, Perera says, "we can pick up intermediate stages that lead toward cancer, instead of knowing somebody's been exposed, then having to wait blindly for 20 years before we know whether or not he's going to get sick."

Molecular Epidemiology at Work

A good illustration of molecular epidemiology at work is offered by studies connected with polycyclic aromatic hydrocarbons (called PAHs for short). By-products of coal combustion, and ubiquitous in heavily industrialized areas, PAHs rank among the world's best-known and nastiest environmental carcinogens. Once they make their way into a human body, they readily form adducts with cellular DNA. Perera, working with Regina Santella of Columbia's School of Public Health, has been using such adducts as indexes of a population's exposure to PAHs. In 1990, for example, they monitored the occurrence of PAH-DNA adducts in the population of Gliwice, an almost apocalyptically polluted town in Poland's highly cancer-prone Silesia region. The air gets worse every winter, as residents spew the by-products of coal heating into Gliwice's already choking ambient industrial smog. Perera found that PAH-DNA adducts in volunteers' blood samples did indeed rise and fall in tandem with the seasonal fluctuations in the town's pall of hydrocarbons.

Studies of Finnish foundry workers over the past ten years have produced results consistent with those of the Poles. The Finns make a good research cohort because the factory closes down every July for a four-week vacation, when everybody simultaneously enjoys a sharp drop in exposure to pollutants. Their levels of PAH-DNA adducts rose sharply in the weeks after their return to work. Similarly, a group of smokers, whose nicotine habit also exposes them to PAHs, showed dramatic drops in PAH-DNA adduct levels within months of stopping smoking. Such results, of course, strongly suggest that PAH-DNA adducts appear in the bloodstream in response to carcinogenic pollutants.

The Connection Between Adducts and Cancer

Still, you may well ask if such adducts are really connected with cancer. Apparently the answer here is also affirmative. In a study at New York's Columbia-Presbyterian Medical Center, Perera's group found significantly higher levels of PAH-DNA adducts in blood samples from lung cancer patients than in people without disease, even when they adjusted their results to account for whether the subjects smoked. Their results suggest that cancer patients are particularly susceptible to genetic damage from tobacco smoke.

All these studies, of course, illuminate only small corners of a vast and intricate picture. The work in Poland and Finland suggests that PAH-DNA adducts mount quickly in your blood when you're exposed to airborne PAHs, and such adducts correlate with precancerous mutations in oncogenes. But no one yet knows how many of the Polish and Finnish workers with elevated PAH-DNA adduct levels will actually go on to develop disease. Nobody knows what level of these adducts in an early blood test constitutes an ignore-it-at-your-peril warning. "Adducts," Perera says, "are just a fingerprint."

Building a Biomarker Library

These uncertainties underline the vast amount of work yet to be done in molecular epidemiology. Perera and her colleagues are busy expanding their arsenal of biomarkers. They've already explored adducts between human DNA and other carcinogens besides PAH. They've also sampled other sorts of indicators that might serve as surrogates, like adducts between carcinogens and the proteins produced by DNA (which are useful because they're easy to find even in very small blood samples).

For a complete molecular epidemiology, of course, you'd need a repertory of markers that reflected every known carcinogen and accurately recorded every stage from first exposure to tumor. They'd need to be consistent, so that a given level in a blood sample would indicate reliably what your chances were of full progression at each stage.

And they'd have to be easy to harvest too, available, for example, from a blood sample—you wouldn't want to part with a chunk of your liver every time you submitted to a shopping mall health screening. Then, in the kind of painstaking and exhaustive statistical research that forms the bedrock of epidemiology, the markers would have to be correlated over time with changes in the cancer status of groups that are big enough to yield significant results.

Perera and her colleagues believe that this effort will ultimately lead to a twofold reward. The earliest probable payoff will be a general one: accurate knowledge about which potential carcinogens most threaten the human population at large. "We'll be able to make better use of animal models; we'll know better what adjustments we have to make in our animal results to apply them to humans. And if we can document the range of genetic or other preclinical damage to humans, we can fine-tune risks to the population at large. We'll have better information on how to set environmental standards."

After that, the rewards may become more personal. "You and I can be exposed to exactly the same amount of a chemical," Perera observes, "and our responses will differ because we metabolize carcinogens differently, because we have different rates of DNA repair, or because of acquired factors like diet. In fact, we've estimated there may be fiftyfold to a hundredfold differences among individuals in the way they respond to a carcinogen."

Molecular epidemiology, in other words, is an enterprise that promises to unite the macro and the micro, the theoretical and the practical. Someday, the researchers dream, their work will give us a simple test that will finally tell you, if you've been exposed to a carcinogen, precisely what you want to know most of all: Are you one of the lucky individuals who can safely ignore it? Or are you the one at risk?

Chapter 3

Preventing and Treating Cancer

Contemporary Issues
Companion

CHANGING THE FOCUS OF RESEARCH TO PREVENTION

Robert N. Proctor

In 1971, President Richard Nixon announced that the American government was declaring a "war on cancer." In the following article, adapted from his book *Cancer Wars: How Politics Shapes What We Know and Don't Know About Cancer*, Robert N. Proctor claims that scientists have been losing that war because they have concentrated research efforts on seeking cures for cancer rather than on ways to prevent it. He calls instead for research on the social forces that perpetuate people's exposure to known carcinogens and for the removal of these carcinogens from the environment. For instance, he recommends that the United States halt its export of tobacco—a potent carcinogen—to the Third World. Proctor is an associate professor of the history of science at Pennsylvania State University in University Park.

> I propose to speak of a monster that is more insatiable than the guillotine; more destructive to life and health than the mightiest army that ever marched to battle; more terrifying than any scourge that has ever threatened the existence of the human race. The monster of which I speak . . . has fed and feasted and fattened . . . on the flesh and blood and brains and bones of men and children in every land. The name of this loathsome, deadly, and insatiate monster is "cancer."
>
> —Matthew Neely, U.S. Senator from West Virginia, in a speech before Congress in 1928

Senator Neely failed to convince the government of his day to ride forth like Saint George to slay the dragon. But within a decade the rising toll from cancer had so frightened people into sharing his apocalyptic vision that the National Cancer Institute was established. In the years since, the NCI has pumped more than $29 billion into cancer research, yet Neely's monster rages more terribly than ever. His words, so feverishly exaggerated nearly seventy years ago, when fewer than

From *Cancer Wars*, by Robert N. Proctor. Copyright ©1995 by Robert N. Proctor. Reprinted by permission of Basic Books, a member of Perseus Books, L.L.C.

100,000 Americans a year succumbed to cancer, are frighteningly apt today. Cancer has become the plague of the twentieth century: one in three Americans alive today will contract the disease, and one in five will die from it. Whereas most other diseases have disappeared or declined, cancer's appetite has never stopped growing. In 1899 a Buffalo physician named Roswell Park noted that cancer was the only disease "steadily upon the increase." That year cancer in the United States claimed about 30,000 lives. In 1994, according to projections by the American Cancer Society, cancer killed 538,000 Americans—twice as many as were killed in the Second World War.

The tragedy is deepened by the fact that nearly everyone agrees cancer is a preventable disease. Its causes are largely known, and have been known for some time. Cigarettes and asbestos cause cancer. Foods high in fat, low in fiber or high in salt can cause cancer. It is dangerous to burn one's skin in the sun or to bathe one's foods in pesticides. Dust in the lungs is bad, whether it comes from the floors one cleans, the hobbies one enjoys or the materials one handles at work. Even unregulated industry can cause cancer. Cancer is the product of bad habits, bad government, bad business and bad luck—including the luck of one's genetic draw and the culture into which one is born.

Knowing what causes cancer, however, has done surprisingly little to help control it. Notwithstanding repeated and glowing pronouncements from the American Cancer Society, treatment has progressed little since President Nixon declared war on the disease in 1971. Five-year survival rates for the majority of cancers (lung, colon, breast and stomach cancers, for example) remain essentially what they were in 1975.

Confronted with such gloomy findings, one can hardly deny that the war against cancer is being lost. Nearly a decade ago the physicians John C. Bailar of McGill University in Montreal, Quebec, Canada, and Elaine M. Smith of the University of Iowa Medical Center remarked in *The New England Journal of Medicine:* "Some 35 years of intense effort focused largely on improving treatment must be judged a qualified failure." In 1977 the commissioner of the Food and Drug Administration, Donald Kennedy, expressed his views on the matter more bluntly, calling America's cancer campaign "a medical Vietnam." To James D. Watson, the codiscoverer of the structure of DNA and one of the nation's most widely respected scientists, the campaign is simply "a bunch of shit."

Why the Cancer War Is Being Lost

What is going on here? How can one of the largest medical efforts in history, carried on by some of the best and brightest minds in the world, have proved so futile? Part of the problem lies in the very belief that a single, universal cure can be found. Physicians in the late nineteenth century, accustomed to battling terrible infectious scourges, devoted themselves to finding a "cancer germ" against which a cancer therapy could be devised. After all, the nineteenth-century German bacteriologist Robert Koch had shown that tuberculosis is caused by the tubercle bacillus, anthrax by the anthrax bacillus and cholera by the bacterium *Vibrio cholerae*. Antibiotics were deployed to fight those germs, and powerful new vaccines eventually enabled millions to live free of the fear of polio, smallpox and other killers.

Comparable heroic acts were expected from investigators who study cancer. As late as the 1950s and 1960s, hopes were still high that cancer viruses might be identified against which a cancer vaccine could be developed.

But cancer is fundamentally different from the infectious diseases—in its mode of attacking the body, in its tendency to grow within the body for thirty years or more without betraying any symptoms, and in its ability to circumvent the body's normal defenses. And even if cancer were an infectious disease, the search for a single cure would have been misguided.

Consider the medical experience of the twentieth century with such diseases as cholera and tuberculosis. Although the antibiotics and vaccines developed against those diseases saved millions of lives, in the long run the diseases were conquered by more mundane measures: improved nutrition and sanitation, shorter working hours and generally improved standards of living. Koch probably saved fewer potential cholera victims than did activists like John Snow, who removed the handle from the public water pump on Broad Street in London in 1854, easing the cholera epidemic that had plagued the city. Physicians attending childbirth ended an era of childbed fever simply by washing their hands; scurvy [caused by vitamin C deficiency] among British sailors was eradicated by rations of lime juice (hence the nickname Limeys).

Prevention Is the Best Hope

Such examples suggest that prevention, rather than cure, is the best hope for most chronic ailments. Yet prevention has languished as a relatively minor part of the American cancer program. Nixon's much celebrated "war on cancer" emphasized research aimed at perfecting radiotherapies and chemotherapies, but it gave little attention to the expertise and political action required for prevention. Most of the funds distributed by cancer-research bodies have gone to efforts either to improve treatment (especially surgery, radiation and chemotherapy) or to understand the biological mechanisms involved in carcinogenesis.

Monies from the public treasury are arguably better spent on cancer research than on ballistic missiles or tobacco and sugar subsidies, but one should not be misled into thinking that basic scientific knowledge is the main thing lacking in the fight against cancer. Basic cancer research has led to some remarkable biological insights, but it has given rise to surprisingly little in the way of successful treatments and even less that is of relevance to prevention. Basic cancer research "is an excellent slush fund for molecular biologists," Samuel S. Epstein, author of *Politics of Cancer*, has written, "but it won't have any impact on cancer." Why, if cancer is so obviously a product of things like smoking, radon and the "industrial way of life," has so little been done to attack the problem at its roots?

Like the war in Vietnam to which Donald Kennedy compared it, the war on cancer has been propelled by a mixture of pride and politics. By 1971, when Nixon declared the war, cancer specialists knew that they were dealing with an enemy far more elusive and resourceful than cholera or tuberculosis. With so many carcinogens already identified, a full-scale preventive campaign was needed. Yet then, as now, cancer prevention suffered from low prestige. A cancer cured was a tangible success; a cancer prevented was invisible, a statistical abstraction. Who would testify on talk shows or before Congress that they were alive and well as a result of a well-planned program of preventive medicine?

At the same time, more and more victims clamored each year for an immediate cure. In an era of unbridled optimism, medical investigators were willing to gamble billions on their ability to provide it: the country that had landed a man on the moon could surely conquer cancer.

Misdirected Research

Nearly a quarter-century later, national optimism has waned appreciably, but heroic medicine is still the order of the day. Prizes and grants abound for high-tech therapies and high-profile research in molecular genetics, but no one will ever win a Nobel prize (and few win major grants) for studies of nutrition, pollution prevention, health education or occupational health and safety. The bias against preventive medicine begins in medical school, where subjects such as diet, public health and environmental policy are neglected in favor of training in surgery, radiology and other curative practices. Most doctors, as a result, are uninterested or at least unskilled in preventing cancer.

The cancer-research establishment would still have people believe that ignorance—symbolized by a shortage of research funds—is the basic cause of cancer. Accordingly, the key to "cancer control" is knowledge, the great scientific breakthrough that will lift the veil of the unknown. Given the inherent uncertainties of the scientific process, it is always possible to delve ever deeper into the mechanisms of pharmacokinetic action [effects of drugs], to elucidate risks with ever greater precision, to demand ever larger animal or human epidemiological studies. It is true that if you do not ask you do not know, and if you do not know, you often cannot act. But it is not necessary to know exactly what causes cancer in order to prevent it.

Taken to an extreme, the unending need for greater accuracy and more knowledge can turn into a call for less action—and specifically, less regulation. The tobacco industry has long applied that paradoxical connection between research and action in its efforts to convince consumers it is premature to conclude that cigarettes cause cancer. A paper issued by the Tobacco Institute titled *The Cigarette Controversy* thus calls for "more research" half a dozen times in as many pages, the purported goal being to resolve a smoking and health "debate" or "controversy." Internal tobacco-industry documents brag about the success of that "brilliantly conceived and executed" strategy for creating "doubt about the health charge without actually denying it."

Such public relations campaigns are now directed by nearly every industry that generates carcinogens, continually urging private and public funders and the research community to chase the red herrings of mechanisms. Had such campaigns been at work during the Irish potato famine, which killed more than a million Irish between 1845 and 1849, they might have engendered studies into the biomechanical processes of famine rather than the social forces that gave rise to it. . . .

Changing Society

Disasters on the scale of the potato famine and cancer cannot be traced to isolated causes or specific biochemical events; they arise from the very structure of a society. The population geneticist Richard Lewontin of Harvard University puts the matter provocatively:

> It is undoubtedly true that pollutants and industrial wastes are the immediate physiological causes of cancer, miners' black lung, textile workers' brown lung, and a host of other disorders. Moreover, it is undoubtedly true that there are trace amounts of cancer-causing substances even in the best of our food and water unpolluted by pesticides and herbicides that make farm workers sick. But to say that pesticides cause the death of farm workers is to make a fetish out of inanimate objects. We must distinguish between agents and causes. Asbestos fibers and pesticides are the agents of disease and disability, but it is illusory to suppose that if we eliminate these particular irritants that the diseases will go away, for other similar irritants will take their place. So long as efficiency, the maximization of profit from production, or the filling of centrally planned norms of production without reference to the means remain the motivating forces of productive enterprises the world over, so long as people are trapped by economic need or state regulation into production and consumption of certain things, then one pollutant will replace another.

One need not be a conspiracy theorist—blaming the neglect of prevention on scientific and industrial self-interest—to recognize that effective prevention requires changes not only in research priorities but also in deeply ingrained personal habits and the logic of business enterprise. That point was made clear in the 1970s, when a leading cancer investigator conceded that although the removal of carcinogens from the environment was the most effective way of conquering cancer, "it may require such a rearrangement of the environment that society cannot or will not allow this to be done except slowly over decades." Governments have been reluctant to curtail tobacco sales because the taxes generated are enormous: more than $13 billion every year in the U.S. alone. Cynics point out that cancer affects the elderly more than it does the young, relieving governments of the cost of social security.

Richard Lewontin may be right in warning that regulated industries will eventually substitute one carcinogen for another. But one must not allow a social reductionism to dissolve specific product accountability. Bans on smoking aboard aircraft, tougher food labeling laws and other measures have gone some way toward legislating prevention, though surely more could be done along those lines.

Stepping Up the War on Tobacco

The war on tobacco, in particular, has been relatively mild compared with the war on drugs, which takes millions fewer lives. The U.S. needs stiffer taxes on tobacco sales, a halt to tobacco subsidies and stricter limits on the substances added to tobacco in the course of its manufacture. The nation needs financial support for tobacco counter-advertising, and support for personal-injury litigation against the tobacco industry. Senator Edward M. Kennedy of Massachusetts has proposed a bill to authorize the federal government to spend $110 million to combat tobacco via a new Center for Tobacco Products; Representative Henry Waxman of California has proposed restricting industry sponsorship of sporting events, eliminating vending machines and banning the use of models and color images in tobacco ads. Both initiatives are worth supporting.

Prevention of cancer caused by tobacco products could include financial support for farmers who want to shift from growing tobacco to producing other, beneficial commodities, such as pharmaceuticals. And prevention must include research into why young people take up smoking and how they can be encouraged to stop once they have begun.

The U.S. needs to learn from creative efforts practiced abroad: the Swedish policy of labeling cigarette cartons with stories of smokers who died from cancer; the 1986 ban on smokeless tobacco in Hong Kong; the former tax of $3.71 on every pack of cigarettes sold in Quebec (reduced substantially when smuggled cigarettes began flooding into Canada from the U.S.). Some encouraging steps in those directions have already been taken. California's five-year effort to curb smoking in restaurants and in the workplace (Proposition 99) has reduced cigarette consumption by 26 percent, according to a 1994 study. New York City's even tougher law banning smoking in almost all public places takes effect in April 1995. And President Bill Clinton's proposed ban on smoking in civilian and military workplaces could turn out to be the most powerful anti-cancer measure in history.

Other Government Steps Toward Prevention

Prevention could include stricter supervision of pesticides, as well as federal support for integrated pest management and other alternatives to petrochemical agriculture. Research aimed at easing the transition from gasoline-powered automobiles to electric-powered ones, and increased support for international limits on chlorofluorocarbons and other ozone-depleting compounds, could help rid the environment of some of its more common carcinogens. Prevention could include stricter regulation of tanning salons; the closing of loopholes that allow nonfood pesticides to be sprayed on crops (such as cotton) that wind up in human foods (cottonseed oil); the paving of dirt roads in areas (such as California) where serpentine, a natural asbestos, forms a major component of the surface rock. And prevention surely ought to include developing the tools needed to identify regions of high radon concentration and empowering the Occupational Safety and Health Administration to regulate indoor pollutants such as radon and secondhand smoke.

The U.S. is the largest exporter of carcinogens in the world, judging from the brisk pace of the tobacco export business and the ongoing practice of "dumping" abroad pharmaceuticals, pesticides and food additives that are banned in this country. Whereas tobacco subsidies have been curtailed at home, tobacco companies have expanded their foreign sales, assisted by trade policies that treat tobacco as an export commodity like any other. (The U.S. today exports more than three times as many cigarettes as any other country.) In 1990 the Council on Scientific Affairs of the American Medical Association attacked U.S. policy in this regard, pointing out that since tobacco worldwide accounts for nearly 5 percent of all deaths, it is perverse for the U.S. to promote smoking abroad. C. Everett Koop, the former U.S. surgeon general, has more aptly recognized the export of tobacco as "a moral outrage." Americans worry a great deal about the import of cocaine and other drugs into the U.S., but little is done to halt the far more deadly export of tobacco into the nations of the third world.

A New Focus for Research

Finally, prevention ought to include a broader search for the causes of cancer—a search that will examine such phenomena as apathy in the face of radon hazards; body machismo in the face of the hazards of steroids and over-exposure to the sun; the social forces that shape dietary habits; and the failure to enforce federal and local environmental policies. If natural carcinogens are contributors to disease, why have plants bred for insect resistance not come under closer scrutiny? If dietary fat presents a danger, why do agricultural policies not encourage a shift away from meat- and dairy-centered production? It is not hard to expand such a list; what is needed in each case is a broader-minded research focus, combined with the political will to translate knowledge into policy.

Each of those investigations would, of course, lead to new questions, a marvelous phenomenon that is the bread and butter of science. But one must not lose sight of the simple measures that are already known to lower the incidence of cancer. One must recognize that things are not always as they seem: that ignorance can be manufactured; that causes can be cultural; that writing checks to scientists is only one of several ways of fighting cancer. Activists who push for "more research" must ask: What kind of knowledge? Knowledge to what end? As citizens, we all need to appreciate not only how ignorance can invite knowledge but also how knowledge can abide ignorance, despite all our efforts to clear a path from one to the other.

LIFESTYLE CHANGES THAT PREVENT CANCER

R. Grant Steen

Many cancer experts believe that about two-thirds of human cancer cases could be prevented if people made certain changes in their lifestyles. R. Grant Steen, who is on the faculty of St. Jude Children's Research Hospital in Memphis, Tennessee, cites twenty-five preventable causes of cancers and lists ten ways to avoid them. For instance, he recommends avoiding exposure to tobacco smoke and increasing the amount of fruits and vegetables in one's diet. "Much of what we know about cancer prevention," he writes, "is common sense." The following article on cancer prevention is adapted from Steen's book *Changing the Odds: Cancer Prevention Through Personal Choice and Public Policy*.

Cancer is probably the most dreaded of all diseases; nearly everyone has close friends or relatives who have fallen victim to it. Cancer is now the leading cause of death for women and the second leading cause of death overall, after heart disease. Cancer has been projected to become the leading overall killer in the United States by the year 2000.

Cancer will probably never be completely preventable. Yet it has been calculated that about two-thirds of all human cancers could be prevented.

In this article, I will compile and rank the major *preventable* cancer risk factors—i.e., those that are not inherited. While hereditary cancers carry a high risk if they run in your family, they are *very* rare otherwise. By focusing on preventable cancer risk factors, we can direct our personal choices and public policies toward achieving the maximum possible reduction in cancer mortality.

The top 25 preventable cancer risks in the United States are listed in Table 1.

Preventable Causes of Cancers

Of the top 25 completely preventable causes of cancer in the United States, about 84% are lifestyle-related. Those few that are not clearly lifestyle-related (such as hepatitis B virus infection, DDT exposure,

Reprinted from R. Grant Steen, "Winning the War on Cancer," *The Futurist*, March/April 1997, by permission of the World Future Society, 7910 Woodmont Ave., Suite 450, Bethesda, MD 20814; (301) 656-8274; www.wfs.org.

and secondhand smoke) nevertheless can have a significant component of lifestyle choice involved. For example, hepatitis B virus (HBV) infection is more prevalent among homosexual men who engage in anal sex, high-level DDT exposure is usually occupational and can be minimized through careful application of the pesticide, and secondhand smoke is often avoidable.

Table 1. The Top 25 Risk Factors for Preventable Cancers

Rank	Risk Factor	Related Cancer
1.	Hepatitis B virus infection	Liver
2.	Tobacco smoking (two packs or more per day, 10 years)	Lung
3.	Human papilloma virus (HPV-16 or -18)	Cervical
4.	High dietary intake of saturated fat	Lung
5.	Low dietary intake of folate	Cervical
6.	Heavy drinking (any alcohol)	Oropharyngeal
7.	DDT in pesticides	Breast
8.	Frequent red meat consumption	Colon
9.	*Helicobacter* infection	Stomach
10.	Highly stressful life events (more than two in last year)	All cancers
11.	Low dietary intake of Vitamin E	Colon
12.	Low dietary intake of Vitamin C	Cervical
13.	Oral contraceptive use (at 40–44 years of age)	Breast
14.	Long-term use of black hair dye	Lymphoma
15.	Low dietary intake of raw fruits and vegetables	Lung
16.	Chronic obesity	Colon
17.	Low carbohydrate intake	Colorectal
18.	Secondhand smoke (more than 22 years)	Lung
19.	High total caloric intake	Prostate
20.	Low activity (less than 1,000 kilocalories per week)	Colorectal
21.	Low dietary intake of selenium	Lung
22.	Low dietary intake of fiber	Colorectal
23.	Never bearing children	Breast
24.	Low dietary intake of peas and beans	Lung
25.	More than 30 years old at first childbirth	Breast

R. Grant Steen, *Changing the Odds: Cancer Prevention Through Personal Choice and Public Policy*, 1995.

At least 48% of the top 25 preventable causes of cancer are related to diet. This shows that the current emphasis on dietary prevention of cancer is not a misplaced effort, since diet is more easily changed than certain other lifestyle risk factors, such as tobacco use or obesity.

At least 28% of the top 25 preventable causes of cancer are specifically related to an inadequate intake of fruits and vegetables. This would seem to be a relatively easy dietary change to make, since modern farming and shipping practices make fresh fruits and vegetables available year-round to virtually everyone in the United States. Many cookbooks provide recipes that make vegetables more palatable, so all that may be required is the impetus to try these recipes. It is hoped that our analysis of cancer risk factors will provide such impetus.

One-fifth of the top 25 preventable causes of cancer are arguably stress-related, since stress can cause an increased intake of tobacco, alcohol, and total calories, and since many people respond to stress by becoming obese. Dealing productively with stress can therefore play a critical role in maintaining a healthy lifestyle and minimizing the risk of cancer. Perhaps the most effective way to deal with stress is to establish a regular routine of exercise.

Other preventable risks are exposure to carcinogenic chemicals, such as tobacco smoke, hair dye, and DDT; HBV, for which a vaccine exists; and of course tobacco, which is known to cause at least 85% of all lung cancers and up to 30% of all other cancers.

Actual Causes of Death

A study examined the actual causes of death in the United States, with the specific goal of identifying the major nongenetic factors that contribute to death. Of the 2.1 million people who died in 1990, death certificates show that more than half a million people died of cancer, and that cancer was the second leading cause of death overall, after heart disease.

But medical terms (e.g., cancer), used to describe the physical condition at death, do not reveal the actual root causes of death. In order to get at the root causes of death in the United States, a large number of separate studies were analyzed in a sort of meta-analysis. The actual (nongenetic) causes of death identified in this meta-analysis were, in descending order of importance:

1. Tobacco.
2. Diet and activity patterns.
3. Alcohol.
4. Microbial agents.
5. Toxic agents.
6. Firearms.
7. Sexual behavior.
8. Motor vehicles.
9. Illicit use of drugs.

Together, these causes accounted for about half of all deaths in the United States in 1990.

Tobacco was the major root cause of death identified in the United States, taking 400,000 lives in 1990. Tobacco is responsible for about 19% of all deaths, 30% of all cancer deaths, 30% of all chronic lung disease deaths, 24% of all pneumonia and influenza deaths, 21% of all cardiovascular deaths, and a substantial fraction of deaths from cerebrovascular disease and diabetes. Without doubt, smoking is the most damaging carcinogen to which humans are regularly exposed.

Diet and activity patterns were the next most important root cause of death identified, taking 300,000 American lives in 1990. Dietary factors are responsible for deaths from cardiovascular disease, cancer, and diabetes, while physical inactivity is responsible for deaths from heart disease and cancer. Together, these factors account for at least 20% of all cancer deaths, 30% of all diabetes deaths, and 22% of all cardiovascular deaths.

Alcohol was the third most important root cause of death identified, taking 100,000 lives. An estimated 18 million people in the United States suffer from alcohol dependence, and 76 million are affected by alcohol abuse at some time during their lives. Alcohol abuse is responsible for at least 3% of all cancer deaths, 60% of all cirrhosis deaths, 40% of all motor vehicle fatalities, and 16% of all other injuries.

More than 20 times as many people died from cancer in 1990 as died from AIDS. Despite the public attention given to HIV/AIDS, various other viruses were far more important as a cause of death in the United States in 1990. Viruses caused about six times as many deaths from cancer as from AIDS in 1990, and the death toll from virally induced cancer is rising at a rate comparable to the death toll from AIDS in the United States. Thus, cancer must remain a major focus of the medical research enterprise.

Ten Steps to Cancer Prevention

1. Stop smoking. No rationale is possible for this devastating habit. Stop those you love from smoking or hound them senseless. Don't allow anyone to smoke in your house or your office, and make it as difficult as possible for smokers to abuse themselves. Smokeless tobacco is really no better than smoked tobacco—it just causes cancers that are somewhat less uniformly fatal than lung cancer.

2. Learn your familial risk factors and be especially vigilant about those cancers that seem to run in your family. Ask your older relatives for as full a description as possible of the cause of death of your deceased relatives, then specifically avoid the risk factors for these cancers.

3. Increase your consumption of fresh fruits and vegetables. A broad variety of each is best, with special emphasis on whatever is freshest in your produce department or store.

4. Decrease your consumption of red meat. This does not mean become a vegetarian, but rather place greater dietary emphasis on white meats, such as chicken and fish. An appropriate dietary modification might be as simple as having red meat fewer than four times per week, or having chicken or fish at least three times per week. Vegetarian dishes or dishes rich in complex carbohydrates (e.g., pasta) can also be substituted for red meat.

5. *Exercise* at least three times per week, for at least 20 minutes each time. This will help to maintain your weight at an appropriate level as well as conferring other benefits.

6. *Get vaccinated against hepatitis B virus* if at all possible and avoid other viral exposures. This may mean using a condom, minimizing the number of different sexual partners, or avoiding intercourse with someone you suspect to be infected with human papilloma virus.

7. *Practice moderation in all things.* Overuse or abuse of alcohol, prescription drugs, and fast foods takes a very high toll in the modern world, as does overexposure to sunlight.

8. *Make a yearly visit to a physician if you are over 40 years old,* and make biannual visits if you are over 30. This will certainly help to diagnose and treat current problems, but may also alert you to newly discovered cancer risk factors. In addition, there are several widely available cancer screening tests that should be used on the advice of your physician, including mammography, Pap test, fecal occult blood test, and prostate-specific antigen screening.

9. *Avoid unnecessary exposure* to the hormones used in estrogen-replacement therapy (ERT). Long-term ERT use by perimenopausal women is associated with an increased risk of breast cancer, especially if estrogen is combined with progestin. However, the benefits of ERT may outweigh the risks, since breast cancer risk may drop rapidly after discontinuation of the therapy.

10. *Learn the 10 warning signs of cancer:* (1) Swelling, thickening, or lump in any soft tissue, but especially the breasts. (2) Persistent or unexplained coughing or hoarseness. (3) A sore that does not heal or a mole that abruptly changes in size or color. (4) Unexplained fatigue. (5) Abrupt weight loss or loss of appetite. (6) Changes in bowel habits, including pain or bleeding on defecation, narrow stools, or constipation. (7) Changes in urinary function, particularly bleeding or difficulty in discharge. (8) Changes in menstrual function, especially unexpected or excessive bleeding. (9) Difficulty in swallowing or a feeling of bloat or fullness. (10) Pallor or abnormal bleeding.

Prevention Is Common Sense

Much of what we know about cancer prevention is common sense. Everyone should eat a balanced diet and practice moderation in all things. It is fair to say that cancer is a disease of abuse or disuse, and moderation may be key to avoiding both extremes.

Whenever possible, people should learn more about their personal risk factors. If there is a family history of cancer, especially if cancer has affected a particular organ in a large number of family members, special care should be taken to avoid known risk factors for that cancer. It would also be wise to be screened for that cancer whenever possible. In the absence of specific screening tests for a particular cancer, regular visits to a family physician can substantially reduce cancer risk. However, there is no substitute for common sense, moderation, and personal knowledge of cancer risk factors.

The Debate over Screening for Breast Cancer

Delia Marshall

Screening tests—routine tests given to seemingly healthy people in the hope of detecting hidden disease—can prevent cancer deaths by finding tumors early in their development, when they are more likely to be curable. Experts sometimes disagree, however, about which screening tests should be given to which groups of people. In the following selection, freelance health writer Delia Marshall examines the debate about whether mammography, an X-ray screening test for breast cancer, should routinely be administered to women between the ages of forty and fifty. Yearly mammograms definitely reduce cancer deaths in women over fifty, Marshall explains, because older women are more likely to develop the disease and the test is more accurate in older women. The benefits of testing younger women are much less clear, Marshall writes, and breast cancer experts and advocates disagree on its usefulness.

Should a 40-year-old woman get a mammogram? It's one of the most controversial questions in medicine today. The debate exploded in December 1993, when the National Cancer Institute (NCI) dropped its recommendation that women 40 to 49 get regular mammograms. Previously, both the NCI and the American Cancer Society had recommended annual or biannual mammograms for women when they reached 40, then yearly mammograms beginning at 50.

An Age Controversy

Fifty is generally recognized as a watershed. At that point, the breast-cancer rate increases and mammograms become more effective, since postmenopausal breasts tend to be less dense and easier to X-ray. But there are many detectable cancers in women 40 to 49, and despite a lower incidence, the clustering of baby boomers in this age group has shifted the numerical balance. "In 1993, there were 28,900 breast cancers diagnosed in the 40-to-49 age group," says Dr. Janet Rose

From "Mammograms Under 50?" by Delia Marshall, which first appeared in *Working Woman*, October 1994. Reprinted with permission of MacDonald Communications Corporation. Copyright ©1994 by MacDonald Communications Corporation.

Osuch, head of the breast-cancer subcommittee of the American Medical Women's Association. "There were only 2,600 more in women 50 to 59."

But the NCI and some scientists insist that there is no conclusive evidence that mammograms for younger women reduce their mortality rate, the criterion for screening tests. Eight clinical trials have been undertaken to evaluate mammography; in them, women were randomly assigned either to a control group or to one that had mammograms. The first trial, begun in the 1960s, studied women 40 to 64 and showed a benefit for those who had mammograms. The following six confirmed these findings. But none had conclusive data on women in the 40-to-49 age group. Still, the overall data were compelling enough to make mammograms common by 1980. In 1987, both the American Cancer Society and the NCI agreed that women 40 and up should be screened. Then, in 1992, the results of a seven-year Canadian study caught the NCI's attention: Routine mammograms for women in their 40s had no effect on their life span.

Critics immediately assailed the Canadian data, pointing out that the groups were not adequately randomized, skewing the results. They added that many of the earlier images were made on outdated equipment, and that some of the radiologists were poorly trained. The researchers countered that these criticisms were unfounded. Moreover, the Canadians were the first to design a study to investigate younger women as a separate group. Still, said critics, while the study didn't establish the effectiveness of mammograms, the evidence wasn't good enough to prove that mammography *wouldn't* benefit women under 50.

Despite the disagreement, the NCI's latest position has an impact on health-care policy. From the cost standpoint, says Dr. Alvin Mushlin, mammogram specialist for the American College of Physicians, "mammography for women in their 40s is not a good investment.". . .

What to Do?

At any age, mammography has its flaws. Although it is the best detection method we have now—capable of spotting a cancer roughly two years before it can be felt—overall the test misses 10% to 15% of cancers. That false-negative rate is higher in women under 50—up to 25%, according to most estimates, 40% according to the NCI. Mammograms may also highlight lumps that after a biopsy turn out to be benign. Surgical biopsy scars, for their part, may obscure tumors on later mammograms.

Few dispute that routine mammograms are beneficial for older women. Everyone agrees that if a woman notices anything suspicious, she should get a diagnostic mammogram immediately, regardless of her age (black women under 45 have an especially high breast-cancer incidence rate). But "we still don't know the answer for women aged

40 to 49, even though this is the most scrutinized test of any in medicine," laments Osuch.

While other studies continue, the lack of a medical consensus leaves many women terribly confused about what to do. The NCI offers the lame suggestion that women decide after talking to their doctors, not a group known for their communication skills. Instead, women simply have to educate themselves. These opinions, culled from experts on the front lines of the battle, may make your decision easier.

Experts' Opinions

Edward Sondik, Ph.D., acting deputy director of the National Cancer Institute, says that the NCI's statement is only an advisory, not a mandate: "The issue boils down to these five facts: (1) We do not have conclusive results that detecting breast cancer in a woman aged 40 to 49 with mammography will prolong her life. (2) A woman in her 40s is less likely than an older woman to get breast cancer: The chances are about 1 in 60 that a woman will get the disease by the time she's 50. (3) The test is not terribly accurate for younger women. Chances are 2% to 5% for a false positive, which means a lot of excess biopsies. (4) In addition, there's a high chance of a false negative. Here's the problem with false negatives: Six months later, a woman might notice a discharge or change in her breast, and she might say to herself, 'Oh, I just had a mammogram, so I have nothing to worry about.' She does indeed have something to worry about, and should go back to see her physician. (5) There is a minimal amount of radiation involved, and radiation can lead to the development of cancer. If a woman decides to be screened and she knows the facts, NCI has no problem with that. If she decides not to get screened, that's fine, too."

Harmon Eyre, M.D., chief medical officer of the American Cancer Society, feels that women should err on the side of caution: "We recommend that all women aged 40 to 49 continue to be screened with mammography every one to two years until we get more or better science. Fewer and fewer younger women are dying from the disease, and most cancer experts would agree that it is in part due to earlier detection. The risks of radiation exposure are tiny: Out of 100,000 women who started at age 40 to have mammograms, perhaps 10 to 13 would develop breast cancer as a result, in part, of radiation."

Susan M. Love, M.D., director of the UCLA Breast Center, says each woman should base her policy on her body: "In your early 40s, get one mammogram and see what your breasts look like. Are they dense and have a lot of tissue? If so, then you might want to wait until you're 50. On the other hand, if they're fatty, mammograms may be more helpful. I'm 46, I have very fatty breasts that you can see through fine, and I have a family history, so I get them every year. By the way, this focus on what younger women should do makes me crazy. Breast cancer is just as tragic for a 65-year-old as it is in a younger woman.

One of my big complaints is that there's no question that mammograms for women over 50 work *great*, and yet only 30% of these women are getting them. But older women don't see themselves portrayed in the public-service announcements and in women's magazines, so they don't get mammograms."

Janet Rose Osuch, M.D., head of the breast-cancer subcommittee of the American Medical Women's Association, dismisses the issue of cost. "AMWA supports beginning screening mammography at age 40. Should a woman 'do the right thing' and not have a mammogram for the greater economic good? No. Society bears the burden of every woman who's diagnosed with breast cancer in many more ways than just taking care of her. There's her family—especially her children, if she's young—the impact on her workplace, her social relationships. I'm 46, and I want to know I've done everything I can to keep myself healthy. If I don't get screened, I'll feel like I had my head in the sand."

Nancy W. Dickey, M.D., a family physician in Richmond, Tex., and the vice chair of the Board of Trustees of the American Medical Association, uses this rule of thumb: "If a patient has no risk factors, it's not unreasonable to ask her to wait till age 50. If breast cancer is high on her anxiety level, for her a mammogram is a well-spent $95 or $125."

Bernadine Healy, M.D., former director of the National Institutes of Health, insists that the government shouldn't decide which tests women get: "Women under 50 should get mammograms every two to three years. Because it's less reliable in younger, denser breasts, and because breast cancer in younger women appears to be more aggressive, we need better mammography for younger women, not less mammography. Of course, picking up cancer earlier is not an economic thing to do: Treatment costs money. But come on—we get on the slippery slope when we start doing this sort of rationing. We should instead be concentrating on better health care."

Cynthia Pearson, program director of the National Women's Health Network, one of the few groups that discourage routine mammograms for premenopausal women under 50, explains the NWHN's view: "There's no evidence that the mammogram will help save a younger woman's life, and there is some evidence that it can be harmful. The frustrating truth is that women under 50 face a significant risk of getting breast cancer, but mammograms cannot detect that cancer early enough to make a difference."

Fran Visco, president of the National Breast Cancer Coalition, is ambivalent about mammograms: "Too often, mammography is referred to as prevention. It does not prevent breast cancer, nor does a negative reading mean a woman is fine. It usually takes about eight years for a breast cancer to get big enough to be seen. Having said all this, I should also point out that mammograms do detect breast cancer in some younger women. I suppose if I were a symptom-free woman in my 40s, I would get regular mammograms. But women should also do self-exams and get good clinical breast exams from their doctors."

Amy Langer, executive director of the National Alliance of Breast Cancer Organizations, supports routine screening by age 40 and insurance reimbursement: "As far as younger women are concerned, unfortunately, we know as much now as we did before any of the trials took place. But many of us in NABCO know from personal experience that mammography offers the best chance we have for survival."

Marie Zinninger, M.S.N., assistant executive director of the American College of Radiology, insists that mammograms are effective and safe: "All mammogram facilities will have equipment accredited by the ACR and other agencies and be certified by the FDA [Food and Drug Administration] as of October [1994], ensuring that the test is as low-dose as possible. Many people advocate breast exams. Well, breast exams lead to as many biopsies as mammograms do, and there have been few clinical trials studying their effectiveness."

GENETIC TESTS: THE DANGERS OF KNOWING TOO MUCH

The Associated Press

Recently developed tests can sometimes reveal whether a person has inherited a damaged gene that is associated with a high risk of a particular kind of cancer. Such tests have the potential to help prevent cancer deaths, but they do not always give clear-cut results, and at present there is little that can be done in most cases to keep cancer from developing after the gene is identified. The authors, from the international news organization Associated Press, describe a dramatic case in which a genetic test spared a woman disfiguring surgery by showing that she had not inherited a cancer gene, but they note that few cases are so easily resolved. People who take the tests need to meet with genetic counselors to receive help in interpreting and acting on the test results, the authors conclude.

Janet didn't need a doctor to tell her something was wrong.

For more than a decade, she had watched as breast cancer stalked her family. Her mother was diagnosed in 1978, at the age of 47. Her aunt was struck a year later. The aunt's 29-year-old daughter was next, then another daughter, then one of Janet's sisters.

The two cousins and the sister died, and in 1992, the shadow fell on Janet. She, too, had breast cancer. She was 40 years old.

By then, Janet's sister Susan—four years younger and free of any sign of disease—could not stand waiting for what she viewed as the inevitable. She decided to do the only thing she could to avoid the tragedy that had befallen her mother, aunt, cousins and sisters: She scheduled surgery to have both her healthy breasts removed.

Janet and Susan—who used assumed names to protect their privacy—told their story in the fall of 1994 to several hundred geneticists and researchers gathered in Montreal for the annual meeting of the American Society of Human Genetics.

As Janet began, the audience fell silent. The sorrow in her voice filled the cavernous hall, where doctors and researchers were beginning to grapple with a problem unlike any they had faced before.

Reprinted from "Confronting the Shadow," Anonymous, *The Blade-Citizen Accent*, June 17, 1995, by permission of the Associated Press.

Hope and Despair

In 1994, the mystery behind the shadow that fell on the women of Janet's family was solved. Researchers identified the gene causing the breast cancer in families like hers.

But the discovery did little to lift the shadow. Instead, it brought with it a fearsome power. For the first time, doctors could predict, decades in advance, which members of those families would get cancer and which would not.

Within weeks of the discovery, Susan became one of the first women to undergo testing. Only days before the scheduled surgery to remove her breasts, doctors notified her of the results: She did not carry the breast cancer mutation.

That meant her risk of developing breast cancer was normal—not astronomical, as it would be if she carried the gene. She canceled the surgery.

"I couldn't believe it," Susan said. "It was the first reason we had for hope."

For many others, however, including other women in Janet's and Susan's family, doctors have only bad news. Many of those women are carrying "genetic markers" indicating they have the mutation. And doctors can do nothing to help them.

Some day, it may be possible to pluck out harmful genetic mutations, to "cure" bad genes. In the meantime, doctors who have identified patients at risk can only watch helplessly as their fates unfold.

"There's that quote from Sophocles—'It is but sorrow to be wise, when wisdom profits nothing,'" said Dr. Francis Collins, the director of genetics research at the National Institutes of Health.

Collins directs the National Center for Human Genome Research, an ambitious effort to identify all the estimated 100,000 genes in humans—including an unknown number of cancer genes.

In 1994, researchers discovered genes that make it possible to identify the individuals at risk in families ravaged by colon cancer. More such genes are sure to follow, Collins said.

"These genes for cancer are getting cloned willy-nilly. Testing would have potential benefits if we knew what to recommend. But we don't."

In 1993, doctors found the gene for Huntington's disease, a crippling and ultimately fatal nerve disorder that killed folk singer Woody Guthrie. They are close to finding a genetic indicator of Alzheimer's disease.

Vexing Questions

Collins is among many geneticists who see a crisis building. Pressure to make testing available is coming not only from patients like Janet and Susan, but also from biotechnology companies, which stand to make a fortune selling test kits.

This new ability to predict cancer raises a host of vexing scientific and ethical questions. How should the tests be interpreted outside the research lab? Should testing be offered to anyone? What kind of psychological support should be provided?

Cancer testing also is likely to have a disastrous impact on patients' health insurance. Insurance companies may drop coverage for people carrying cancer genes. And as the ability to test for such genes grows, the pool of people excluded from coverage could grow.

A further problem is that the government hasn't decided what it should do to assure the accuracy of the new gene tests and ensure they aren't misused.

The Food and Drug Administration has the authority to regulate genetic tests, but has not exercised it so far. Companies promoting the tests have not been submitting them to the FDA for approval, the National Academy of Sciences warned in a 1993 report.

The emotional consequences of testing can be so overwhelming that the tests must be nearly 100 percent accurate, the academy said. At present, they aren't.

Inconclusive Results

Mary-Claire King, a geneticist at the University of California in Berkeley, did the groundbreaking work leading to the discovery of the breast cancer gene. Breast cancer runs in King's family, as it does in Janet's and Susan's.

Few people understand the significance of the test and its implications better than King. And she has decided not to take it.

The genetic link to breast cancer in her family is weaker than in Janet's and Susan's family; in King's family, the tests might not provide conclusive information on risks.

Many other families are in similar circumstances. Few families are hit as hard as Janet's and Susan's, so King pleaded with women in those families to wait before seeking testing. "Give us time to sort out the biology," she said.

When the biology is sorted out over the next few years, testing may become routine. But that in turn will create another problem. Genetic testing does not produce yes-or-no answers. The results are expressed in terms of probabilities.

In Janet's and Susan's family, the probability for any individual woman is either very high or very low, making the results relatively simple to understand. But what happens when a woman has a slightly elevated probability of getting breast cancer, or double the usual risk? What if a young man is told he is at high risk of getting Alzheimer's disease in his 60s?

There will be an urgent need for genetic counselors, professionals who can interpret test results and provide guidance.

Providing Emotional Support

Robert Buckman

A diagnosis of cancer and the treatment that follows can be devastating, and the support of family and friends is essential in helping a person survive these ordeals. Yet, as physician Robert Buckman explains in the following excerpt from his book What You Really Need to Know About Cancer: A Comprehensive Guide for Patients and Their Families, *cancer patients' loved ones often fear that they will not know the right thing to say and therefore hesitate to discuss the disease at all. In fact, Buckman maintains, what people say is far less important than how well they listen. Cancer patients, he writes, frequently find immense comfort in being able to talk honestly and freely about their concerns and fears. Buckman offers advice on how to be a good listener when a friend or family member needs to talk about experiences with cancer.*

Everyone feels somewhat stuck, sometimes almost paralyzed when a friend receives some bad news (even if things later work out much better than we feared at first), and we all tend to feel that we don't know what to say.

To make things worse, we probably think that there are things we *should* be saying or doing that would automatically make things easier for the person with cancer if only we knew what they were....

No Magic Formulas

Perhaps the most important thing to realize is that there are no magic formulas or phrases or approaches, no "Correct Thing" to say or do that covers all circumstances. There is no magic set of words or attitudes, no Universal Phrase that everybody but you knows. If you really want to help your friend, your own desire to help is the really vital ingredient, not some perfect script that you're supposed to follow word for word.

Another important point is that it's not what we *say*, it's how we *listen*. Sometimes the single most important thing you can do for your friend or relative with cancer is to listen. Once you've learned a few simple rules of good listening, you can be of great help and support,

Reprinted from Robert Buckman, *What You Really Need to Know About Cancer: A Comprehensive Guide for Patients and Their Families*, pp. 307–14, ©1995, 1997 Robert Buckman, by permission of The Johns Hopkins University Press.

and communication will improve from there on. The secret is to start. Learning how to be a good listener begins with understanding why listening (and talking) are so valuable.

Before we can listen effectively, however, we need to recognize the unique atmosphere of dread and foreboding associated with the word "cancer" in our society. It is true that large numbers of patients with cancer will be completely cured, and that number is increasing slowly and steadily all the time. Nevertheless, for many reasons and despite those good statistics, the word "cancer" has a more paralyzing and numbing effect than most other diagnoses. . . .

Why Talk, Why Listen?

You want to help, but you're not sure what is the best thing to do. Well, perhaps the most logical place to start is with what you're trying to achieve for your friend—the objectives of conversation and dialogue. There are excellent reasons for talking (and, of course, listening).

There are many different ways of communicating: kissing, touching, laughing, frowning, even "not talking." (You may have heard the story of the man who wanted to know why his wife hadn't spoken to him for three days, and his psychotherapist replied, "Perhaps she's trying to tell you something.") Talking is, however, the most efficient and the most *specific* way that we have of communicating. Other methods of communication—hugging, touching, and all nonverbal communications—are very important, but for them to be of use we usually have to talk first.

Talking and Listening Relieve Distress

There are many things that a conversation can achieve. In other words, there are many reasons for us to talk. There are obvious ones, such as telling the children not to stick their fingers in the fan, telling a joke, asking about the results of the game or the horse race, and so on. There are also less obvious reasons for talking, one of which is the simple desire to be listened to. In many circumstances, particularly when things go wrong, people talk in order to get what is bothering them off their chest and to be heard. You can see this quite often in the behavior of children. If you have an argument with your child, you may often hear your child later grumbling to his or her teddy bear or even telling the bear off in the way you told the child off. Although this is not exactly dialogue or conversation (since it's one-way), it serves a useful function in releasing a bit of pressure. Human beings can stand only so much pressure. There is relief to be found in talking, which means that there is a relief that *you* can provide for a sick person by listening and by simply *allowing* him or her to talk. That, in turn, means you can help your friend, even if you don't have all the answers.

In fact, simply doing "good listening" is known to be effective *in itself.* In an interesting research study done in the United States, a number of totally untrained people were taught the simple techniques of good listening, and volunteer patients came to see them to talk about their problems. The listeners in this study were not allowed to say or do anything at all. They just nodded and said "I see" or "Tell me more." They weren't allowed to ask questions of the patients or say anything at all about the problems that the patients described. At the end of the hour, almost all the patients thought they had got very good therapy; some of them called the "therapists" to ask if they could see them again, and to thank them for the therapy. Remember, then: You don't have to have the answers. Just listening to the questions will help a bit.

Releasing Feelings

One of the arguments friends and family put forward in order to *avoid* talking to the patient is that talking about a fear or an anxiety might create that anxiety, even if it didn't exist before the conversation. In other words, a friend might say to herself: *"If I ask my friend whether he's worried about radiotherapy and he wasn't worried about it, I might make him worried about it."* Well, that doesn't happen. There is very good evidence from studies done by psychiatrists talking to patients with terminal illnesses (in Britain in the 1960s) that conversations between the patients and their relatives and friends did not create new fears and anxieties. In fact, the opposite was true: *not* talking about a fear makes it bigger. Those patients who have nobody to talk to have a higher incidence of anxiety and depression. Several other researchers have shown that when people are seriously ill, one of their biggest problems is that people won't talk to them. The resulting feelings of isolation add a great deal to their burden. In practice, a major anxiety occupying a patient's mind frequently makes it difficult for that patient to talk about anything at all.

One reason why bottled-up feelings may cause damage has to do with shame. Many people are ashamed of some of their feelings, particularly of their fears and anxieties. They may be afraid of something but feel they aren't "supposed" to be, and so they feel ashamed of themselves. One of the greatest services you can do for your friend is to hear his or her fears and stay close when you've heard them. By not backing away or withdrawing, you show that you accept and understand them. That in turn will reduce the fear and the shame and help the patient get back a sense of perspective.

In short, you have everything to gain and nothing to lose by trying to talk and listen to someone who's just been told that she or he has cancer. . . .

There are ways of making yourself available for listening and talking without thrusting your offer down the patient's throat, just as there are ways for you to work out whether the patient needs to talk or does

> **Effective Listening: The S-C-A-N-S Mnemonic**
>
> **S—Setting**
> Get the setting right. Sit down with your eyes on the same level as the other person. Look as "at ease" as you can (for example, drop your shoulders).
>
> **C—Communication skills**
> Don't talk over the other person (that is, keep quiet while he or she is talking). Use simple techniques such as nodding, smiling, and using one word from the person's last sentence in your first sentence (to demonstrate that you were listening).
>
> **A—Acknowledgement**
> Always acknowledge the existence of the other person's emotion (for example, *"It must be very frustrating having to wait for the results. . . ."*).
>
> **N—Negotiating**
> Clarify what it is that the other person wants (for example, practical help, information, emotional support). Then clarify what it is that you can do and are good at. Then do the things on your list that seem to fit the other person's list.
>
> **S—Summary**
> Always end a discussion summarizing the main two or three points that you've been talking about together. Ask if there are other important issues. End with a clear "contract," which can be as simple as *"I'll see you on Friday"* or *"I'll phone you next week."*

not. . . . You can encourage free conversation and avoid awkward communication gaps by following a few simple rules or techniques of good listening. Both physical and mental techniques are important. The most important components of good listening are summarized with a mnemonic (S-C-A-N-S) that makes them easier to remember.

Get the Setting Right

The physical context is important. Get comfortable, sit down, try to look relaxed (even if you don't feel it), and signal the fact that you are there to spend some time (for instance, take your coat off!).

Keep your eyes on the same level as the person you're talking to. This almost always means sitting down. As a general rule, if the patient is in the hospital and chairs are unavailable or too low, sitting on the bed is preferable to standing. All kinds of things conspire against us in circumstances like that. I've sometimes found, on ward rounds, that if I can't sit on the bed because of obstacles, the only available chair is a commode. It causes minor embarrassment, but as long as you acknowledge the circumstances, it's better than trying to talk to someone while towering above the person. In other circumstances, you should try to keep as "private" an atmosphere as possible: don't try to talk in a corridor or on a staircase. That seems obvious, but actually conversations often go wrong because of these simple things. So do try to create the right space. Of course, no matter how hard you try, there will always be interruptions: phones and doorbells ringing, children coming in, and so on. But do your best to keep the atmosphere as intimate as possible.

Keep within a comfortable distance of the patient. Generally there should be one to two feet of space between you. A longer distance makes dialogue feel awkward and formal, and a shorter distance can make the patient feel hemmed in, particularly if he or she is in bed and unable to back away. Try to make sure there are no physical obstacles (desks, bedside tables, and so on) between you. Again, that may not be easy, but if you say something (like, *"It's not very easy to talk across this table; may I move it aside for a moment?"*), it helps both of you.

Keep looking at the person while he or she is talking and while you talk: eye contact tells the other person that the conversation is solely between the two of you. If, during a painful moment, you can't look directly at each other, at least stay close and hold the person's hand or touch the person if you can.

Gently Encourage Talking

The other person simply may not be in the mood to talk or even may not want to talk to you that day. Try not to be offended if that's the case. If you're not sure what the patient wants, you can always ask (*"Do you feel like talking?"*). Asking is always better than trying to start a deep conversation (*"Tell me about your feelings."*) when the person may be tired or be "talked out" from a previous visit.

When the patient is talking, try to do two things. First, listen to the person instead of thinking about what you're going to say next. Second, *show* that you're listening.

To listen properly, you must be thinking about what the patient is saying. You should not be rehearsing your reply (doing so would mean that you're anticipating what you think the patient is *about* to say and not listening to what he or she *is* saying). Try not to interrupt the patient. While the patient is talking, don't talk yourself but wait for him or her to stop speaking before you start. If the patient interrupts you while *you're* talking, with a *"But . . ."* or an *"I thought . . ."* or something similar, stop and let the patient speak.

Good listening doesn't mean just sitting there like a running tape recorder. You can actually help the patient talk about what's on his or her mind by encouragement. Simple things work very well. Try nodding or saying affirmative things like *"Yes," "I see,"* or *"Tell me more."* These all sound simple, but at times of maximum stress it's the simple things you need to help things along.

You can also show that you're listening—and hearing—by repeating two or three words from the patient's last sentence. This really does help the talker to feel that his or her words are being taken in. When medical students are shown this technique, they invariably report that using it at home with their friends and family members always moves the conversation along and makes the listener suddenly appear more interested and involved.

You can also reflect back to the talker what you've heard, partly to check that you've got it right and partly to show that you're listening and trying to understand. (You can say things like, *"So you mean that . . ."* or, *"If I've got that straight, you feel . . ."* or even, *"I hear you,"* although that last one might sound a bit self-conscious if it isn't your usual style.)

Use Silent Communication

If someone stops talking, it usually means that she or he is thinking about something painful or sensitive. Wait with your friend for a moment—hold the person's hand or rest your hand on his or her arm if you feel like it—and then ask what he or she was thinking about. Don't rush it, although silences at emotional moments do seem to last for years.

When there's a silence, you may find yourself thinking, *"I have no idea what to say."* On occasion, this may be because there isn't anything *to* say. If that's the case, don't be afraid to say nothing and just stay close. At times like that, a touch or an arm around the patient's shoulder can be of greater value than anything you say.

Sometimes nonverbal communication tells you much more about the other person than you might have expected. Here's one example from a doctor's experience.

Recently I was looking after a middle-aged woman named Gladys who seemed at first to be very angry and uncommunicative. I tried encouraging her to talk, but she kept very "wrapped up." During one interview, while I was talking I put my hand out to hers, rather tentatively because I wasn't sure it was the right thing. To my surprise, she seized it, held it tightly, and wouldn't let go. The atmosphere changed instantly, and she instantly started talking about her fears of further surgery and of being abandoned by her family. The message with nonverbal contact is "try it and see." If, for example, Gladys had not responded so positively, I would have been able to take my hand away, and neither of us would have suffered any setback as a result of it.

Other Good Communication Tools

You are allowed to say things like, *"I find this difficult to talk about"* or, *"I'm not very good at talking about . . ."* or even, *"I don't know what to say."* Students are often taught this when they learn communication skills. One of them said to me later, *"I tried what you told me—telling the patient that I found it awkward—and it really worked."* The student was pleasantly surprised, and so will you be.

If you are sure you understand what the patient means, you can say so. Responses such as, *"You sound very low"* or, *"That must have made you very angry"* tell the person that you've picked up the emotions he or she has been talking about or showing. But if you're not sure what the patient means, then ask, *"What did that feel like?" "What do you think of it?" "How do you feel now?"* Misunderstandings can arise if you make assumptions and are wrong.

It's certainly advantageous when you instinctively pick up what the patient is feeling, but if you don't happen to do that, don't hesitate to ask. Something like *"Help me a bit more to understand what you mean"* is quite useful.

If your friend wants to talk about how rotten she or he feels, let the person do exactly that. It may be difficult for you to hear some of the things being said, but if you can manage it, stay with the person while he or she talks. If you find it too uncomfortable and think you just can't handle the conversation at that moment, then you should say so and offer to try to discuss it again later (you can even say very simple and obvious things like, *"This is making me feel very uncomfortable at the moment. Can we come back to it later?"*). Don't simply change the subject without acknowledging the fact that your friend has raised it.

Ideally no one should give advice to anyone else unless it's asked for. Nevertheless, this isn't an ideal world, and quite often we find ourselves giving advice when we haven't quite been asked. Try not to give advice early in the conversation because doing so stops dialogue. If you're bursting to give advice, it's often easier to use phrases like *"Have you thought about trying . . ."* or (if you're a born diplomat), *"A friend of mine once tried. . . ."* Those are both less bald than *"If I were you, I'd . . . ,"* which makes the patient think (or even say), *"But you're not me,"* which really is a conversation stopper.

Respond to Humor

Many people imagine that there can't possibly be anything to laugh about if you are seriously ill or dying, but that is to miss an extremely important point about humor. Humor performs an essential function in helping us cope with major threats and fears: it allows us to *ventilate,* to get rid of intense feelings and put things in perspective. Humor is one of the ways human beings deal with things that seem to be impossible to deal with. If you think for a moment about the most common subjects of jokes, they include mothers-in-law, fear of flying, hospitals and doctors, sex, and so on. None of those subjects is intrinsically funny. An argument with a mother-in-law, for instance, can be very distressing for all concerned; but an argument with the mother-in-law has been an easy laugh for the stand-up comedian for centuries, because we often laugh most easily at the things we cope with least easily. We laugh at things to get them in perspective, to reduce the size of the threat they represent.

One patient I particularly remember was a woman in her early sixties who had had a mastectomy for breast cancer many years before I met her. She had an external prosthesis (the kind that is worn under a brassiere or bathing suit). She told me (proudly) that she was swimming with her friend when the prosthesis fell out of her bathing suit and floated off toward the shallow end while she was headed for the deep end. Her friend saw it first and pointed out the loss. Whereupon my patient, to her everlasting credit, covered the embarrassment by saying, *"Oh there it goes, doing the breast stroke on its own."* In telling me the story, she was justifiably proud of the way she had coped with potential embarrassment, and it demonstrated, I think, her true bravery and desire to rise above her physical problems. For her, it was very much in character.

From this experience and many others that I have shared with patients, I have become convinced that laughter helps patients get a different handle on their situation. If the patient wants to use humor—even humor that to an outsider might seem black humor—you should certainly encourage and go along with it. It's helping him or her to cope. This does not mean that you should try to cheer the patient up with a supply of jokes. That simply doesn't work. You can best help your friend by responding sensitively. That means responding to his or her humor rather than trying to set the mood with your own.

Understand What Your Friend Is Facing

The objective of sensitive listening is to understand as completely as you can what the other person is feeling. You can never achieve complete understanding, of course, but the closer you get, the better the communication between you and your friend will be. *The more you try to understand your friend's feelings, the more support you are giving.* There are, of course, dozens—if not hundreds—of different aspects that induce fear with any illness, and when the diagnosis is cancer, those fears may be more numerous and may loom larger. Understanding some of the most common concerns can help you encourage your friend to talk about her or his feelings.

The Threat to Health. When we are in good health, the threat of serious illness seems remote, and very few of us think about it before it happens. When it happens to us, we are shocked and confused and often angry or even embittered.

Uncertainty. A state of uncertainty may be even harder to tolerate than either good news or bad news. Not knowing where you are and not knowing what to prepare for is a very painful state in itself. You can help your friend a lot by simply acknowledging the unpleasantness of uncertainty.

Unfamiliarity. With cancer therapy there are often many different disciplines involved in the treatment, each with its own expertise and rules or regulations. Often the patient feels, however mistakenly, unskilled and foolish among the skilled and busy staff. You can help by reinforcing the fact that nobody is "supposed" to know all the details in advance. You can also help by getting some of the patient's questions answered.

Physical Symptoms. Physical symptoms are of paramount importance. The patient may, at various stages in the treatment, have a variety of symptoms (including pain or nausea). Don't hesitate to allow the patient to talk about the symptoms.

Visible Stigmata of Treatment or Disease. The same is true of outward signs of cancer or its treatment. The most obvious is hair loss due to chemotherapy (or radiotherapy to the head). You can help the patient feel less self-conscious by being matter-of-fact about the selection of wigs or scarves.

Social Isolation. Most serious diseases, particularly cancer, seem to put up a social barrier between the patient and the rest of society. Visiting the patient and encouraging mutual friends to do the same are good ways to help reduce that barrier.

The Threat of Death. Many patients are cured of cancer, but the threat of dying of it is always present (and sometimes haunts even those who are truly cured). Naturally you can't abolish that fear, but you can allow the patient to talk about it and, by listening, reduce the impact and pain of that threat. Remember: *"You don't have to have all the answers. Simply listening to the questions will help a lot."*

This is only a partial list, but it will at least give you a glimpse of what may be going through your friend's mind. All of these fears and concerns are normal and natural; what is "wrong" or "unnatural" is not having anybody to talk to about them. That is why you can be so important to your friend.

Informed Decisions: Taking Charge of a Treatment Program

Leslie Laurence

A generation ago, Leslie Laurence relates in the following selection, women with breast cancer usually allowed their doctors to make all the decisions about their treatment. This is no longer the case, Laurence writes: Instead, women extensively research their disease and possible treatments, go to doctors' appointments with notebooks or even tape recorders in hand, and demand honest answers to their questions and an active role in determining which treatments they will have. According to Laurence, one woman even designed custom cuts for her surgeon to make in removing her tumor. This change in patients' roles is related to a growing political activism among breast cancer survivors, she maintains. At both an individual and a group level, she asserts, increased knowledge brings increased power to women with breast cancer. Laurence, a health and science journalist, writes the nationally syndicated column "Her Health." She is also the coauthor of Outrageous Practices: The Alarming Truth About How Medicine Mistreats Women.

Janine Jacinto Sharkey had barely learned she had breast cancer when her surgeon began booking an operating room for a mastectomy. In a state of shock, Sharkey, a 41-year-old partner in an Aspen, Colorado, real estate company, asked her doctor if she should be lining up a plastic surgeon. "Oh, no," he said. "That's not necessary."

Sharkey caught her breath and consulted a female oncologist. "Absolutely do not schedule surgery immediately," the doctor told her. "You can take two weeks to research this. And definitely get yourself a plastic surgeon."

A Decision Based on Information

Sharkey plowed through fourteen books and numerous articles in magazines and medical journals. Then she organized all her research in a three-ring notebook. The first section listed the names and phone

Reprinted from Leslie Laurence, "The Proactive Patient," *Town and Country*, October 1994, by permission of the author.

and fax numbers of her entire medical team—her surgeon, plastic surgeon, oncologist and second-opinion doctors—as well as those of a support group. She put together sections on surgery, reconstruction, chemotherapy, lab work and insurance, and assembled a complete medical history. As questions or concerns arose, she faxed them to her doctors, who she knew would be hard to reach by phone.

Two weeks later, Sharkey made her decisions. Because she had a very aggressive tumor—and because a lumpectomy would entail radiation, which can damage the skin around the breast—she opted for a mastectomy with immediate reconstruction. When her surgeon described the types of incisions he could use—both of which sounded too mutilating—she responded, "Neither is acceptable to me." Well-endowed, Sharkey was not about to give up wearing low-cut dresses. Instead, she devised custom cuts so that her scars would not interfere with her fashion sense. (Sometimes, however, the location of the tumor dictates where the incision must be made.) Sharkey even selected the music to be played in the operating room: classical.

"This was the only way I could cope," says Sharkey. "I'm not the kind of person to sit there and allow someone to dictate to me. I question. I'm involved. I want to know what's going on with my body."

A New, Active Role

Sharkey's informed decision making exemplifies the new role of women in their breast cancer treatment. Today, it's not uncommon for women to meet with their doctors armed with tape recorders and notebooks so they can review the onslaught of information later on. One woman went so far as to videotape her physician, Dr. Marc Lippman, director of the Vincent T. Lombardi Cancer Center at Georgetown University in Washington, D.C., as he discussed her case with her. Nor do women have qualms about asking their doctors for bone scans and other tests. They help select their chemotherapy regimens and, like Sharkey, tell their surgeons, when possible, where they'd like them to cut.

By the time these women have chosen their team of doctors, many are also fluent in all the medical terminology. They know about estrogen receptor tests, used to determine whether a tumor is sensitive to estrogen. (Tumors that are sensitive can often be treated with such hormone therapy as tamoxifen, a drug that blocks the action of estrogen in the breasts.) They're familiar with the S-phase fraction (which indicates how aggressive a tumor is) and flow cytometry, which measures the DNA in a tumor to determine whether it is diploid (with the normal amount of DNA) or aneuploid (with an abnormal amount). They ask how many lymph nodes will be taken and whether the small intercostobrachial nerve (a sensory nerve to the underarm) will be spared.

Their newfound expertise is no mere intellectual exercise. Women are aware more than ever that their lives depend as much on *their* decisions as on their doctors'. And with treatment options more varied and complicated than ever, it's all the more important for them to ask questions and demand answers. Knowing that 182,000 women will be diagnosed with breast cancer this year, and that another 46,000 will die from the disease, makes their task that much more daunting.

The Old Days: Following Orders

"There's no question women are much more involved in decision making when it comes to breast cancer," says Fran Visco, president of the National Breast Cancer Coalition and a Philadelphia attorney who was diagnosed with breast cancer in 1987, at age 39. "They're no longer willing to turn themselves over to the medical community without question."

This is in sharp contrast to the breast cancer patient of a generation ago, who rarely asked questions and followed her doctor's orders to the letter. Dr. Janet Osuch, medical director of the Comprehensive Breast Health Clinic at Michigan State University in East Lansing, shudders when she recalls the one-step procedures of the 1970s, in which women admitted to the hospital had to sign an agreement for a biopsy as well as a possible mastectomy only to "wake up with their breast there or not there," she says. "That was the most disenfranchising approach to the treatment of a disease."

The landscape began to change in the mid-Seventies, when breast cancer patients Betty Ford and Happy Rockefeller went public. Medical writer Rose Kushner, also stricken with breast cancer, pioneered the movement that urged women to be involved in their care. Instrumental in getting the medical community to retire the Halsted radical—an extreme operation that involved removal of the breast, the underlying muscles on the chest wall and the lymph glands under the arm—Kushner lobbied for breast preservation and more funds for breast cancer research. "Rose was light-years ahead of the rest of us," says breast cancer survivor Rosemary Locke, who cofounded a chapter of the Y-Me National Breast Cancer Organization, an information/support/advocacy group based in Chicago.

Indeed, it was trailblazing by women like Kushner that led to a heightened political consciousness among women and the rise of the breast cancer activist movement. In 1976, the book of record was Betty Rollin's *First, You Cry*. In 1994 it's Joyce Wadler's *My Breast*. The titles alone show how far we've come. In Rollin's day, a breast cancer diagnosis was so stigmatizing that a woman often kept her illness hidden from even her closest friends. Now, almost two decades later, Wadler has unabashedly lifted the veil of shame and brought breast cancer out of the closet.

But the '90s have also brought about a new range of complex medical decisions for breast cancer patients to face. Most women have a choice between lumpectomy and mastectomy, with or without reconstruction. If they opt for reconstruction, they must decide whether to use their own tissue or implants—either saline or silicone (the latter is currently not approved by the Food and Drug Administration [FDA] for breast augmentation but is allowed for reconstruction). Then there are the treatment decisions: radiation therapy, chemotherapy, tamoxifen, Taxol (an antitumor drug) or, for advanced cancers, high-dose chemotherapy with a bone-marrow transplant.

For women who decide to get actively involved in their care, "It's a brave new world," says Dr. William Shaw, professor and chairman of the department of plastic surgery at the University of California at Los Angeles (UCLA) Medical Center. "You need to think for yourself, take charge of what's going on, decide what's important and go get it."

Shaw's point was driven home in 1994 with the discovery of falsified data in this country's largest lumpectomy-versus-mastectomy trials, coordinated by a University of Pittsburgh research group. While recent reanalyses of the original, untainted data have suggested that the studies' results still stand, women were reminded that they cannot afford to place blind faith in their doctors or in the medical establishment. The onus is on all women to be activists, at least on their own behalf. As Nancy Brinker, founding chairman of the Susan G. Komen Breast Cancer Foundation, says, "This is a disease for which it's very hard to have peace of mind."

Leaving Cancer Behind

Women must not rely on medical facts alone but look into their own hearts for answers as well. Mimi Bowen, 50, is a case in point. The owner of a designer sportswear boutique in New Orleans, Bowen was satisfied with her choice of a lumpectomy after being diagnosed in July 1992. When her cancer recurred a year later, no one questioned her decision to have a mastectomy with immediate reconstruction. But Bowen stunned her doctors when she said she wanted her other breast removed as a preventive measure.

Her husband, Dr. John Bowen III, chief of surgery at the Ochsner Foundation Hospital in New Orleans where she would have the operation—and who has himself performed breast surgery—thought the second mastectomy was unwarranted, although he said he'd support whatever decision she made. Mimi Bowen's surgeon, too, insisted there was no reason to remove her healthy breast, that her chances of getting cancer in the other breast were small. What's more, a prophylactic mastectomy does not rule out a future incidence of cancer, because the small amount of remaining tissue is still susceptible to disease. Nonetheless, Bowen felt that getting rid of her breasts was the only way to put cancer behind her and go on with her life. Her attitude was, "Look, I don't want to be back on your table next year for the next one." She prevailed and had a double mastectomy.

Author Joyce Wadler had another way of exorcising her tumor. She asked her surgeon if she could see it once it was removed. It turned out to be a grayish-whitish-pink glob the size of a robin's egg. "It really demystified it," she says. "It was a lump lying there in a tray. I could see it was encapsulated, which is supposed to be good. Maybe there were microscopic cancer cells doing the cancan and jeering at me, but I couldn't see them. It gave me a great feeling that this was out."

A Long Road to Recovery

Surgery, of course, is only the first step along the road to recovery. Women who have lumpectomies need radiation, and premenopausal women—and some postmenopausal women—with tumors larger than one centimeter are generally advised to undergo chemotherapy to kill cancer cells that might have traveled to other parts of their bodies. While the drugs used vary depending on the size and stage of the tumor, women often have a choice of regimens. Fran Visco and Janine Jacinto Sharkey both selected a less toxic treatment known as CMF, a mixture of the drugs Cytoxan, methotrexate and 5-fluorouracil, which is less apt to cause nausea, hair loss and premature menopause. For Visco, "It was a quality-of-life issue."

Some women go even further, entering clinical trials—scientific studies to test promising new therapies—both out of a sense of altruism and because they believe they will get state-of-the-art care. Doctors concur. "One way women can make sure they're getting the absolute best care is to be monitored by a whole group of people, as they are in a clinical trial," says Dr. William Wood, chairman of the department of surgery at the Emory University School of Medicine in Atlanta, Georgia.

Laura Marblestone, 44, of Bucks County, Pennsylvania, was 40 when she was diagnosed with breast cancer. Concerned about her prognosis—her cancer had spread to one lymph node—she felt her best option was to participate in a clinical trial at the Fox Chase Cancer Center in Philadelphia, where she was being treated. She was not thrilled, however, to learn that she would be randomly assigned to one of three groups: The first would get CAF (Cytoxan, Adriamycin and 5-fluorouracil), a standard treatment; the second, CAF plus Zoladex, a drug that works on the pituitary gland to make premenopausal women postmenopausal; and the third, CAF, tamoxifen and Zoladex, potentially the most promising regimen. Marblestone decided that if she wasn't randomized to the third group, she would pull out of the study and take the drug combo on her own, an option she knew was available to her. "It turned out I got all three treatments," she says happily. "It's a security blanket. I feel like I'm getting the best treatment possible at this time."

In order to make such informed decisions, women need detailed information about their tumors. If their doctors don't provide it, some women have actually ordered up tests themselves. Carol Wall, 43, of

Montclair, New Jersey, had been reading about the so-called HER-2/Neu genetic marker, which, when present, is associated with relapse. Wall phoned Dr. Dennis Slamon, a UCLA researcher who had done pioneering work in the area, and sent him her slides. Then she flew to UCLA to meet with him. "I really felt better," she says. "When you have a life-threatening illness, it's important to assess how aggressive you must be. Being node-negative and estrogen- and progesterone-receptive were major indicators that my tumor was not rapidly proliferating."

Knowledge Is Power

Doctors generally applaud this proactive role, and some even encourage it. At Columbia-Presbyterian Medical Center in New York, for instance, Dr. Alison Estabrook, chief of the breast service, makes sure all patients get copies of their pathology reports and other medical records. And only rarely are women in such denial that they use information gathering as a way to avoid making decisions. "As long as I feel the patient has been well educated and really knows what's going on, then whatever decision she makes is okay with me," says Dr. Susan Love, director of the UCLA Breast Center. "After all, I'm not God."

Most importantly, patients who participate in decision making gain a sense of control, which makes them more likely to follow through with their treatment plan. "Women who are most informed and take charge feel good about their care. Knowledge definitely is power," says Evelyn Lauder, senior corporate vice-president at Estée Lauder, Inc. Lauder has raised $17 million to build the Evelyn H. Lauder Breast Center at Memorial Sloan-Kettering Cancer Center in New York City, which opened in 1992, and in 1993 established the Breast Cancer Research Foundation to fund research into the causes and treatment of the disease.

Knowledge was indeed power for Carol Wall. Her treatment complete, Wall has become something of an activist. She now devotes much of her time to the National Breast Cancer Coalition and travels to Washington to lobby members of Congress for increased funding for breast cancer research. In fact, it's become a family affair. Carol's husband, Terry Wall, CEO of Vital Signs, a New Jersey manufacturer of medical devices, helped her with a petition drive in 1993. And the Walls' family foundation has become a major donor to the coalition.

Women's progress in orchestrating their care and in nurturing one of this country's biggest advocacy movements delights Rosemary Locke. Her thoughts turn to her friend and role model, Rose Kushner, the original breast cancer activist, who finally succumbed to her disease. "Rose," she says wistfully, "must be smiling down on us from somewhere."

The Chief Methods of Treating Cancer

Gerald P. Murphy, Lois B. Morris, and Dianne Lange

The following selection is taken from *Informed Decisions: The Complete Book of Cancer Diagnosis, Treatment, and Recovery*, a handbook about cancer authorized by the American Cancer Society. Gerald P. Murphy, Lois B. Morris, and Dianne Lange describe the most common methods of treating cancer—surgery, radiation, and chemotherapy—as well as some newer approaches. They also explain the aims of treatment and the factors a doctor considers in deciding which treatment or combination of treatments will work best for a particular person with cancer. The authors point out that a person has a right to be fully informed about the treatments he or she will receive and to help to choose or even refuse treatment. Murphy is the director of research at the Northwest Hospital and the Pacific Northwest Cancer Foundation in Seattle, Washington, and a former chief medical officer of the American Cancer Society. Morris and Lange are medical journalists.

Decisions concerning how best to treat a cancer are based on many aspects of a person's life, but the main concern and primary goal is choosing what will work....

The Aims of Treatment

Cancer treatments are based on the following principles:
- to remove all known tumors;
- to prevent the recurrence or spread of the primary cancer;
- to balance the likelihood of a cure of the cancer against the side effects of the treatment.

If the cancer has recurred or is growing rapidly, the principles for treatment shift slightly to include
- a direct, antitumor approach to controlling the cancer as long as possible;
- the treatment and relief of symptoms if all reasonable curative approaches have been exhausted....

From *Informed Decisions*, by Gerald P. Murphy, Lois B. Morris, and Dianne Lange. Copyright ©1997 by The American Cancer Society. Used by permission of Viking Penguin, a division of Penguin Putnam Inc.

How Treatment Is Chosen
When weighing the options, the physician considers such factors as the following:
- The type and stage of the cancer;
- Your general health;
- Quality of life for you and your family;
- Your financial status, insurance coverage, and managed care options;
- Logistics of travel for treatment;
- Effectiveness of the therapy;
- Side effects of the therapy.

Cancer Stages. The method of treatment your doctor recommends depends on where the cancer is, its size, whether or not it has spread, and how aggressive it is known to be. Oncologists consider these characteristics—known as the type and stage of cancer—in selecting treatment options.

Overall Health. Your health status can be the determining factor in how aggressively the cancer will be treated. Among the many factors that the physician evaluates are:

• *Age.* The general rule has been that children and young adults tend to handle the stress of aggressive treatments better than older people do, but recent studies suggest that many elderly people can tolerate such treatments.

• *General activity level.* Active people may be better able to cope with various therapies than can those whose activity is limited. One system for assessing activity is called *performance status* (PS), which rates activity on a scale from 0 (normal) to 4 (bedridden).

• *Condition of specific organs and systems.* Kidney, heart, and lung function must be assessed before the treatment begins. Certain chemotherapeutic agents can damage these organs, and radiation therapy to the chest can affect lung function. Also, older people may have other serious illnesses.

Personal and Quality-of-Life Issues. To tailor the treatment to your individual needs, and to help you make the right choice considering all the circumstances of your life, doctors must ask many personal questions, and both you and your family need to air your hopes and concerns. Don't be surprised if your doctor wants to know: What are your hopes and dreams at the time the illness is diagnosed? How will the various treatments affect, for example, plans for marriage or hopes for bearing children? How will you take care of young children or other family members? Is extending life worth a great risk to you? Are you frightened of cancer treatments and apt to reject the suggestions most likely to help? Do you have a strong support system?

Financial Status. In a perfect world the issue of finances would not be such a crucial part of health care. However, in these times of shrinking insurance coverage, larger copayments for third-party reimbursements, restrictive health plans, and life circumstances that sometimes catch people without adequate health insurance, expense is a factor. For most people, though, whether they have coverage for a given treatment will be a deciding factor. Cancer treatment can be financially devastating to a family, so information about treatment costs, insurance coverage, and health plan particulars must be obtained, and how the family plans to meet the uncovered costs needs to be discussed.

Logistics of Treatment. Sometimes the type of therapy recommended is appropriate for all reasons except one: You cannot get to the hospital or clinic. This is a common problem for elderly people who live alone or for people who must travel long distances to treatment centers where more advanced options are available or to research institutions for experimental therapies. For instance, the distant travel and long-term hospitalization often required for a bone marrow transplant can put enormous strains on a family's resources.

Will the Treatment Work? Your doctor may offer you one or more treatment options based on the therapies' track record in large clinical trials, current reports in the scientific literature, the most up-to-date standard of care, and his or her own training and experience. In some cases, the likelihood of a treatment curing your particular kind of cancer is well established. In others, the odds of cure are still under study. Along with knowledge of the healing potential of the various options, your physician also weighs specific information about your particular type and stage of cancer and your physical condition. For example, you may not be able to tolerate the most effective therapy for your condition because you are in a poor physical state.

Because every person's cancer is unique, exactly how your tumor will respond to any therapy is not entirely predictable. Doctors balance the pros and cons of many treatment possibilities, narrowing the possibilities down to those they believe have the best chances of extending your life.

Side Effects. Some cancer treatments have uncomfortable, sometimes toxic, side effects. The more common ones, such as hair loss and nausea following chemotherapy, are temporary, and new antinausea drugs have made chemotherapy treatment much more comfortable. However, some side effects last longer and may be permanent. The possible loss of 30 percent of lung function after massive radiation doses for a person preparing for a bone marrow transplant, for instance, must be weighed against the consequences of less intensive therapy.

Conventional Treatments

When considering different treatment approaches, it is helpful to keep in mind the general principles: to remove all the primary tumor, if possible; to prevent its recurrence; and to preserve the integrity of your organs, physical functions, and immune system as much as possible.

Most cancer treatments include surgery to remove a tumor and often radiation or chemotherapy as well. Seventy to 85 percent of all people with cancer receive some combination of treatments, as either the primary therapy or the therapy for a recurrent tumor.

It is believed that a combined approach best prevents the recurrence of cancer. Cancer specialists believe that reducing, by radiation or chemotherapy, the number of cancer cells in certain tumors before surgery may reduce the possibility of its spread or recurrence.

Surgery

Most people with cancer have surgery, whether it is to obtain a biopsy, to determine the stage of a particular cancer, or to remove a growth and perhaps some of the surrounding tissue. Many surgeries for early tumors are curative, determining both the stage and removing the tumor in one procedure.

The recovery and adjustment period after surgery depend on how large the tumor is, where it is located, and how much normal tissue must be removed along with the malignancy. Sometimes the surgery is so extensive that it affects the function of certain organs and interferes with normal life. In this case, you will need rehabilitation and some adjustments in your daily life. Occasionally, the surgery is disfiguring, and you will benefit from psychological help to adjust to the change.

Most serious and/or long-term or permanent effects can be predicted, so considering them is part of the decision to have surgery or not. In the event that the extent of the surgery is unknown beforehand, talking about all possible outcomes is part of the informed-consent process.

Chemotherapy

Chemotherapy is a *systemic* treatment, since it attacks cancer cells wherever they are in the body. Malignant cells divide more rapidly than do most normal cells, and chemotherapy works by destroying cancer cells during their dividing phase when they are more vulnerable. Unfortunately, however, the cells of some organs (such as hair follicles and the lining of the stomach and intestines) also divide rapidly, so these organs are susceptible to the side effects of the anticancer drugs.

More than 50 anticancer drugs are now in use. They are given by mouth or injected into muscle or directly into the bloodstream. Chemotherapy is used alone as a definitive treatment for cancers such as Hodgkin's disease, in combination with another approach such as surgery, or as an *adjuvant* therapy (meaning that it is "added" before or after surgery or radiation therapy) to deal with any known or suspected spread of the primary tumor.

People receiving chemotherapy often receive a combination of drugs, with some designed to target the malignant cells at specific points in their division cycles. Using drugs in combination in this way helps minimize the toxic side effects.

The maximum chemotherapy dosage is based on the amount needed to destroy cancer cells versus the amount of damage that the rapidly dividing healthy tissues in the body can sustain.

Radiation Therapy

About 60 percent of people with cancer receive some sort of radiation therapy during their treatment. Like surgery, radiation therapy is considered a local treatment. A precise dose of radiation is targeted to a specific tumor to eradicate the cancer cells while sparing the surrounding healthy tissue. Radiation damages the diseased cells' DNA, making them less able to reproduce. Because cancer cells divide more quickly than do those of healthy tissue, they are more vulnerable to radiation, just as they are to anticancer drugs.

Radiation may be used alone, as the primary therapy, or following surgery, as a way of eliminating any stray cancer cells in the area and preventing the local recurrence of a tumor.

The equipment used to deliver radiation therapy has become quite sophisticated, allowing tumors deep within the body to be targeted without damaging the surrounding tissues. Dosages are calculated according to the tumor's sensitivity to radiation and the normal, adjacent tissue's ability to tolerate exposure to radiation.

Experimental Therapies and New Approaches

Some people initially choose to try an experimental treatment, especially when they have a type of cancer that has not responded well to conventional therapies. Other physicians recommend this option only for treating recurrent cancer or advanced disease.

Experimental therapies are studied in *clinical trials*—studies that are usually carried out in connection with a medical school or in one of the National Cancer Institute's (NCI) comprehensive cancer centers. Clinical trials are designed to incorporate the best available care with new approaches in cancer treatment.

Some of the following therapies are better established than others; that is, the results of some studies are promising enough that they may already be considered "conventional" treatment for certain cancers although still under study for others.

Immunotherapy. The objective of immunotherapy is to "turn on" the body's own defense against cancer cells. Among the many agents currently being tested are *biologic response modifiers (BRMs),* which include monoclonal antibodies, interferons, interleukin-2, and colony-stimulating factors (CSFs). These agents are not without temporary side effects. CSFs, for example, cause fatigue, fever, rashes, and diarrhea.

Bone Marrow Transplant. At first, bone marrow transplant (BMT) was used primarily for leukemia and lymphoma, but now it is being studied as a supportive therapy for people undergoing high-dose chemotherapy for solid-tumor cancers, such as breast cancer.

The idea is to replace the bone marrow that has been damaged by chemotherapy or radiation with whole bone marrow or, in some cases, immature blood cells from bone marrow taken from a healthy person. This ability to transplant bone marrow makes it possible for you to receive high doses of anticancer agents that otherwise would be fatal.

The process, however, is difficult, and some of the side effects may be life-threatening and can create long-term, even lifelong, problems. Also, like their policies for other experimental treatments, many insurance companies' and managed care plans will not pay for bone marrow transplants for certain types of cancer.

Gene Therapy. If the cancer is triggered by a genetic defect, and scientists believe that some cancers are, then finding and correcting the defective gene is less damaging and more cost-effective than chemotherapy. Gene therapy consists of delivering genes via viruses to human cells, where they can redirect the genetic messages, thereby replacing the malignancy message with a normal one. . . .

The Right to Choose

Discussing the risks and benefits [of a treatment] is part of a process called informed consent, which is a legal standard that means a person has been told enough about the risks and benefits of a treatment or procedure to decide whether he or she wants to proceed. If the person cannot sign a written consent form, permission can be granted by the court. Informed consent is required before you undergo any cancer treatment.

Physicians are trained to heal. But most cancer specialists would agree that the wishes of the person they are treating also must be honored. For example, Sarah, 83, was told she had advanced pancreatic cancer. When she learned that her cancer was fast moving and aggressive, she requested that her doctor not treat the cancer itself but rather help her to remain as comfortable as possible. She discussed her decision with her family, who initially wanted her to put up more of a "fight." They all spoke with hospital social workers and a psychiatrist, and all ultimately agreed her decision was well thought out. Sarah made final legal arrangements for her property, spent time with her children and grandchildren, and stayed at home for the duration of her illness.

Sometimes it is appropriate not to undergo treatment or to direct the treatment toward relief of the symptoms only, such as when a person has already been treated unsuccessfully or when disease has advanced so far that it cannot be cured.

In cases like these, there are legal issues that must be addressed by everyone involved. When the disease is advanced or the cancer has progressed and all treatment possibilities have been exhausted, it is important to establish the wishes of the person with cancer. For instance, a "Do Not Resuscitate" order must be in the medical chart if life-saving or life-support steps are not to be taken. Although the legal requirements vary from state to state, the law generally requires a signed document (a so-called living will and/or power of attorney for a family member) specifying the patient's wish to stop attempts at curative treatment.

NEW ACCEPTANCE OF ALTERNATIVE CANCER TREATMENTS

Doug Podolsky

U.S. News & World Report writer Doug Podolsky reports that up to half of all cancer patients make some use of alternative treatments, which are not fully sanctioned by conventional Western medicine. Alternative treatments used for cancer range from herbs and acupressure to hypnosis and relaxation techniques, Podolsky writes. Many doctors formerly rejected such treatments outright, according to Podolsky, but growing numbers of cancer centers now accept and even encourage at least some alternative techniques—provided that patients use them along with, rather than instead of, the standard cancer treatments of surgery, radiation, and chemotherapy. Whether or not it directly affects their disease, such "complementary care" can make patients feel better and can help them to handle pain and stress, Podolsky concludes.

Jon Seskevich's hands hover over Kathleen Beil's abdomen, chest, throat and head. "I'm able to sense a disturbance in the energy field," he says. Using spiritual energy, Seskevich tries to "unruffle" her field and so aid in the 53-year-old cancer patient's recovery. Beil, who is recuperating from surgery for early ovarian cancer, says Seskevich's "healing touch" therapy makes her feel peaceful.

By one estimate, half of cancer patients turn to unorthodox treatments—from therapeutic touch to herbal treatments and shark cartilage. But Beil, a homemaker from Durham, N.C., didn't seek out Seskevich's healing hands. Seskevich, a nurse clinician at Duke Comprehensive Cancer Center in Durham, approached *her*, with the approval of her doctor, John Soper, during Beil's hospitalization for cancer surgery. "I think it's calming, if nothing else," says Soper, a professor of gynecologic oncology. "You can convey a lot of reassurance by the old laying on of hands even if scientifically you can't prove the benefit."

When the war on cancer started, it was improbable that Duke—or any mainstream hospital—would offer such treatments, concedes O. Michael Colvin, the center's director. "We're comfortable with it as

Reprinted from Doug Podolsky, "A New Age of Healing Hands," *U.S. News & World Report*, February 5, 1996, with permission. Copyright, 1996, U.S. News & World Report.

long as patients understand that it's not going to cure their cancer in and of itself," Colvin says. "It's not designed to offer false hope but to help patients deal with the stress of cancer and conventional treatments." At a growing number of premier hospitals, treatments long scoffed at by mainstream doctors as "alternative medicine" are now being offered to cancer patients. In fact, among physicians, the new buzzword is "complementary care," implying that some New Age treatments may be useful as adjuncts to surgery, radiation and chemotherapy.

For instance, some cancer patients treated conventionally at Duke also receive guided imagery (patients imagine their tumors shrinking), meditation, biofeedback and prayer. In another flick at New Age therapy, Memorial Sloan-Kettering Cancer Center in New York teaches some patients the Japanese tea ceremony to help relieve anxiety and bring balance to their lives. Columbia Presbyterian Medical Center in New York offers hypnosis, reflexology (massaging specific spots on the foot is said to unblock clogged "energy channels"), therapeutic touch (energy field manipulation), yoga and acupressure (acupuncture without needles).

It's a dangerous trend, says William Jarvis, head of the National Council Against Health Fraud. Mixing standard medicine with "pseudoscience," he says, will only confuse patients. He worries that doctors are "putting a stamp of legitimacy" on unproven treatments that patients may later turn to instead of traditional cancer care.

Types of Alternative Therapies

Good national data on insurance coverage for such treatments don't exist. But experts say insurers are most likely to pay when complementary care is ordered during hospitalization—since it's done under doctors' supervision. Here's a roundup of some of the most intriguing mind-body cancer therapies.

• *Meditative methods.* There's now sufficient data on the effectiveness of hypnosis, biofeedback and meditation for the relief of cancer pain, a technology assessment panel of the National Institutes of Health concluded in November 1995. Of the three, hypnosis works best. And behavioral therapy may even influence cancer's course. The most convincing evidence appears in two small but well-done studies by researchers at the UCLA School of Medicine in *Archives of General Psychiatry:* One six-month study found that malignant melanoma patients trained in relaxation techniques showed significant increases in the number and activity of cancer-slaying natural killer cells; the six-year follow-up found higher mortality among the untrained group.

• *Therapeutic massage.* Energy field manipulation is still unproven, though in 1994 an influential scientist at the Karolinska Institute in Stockholm published a paradigm for its basis. Energy from "electric circuits" in the body, he theorized, might affect the structure and function of biological systems. ("A legitimate area of theory and research," says fraud hunter Jarvis, "but not for patient care.")

• *Herbal potions.* Scientific findings on herbal supplements as cancer treatments are scant, with no definitive conclusions yet. But in 1995, investigators at the University of Heidelberg published some provocative results on a Chinese herbal extract that they call Herba Epimediia glycoside icariin. In test-tube experiments, the herb stimulated healthy cells to produce an anticancer substance called tumor necrosis factor-alpha. An appropriate dose, they reported, could some day prove useful against cancer.

• *Unapproved medicine.* Anecdotal reports of remarkable recoveries by patients of Houston cancer doctor Stanislaw Burzynski make his antineoplaston treatment the most prominent of the unconventional medical therapies. Good data on the usefulness of the non-FDA-approved drug, which consists of synthesized amino acid derivatives, may be a year away—perhaps more if legal problems land Burzynski in prison. In November 1995, he was indicted by a federal grand jury on 75 counts alleging violation of federal drug laws, mail fraud in dealing with insurance companies and contempt of a federal court ban on shipping drugs across state lines. [In 1996,] Burzynski denie[d] all the charges and vow[ed] to continue treating patients as long as he [was] able.

• *Prayer therapy.* A news item in the *Journal of the American Medical Association* in May 1995 reported on doctors' renewed interest in spirituality's role in health. In a review of 27 studies, one researcher reported that in 22 of them, religious involvement had a positive effect on good health, including cases of cancer. As complementary care options go, it's one that can't hurt and might just work miracles.

HOW TO EVALUATE ALTERNATIVE TREATMENTS

Barrie R. Cassileth

In the following selection, Barrie R. Cassileth examines several types of alternative cancer treatments, including special diets and treatments that attempt to strengthen the immune system. Even though these treatments may be useful in helping patients feel better, Cassileth maintains, they have not been scientifically proven to destroy cancer. She warns against accepting the unsupported personal claims of "miraculous" cures that often form the core of advertising for alternative treatments, and she provides standards and sources of information that can help people with cancer and their families to evaluate the effectiveness of such treatments. Cassileth, a psychosocial oncologist at Duke University in Durham, North Carolina, is the author of *The Alternative Medicine Handbook: The Complete Reference Guide to Alternative and Complementary Therapies.*

Surgery, radiation therapy and chemotherapy have been "accepted" cancer treatments for a long time. They are accepted because they were developed after years of study with animals and then humans. The studies were based on logical, scientific principles, and the treatments were then shown to be effective against the growth of tumors in thousands of people.

These conventional cancer treatments are responsible for dramatic improvements in survival over the past few decades. Where few people used to survive for long after a cancer diagnosis, about half of all diagnosed patients are now cured.

"Miraculous Cures"

Every few years or so, the media present a startling report on some new way to treat cancer. The treatment is typically described as resulting in "miraculous cures" or as being able to prolong lives in some extraordinary fashion. The exact formula or chemical content is usually unknown or is kept secret by the practitioner promoting this new method. Knowledge of the treatment often spreads only by word of

Excerpted from Barrie R. Cassileth, "Questionable and Unproven Cancer Therapies," in *Everyone's Guide to Cancer Therapy*, by Malin Dollinger, Ernest H. Rosenbaum, and Greg Cable, 2nd rev. ed., Somerville House Books, Toronto. Reprinted with permission.

mouth or by being publicized in certain types of popular magazines and tabloid papers.

These "cures" are not reported in the scientific literature, however, nor are they backed by the extensive data and research information that accompany reports of new medical tests and therapies. There are two reasons why reports on these cures never show up in scientific journals.

The most common reason is that the practitioners promoting the unorthodox method did not actually study it and so never prepared any report to send to scientific publications. Typically, these practitioners say they are too busy treating patients to spend time on evaluation or research, even though it is only through rigorous evaluation and research that the worth of a treatment can be known.

The other reason is that a report may have been sent to a journal's editorial board, but that its publication in a medical journal was considered not warranted because the quality of its data was so poor or because it lacked accurate information.

Most unproven methods have never been studied at all. The only "proof" their developers usually offer is the display of people who—the practitioners say—have been cured by their therapy. The "beneficiaries" of the miracle treatment may be displayed live during some publicity event. Or they may testify to the worth of the treatment in writing, often in a brochure. Of course, it is not possible to know from these kinds of displays whether people were cured by the unproven method, whether they received conventional treatment before or at the same time as receiving the unproven treatment or if they were, in fact, ever diagnosed as having cancer at all.

Stories told by or about a patient are called anecdotal reports, and they can sound very impressive and persuasive. Even assuming they are true, however, no faith can be placed in anecdotal reports about one or even a few patients. Careful study of many clinically similar patients is required before a legitimate conclusion can be drawn about any new therapy.

The Appeal of New Methods

To people with cancer and their families, unproven treatments can look very appealing, especially when no conventional treatment is left to be tried. They may be drawn to some unorthodox remedy even if there is no solid evidence that a product or procedure is beneficial. Patients and families may be ready to try anything, feeling that they have nothing to lose.

But there *is* something to lose. The financial losses can be considerable for anyone who pursues a useless treatment, usually at an expensive private clinic. For those who are terminally ill and beyond the help of conventional treatment, false hope can also rob them of the good use of what time they have left. When patients can still benefit from conventional treatment and there is a possibility of a long remission or even cure, what can be lost is a life.

It is understandable that you or your family may be attracted to some unproven therapy. The best physical and financial protection, however, is to become an educated health care consumer. Develop a basic understanding of medical procedures and services, including unproven methods. . . .

The questionable cancer remedies now getting the most attention range from those that are based on misinterpretations of scientific data to those that are downright fraudulent. All are good examples of why cancer patients and their families must become *educated* health care consumers. The principles or concepts on which unproven methods are based must be reviewed critically so that their logic and accuracy can be evaluated.

Complementary Treatments

The standard treatments—surgery, chemotherapy, radiation therapy and biological therapy—are all designed to remove or kill tumor cells. But cancer specialists and other doctors may also recommend other types of treatment that are not designed to kill tumor cells. Instead, these treatments aim to bring about some overall improvement in general health and well-being. They are often called complementary or adjunctive treatments because they are used along with the standard therapies.

Nutritional therapy, relaxation therapy, a focus on emotional wellbeing, the provision of effective support systems, yoga and so on all fit into this category. When used in conjunction with standard therapies, these are legitimate therapeutic approaches. They are helpful in recovery or rehabilitation.

But sometimes these adjunctive or complementary therapies are advertised as having the power to cure cancer on their own. Nutritional programs are promoted as dietary "cures." Relaxation therapy or imagery are promoted as essential to developing the right attitude that will make cancer go away.

Many people are drawn to these "cures" because they are claimed to be free of the sometimes unpleasant side effects of conventional treatments. But this is a very destructive and unfortunate misuse of otherwise helpful activities. When cancer patients look on these complementary therapies as cures, they may decide—or even be encouraged—to stop their conventional treatments. Some may assume that they no longer have to see their oncologist or receive chemotherapy. If that happens, they may lose their chance for remission or cure.

Immune-Enhancing Therapies

After a long period of intense and well-publicized scientific study of the immune system, a number of unorthodox practitioners developed therapies aimed at improving cancer patients' immune systems. Several unorthodox approaches work toward this goal. One aims to stimulate immune function through injected vaccines. Another aims to enhance the immune system through mental imagery and attitude.

These therapies sound legitimate because they address an issue—the immune system—that is a subject of legitimate scientific investigation. Because the terminology sounds scientific and the rationale appears to be a great deal more accurate than it really is, it is important to understand some background information before evaluating these therapies.

There is some scientific experimental evidence showing that the immune system plays a role in the body's defenses against cancer. There is very little evidence indicating that the system is helpful against metastatic disease once cancer has developed. But there is no scientific proof that mental imagery or adopting a new emotional attitude influences the immune system in a way that affects the growth of tumors.

Many immune-stimulating agents have been studied in clinical trials. These include the tuberculosis vaccine, BCG, as well as a variety of chemicals that have been shown to stimulate immunity in animals. One immune stimulant—Levamisole—was approved by the National Cancer Institute in late 1989 for use in combination with standard chemotherapy for one stage of colon cancer because this combination produced better results than chemotherapy alone. BCG has also been approved for the treatment of early bladder cancer. Yet very few immune-enhancing substances are known to improve disease in humans. Ongoing studies with other cancers have not yet shown much benefit from immune-enhancing techniques.

Metabolic Treatments

These are offered by many practitioners and clinics in the United States and in Tijuana, Mexico. Metabolic procedures vary according to the practitioner, but they generally include:
- "detoxification," typically through cleansing of the colon
- special diets
- vitamins
- minerals
- enzymes

Metabolic treatments sound appealing. They emphasize "natural" therapy with treatment directed at "cellular detoxification and restoration." But these treatments are neither natural nor safe. Many people have been harmed by them. Like most unproven treatments, metabolic therapy is based on an invented principle: that toxins and waste materials in the body interfere with metabolism and healing. Cancer and other chronic illnesses are seen as the result of degeneration of the liver and pancreas or of the degeneration of the immune and "oxygenation" systems.

The educated consumer will know that there is no such thing as an oxygenation system. Nor is there any such thing as cellular detoxification and restoration.

Special Diets

The "miracle diet" that cures cancer is a staple of the tabloid press. You can read about these diets at the checkout counter of any supermarket, but not in many other places.

Such diets are a good example of the faulty logic that often accompanies a misunderstanding of scientific information. People read or hear that low-fat diets may help prevent some cancers. Eating a low-fat, high-fiber diet, for example, can lower the risk of developing some kinds of cancer. But some people then make an illogical leap from prevention to cure and assume that these same dietary measures can cure a cancer once it has started to grow.

Following a special diet or eating certain foods will not make cancer go away. Yet many dietary "cures" are promoted in North America today and they are often accepted at face value. Little attention is paid to how they may rob the body of necessary nutrients or that they may be based on false, illogical concepts. The popular macrobiotic diet, for example, is based on a fanciful and completely faulty concept of how the human body works.

The special diets are usually "practitioner-specific." This means that each promoter offers a different approach to cancer therapy through a different type of diet. Oriental herbal remedies recently joined various diets as popular cancer treatments or cures.

None is known to be helpful. Many result in nutritional deficiencies, a situation cancer patients should avoid at all costs. Moderation is still the best approach to diet for all medical problems. Taking excessive amounts of vitamins, minerals or "health food" substitutes may do more harm than good.

The Newest Fads

Consistent with the shifts and trends that characterize unconventional cancer medicine, several products and approaches recently have attained special prominence. Among the most popular are two very different methods: efforts to harness mind-body power, and the use of shark cartilage as a cancer cure.

Advocates of the first method claim that happiness, positive attitudes, a strong will, meditation, mental imagery and other psychological or mental efforts can cause cancer to regress or disappear. These claims are groundless. Emotions do not influence cancer outcome (nor is there any evidence that they play a role in the development of cancer in the first place). Attitude, meditation and so on can enhance quality of life—an important goal in itself—but they do not cure cancer.

The shark cartilage cancer cure fad stems from a recent book with an untrue title, *Sharks Don't Get Cancer*. Powdered cartilage is sold in health food stores, thus avoiding the clinical proof of effectiveness and safety that proper research provides, and to get around the Food and Drug Administration (FDA) review necessary before a product or treatment can be approved for use as medicine. There is no acceptable evidence to show that shark cartilage works.

Standards for Sound Treatments

To make educated decisions about a treatment, it is necessary to go beyond testimonials and promises. You have to understand what the unproven method is all about, the concepts on which it is based and what its track record is.

A legitimate treatment method meets the following standards. A dubious or questionable treatment does not meet any of them.

• The method was studied scientifically and shown to be more effective than no treatment at all.

• The benefits of the method clearly exceed any harm it might do.

• Studies of the method have been properly conducted. That is, an appropriate research design has been used, the studies have been subject to review by others knowledgeable in the field and a human studies committee has given the study its approval.

If you have any doubt about a therapy, examine it critically against these three standards. Check the brochure or any other available literature to see if the method was studied and found to be better than nothing. The brochure will certainly note the "benefits" of the method, but you will have to look for or ask about any problems.

The third point is the easiest to determine. Legitimate treatment methods are *always* evaluated with the participation of other scientists. They are *always* reviewed and approved by a human subjects committee in an established, reputable medical institution.

Warning Signs

"Secret" cures or treatments that are said to work only in the hands of one practitioner are questionable by definition. New scientific therapies are always made available through meetings, talks and publications to the entire community of scientists and researchers. The worth of the treatment can be confirmed only when the results of research can be reproduced by others.

An in-depth, critical evaluation of an unproven program can tell you whether the "cured patients" offered as proof of its worth actually had a diagnosis of cancer confirmed by a tissue biopsy. It can tell you whether the "cured patients" received conventional treatment along with the questionable therapy, even if all credit 'is given to the unproven method. It will indicate what the problems and toxicities associated with the unproven treatment might be.

Sources of Information

Your oncologist can help supply this information and should be your major source for information and assistance. He or she best understands your illness and knows which treatments are useful for you. You can also contact your local offices of the American Cancer Society or the American Medical Association. . . .

In 1991, the Office of Alternative Medicine was established by the United States Congress. Part of the National Institutes of Health, the major goal of this office is to evaluate the merits of complementary techniques and promising alternatives in effecting cure or alleviating the symptoms of illnesses, including cancer. A range of alternatives, including homeopathy, meditation and other mind-body techniques, and acupuncture, will be evaluated. Regardless of their outcome, such investigations will provide extremely important information.

That information, your physician's advice and the resources noted above will help you and your family become educated health care consumers able to consider helpful adjunctive or complementary therapies and avoid treatments that have no benefit. You will certainly save financially. You will spare yourself much anguish. You may gain yourselves precious moments together. And, if there is still a chance for remission or cure, you may also prevent a tragedy of the highest order.

CHAPTER 4

COPING WITH CANCER: PERSONAL VIEWS

Contemporary Issues
Companion

Sharing Cancer Information on the Internet

Glenn Fleishman

Glenn Fleishman is very familiar with computers—he has co-founded a company that develops Web pages and has worked as the catalogue manager for an online book order service, Amazon.com. Therefore, when Fleishman learned that he had cancer, he turned to the source of information he knew best, the Internet, to find out about possible treatments for his condition. In the following selection, Fleishman relates how he used the Internet to learn about treatments and their side effects, the survival rates for his particular kind of cancer, and other information that helped him work with his doctor to decide on the best treatment for him. In addition, he found home pages in which other people with cancer shared their personal experiences. Fleishman was inspired to set up his own Web page, he says, both to keep his friends up to date on his progress and to provide information that might help other cancer patients. After several months of treatment, Fleishman writes, his cancer is in full remission and he is optimistic about the future.

Cancer was not the diagnosis I had hoped for. But it did expose the root of a baffling year and a half of poor health.

In the fall of 1996, I had taken the coolest job in the world, catalogue manager at Amazon.com, knowing that long hours would be the norm. I had worked 60 or 70 hours a week most of my adult life. But after just a few months, I couldn't continue on that schedule and left the position.

Unfortunately, moving into the slow lane on the Infobahn [Information Superhighway] wasn't the solution. I started to get weary every afternoon and began lying down for two or three hours. Near the end of a trip that my girlfriend, Lynn Warner, and I took to Connecticut in December 1997 to visit her parents, I had a 24-hour flu with a fever of 102 degrees. The fever subsided but wouldn't stay away.

On a rare snowy day in mid-January 1998, when less than an inch

Reprinted from Glenn Fleishman, "Turning to the Net to Lift the Shadows of Cancer's Dark Days," *The New York Times*, July 9, 1998, by permission. Copyright ©1998 by The New York Times.

of powder kept most Seattle drivers off the road (the absence of Seattle drivers making it the safest driving day of the year), my Utah-reared doctor, Garrison Bliss, made it into his office for our appointment. He listened carefully, took chest X-rays, did an exam and made a preliminary diagnosis of lymphatic disease, probably lymphoma. One CAT scan and a biopsy later, the diagnosis was confirmed: Hodgkin's disease (also known as Hodgkin's lymphoma), nodular sclerosing subtype.

My only truly bad day followed as Lynn and I absorbed the news. I knew little about Hodgkin's disease besides knowing about a couple of people who had had it. Paul Allen, Microsoft's co-founder and a local billionaire, had beaten it in the mid-1980s, leaving his company to fight the disease. And a talented college acquaintance, Dave Saltzman, an author and illustrator of children's books, died of it eight years ago.

Dr. Bliss is not, he stressed, a cancer specialist, and he suggested that I hold my questions until I could meet a week later with an oncologist, Dr. David White of the Polyclinic in Seattle. But, with no real knowledge at hand, and my stomach dancing the fandango, I found it impossible to wait for answers.

Seeking Answers on the Internet

The place I would turn for information was obvious: I had used the Internet and other networks since 1986 and had spent most of my days and nights on the modern Net since 1994, when I co-founded the Point of Presence Company, a commercial Web site developer (which I sold to join Amazon).

An Infoseek search for "Hodgkin's" and "disease" in close proximity turned up thousands of pages. Some seemed unquestionably credible: Onco Link (oncolink.upenn.edu) at the University of Pennsylvania was vouched for by its address. But a click away from the most serious cancer institutions were sites promoting laetrile, herbs and obscure Hawaiian fruits as sure-fire cancer cures.

I lacked the knowledge to evaluate those sites. Just like a high-school student who cannot find Africa on a map of the world, I couldn't even point to my liver on a map of the internal organs. Onco Link and similar resources educated me rapidly about my disease and the chances for remission and long-term survival. (They also confirmed my suspicions about laetrile.)

Information Brings Power

My Internet readings led me to the two main chemotherapy regimens for treatment of Hodgkin's disease, both of which involved four drugs and about six months of every-other-week treatments. One treatment was disturbing because it includes mustard gas, mechlorethamine, as a cell-killing element (I pictured World War I doughboys in gas masks laid out in medical examining rooms), and it almost always causes sterility. The alternative treatment, which has a similar rate of success, can cause heart and lung damage, but patients have a much better chance of remaining fertile.

This reading and surfing led Lynn and me to think that the second treatment was the better option. I found several sites explaining the regimen and the administration and even nailed down a site listing the wholesale prices for all the medications I would take.

My first meeting with Dr. White must have taken him aback: Lynn and I had two pages of questions prompted by our reading. He didn't show any surprise or impatience, though, and spent almost three hours giving us answers and options. His recommendations coincided fairly closely with the course of treatment I had hoped to go through.

Personal Web Sites

Just after getting a definitive diagnosis, I had sent out dozens of E-mail messages to friends and business colleagues. Because of my slightly peripatetic career, my friends are scattered around the country and the world. I explained my disease, how I felt and how optimistic I was about a positive outcome.

As I started treatment and began experiencing side effects like nausea, hair loss, weight gain and clotting problems, I found that there was a gap between the more technical information at sites like Onco Link and the practical patient-education manuals that the National Cancer Institute and nonprofit cancer societies hand out. That gap is filled by personal Web sites set up by people who are going through or have gone through treatment as a way of sharing their experiences. While Onco Link describes alopecia (hair loss), and the National Cancer Institute literature reminds you that wigs bought for chemotherapy-induced hair loss may be tax deductible, it is the personal sites that have links to on-line wig stores and give advice on what kind of wigs look best.

The personal sites also provide more descriptive details about some of the more bizarre side effects. Without finding the informally named Mike's Lymphoma Resource Pages—an incredible, well-organized descriptive list run by Mike Barela, comprising hundreds of links—I might have screamed when I saw red urine after my first chemotherapy treatment. I would not have known that one drug I was taking, Adriamycin, can cause urine to turn red for hours or days. More directly, a list called the Hodgkin's Disease Mailing List linked me to people who have the disease or have family members with it; others on the list went into remission as long as decades ago and stay on the list to offer encouragement and information.

Setting Up a Web Page

A few treatments into the process, I decided to set up my own Web page, just as many others had done. Putting my health out there for anyone to read might seem strange, but a Web page would make it easier for those who cared to find out about my progress without feeling compelled to call or write. It would make it easier for me, too, as I was not sure how much E-mail I would be able to respond to, and it would help comfort those particularly concerned.

I had first thought that I might keep a real diary on the Web, but I realized that there were plenty of issues—fertility, for example—that I didn't want to share with the world. Other issues, like the experience and joy of having an intravenous catheter and port put in, were easier to share.

Some friends have said that they have used the links I provided to go out and research the disease themselves to assuage their own fears about the disease. By checking Web logs, I see that a number of people search for "lymphatic cancer" at Alta Vista or another search engine and wind up at my site.

I didn't end up posting daily, as I didn't always have enough news. ("Feeling great! Walked three miles! Ate lunch!") I had some bad days, the worst of which was after the surgery for my intravenous catheter and port about a month after starting chemotherapy. I had the surgery and chemotherapy on Friday, and I was injected with GCSF (granulocyte colony stimulating factor) on the following Monday to improve my white-cell counts. Feeling depressed for the first time since getting the diagnosis, I put off writing about it until I'd bounced back.

Posting my own site also resulted in more interesting phone conversations: the people who called were up-to-the-minute on my status, and we talked of other things. The most draining task after the diagnosis has been explaining the disease to every new person who finds out about my condition. The number of people who see a bald head and say, "What, you in chemo or something?" is staggeringly high.

Posting Good News

After a few treatments, my health began to improve. My immune system stopped trying to throttle me, and the miracle drug Zofran almost entirely suppressed the chemotherapy-induced nausea. At that point, the Hodgkin's list started to freak me out. It had too many posts from folks with terrible side effects, extreme cases or just no hope. Even reading about other people's chemotherapy could nauseate me, despite the drugs I had at hand. After just a few weeks, I had to unsubscribe from the list, planning to return after chemotherapy to put something back into the kitty I had drawn from.

By April 1998, I was updating my health page less frequently, as the news was uniformly good. The lymphoma had started retreating almost immediately after chemotherapy began and I felt better and better. X-rays taken at 6 weeks and 12 weeks into treatment confirmed what I was already feeling. Fatigue never really hit me, although my mental abilities had turned a little sluggish. A Bugs Bunny marathon on Comedy Central struck me as a bit funnier than it would have a few months before. (Posts to the Hodgkin's mailing list assure me that this effect is temporary.)

In late May, an M.R.I. scan showed no traces of the disease; I was in full remission, right on schedule. When I padded out of the magnetic resonance imaging machine in my socks and a hospital gown and the imaging technician pinned up the image of my insides—my cancer-free insides—I could point to the liver without any hesitation.

An Opportunity for Growth and Learning

Georgia Brown

In the following selection, Georgia Brown writes that the major event of 1997 in her life was the discovery that she had cancer. Brown describes how she overcame the fear that the diagnosis produced, called upon the love of family and friends during the difficult time of her treatment, and found additional support from other cancer patients. According to Brown, the greatest gain from her cancer experience was an improved ability to see the "big picture." She feels that she now has a better understanding of what is really important to her and is much less likely than before to waste energy fretting about the details of daily life.

As the year draws to a close, it's time to take stock as well as look forward. It's useful to look back and assess events and goals planned, made or failed, as the case may be, then use the product of this process in setting objectives for the year to come.

Many of my goals were met this year. Some still are in flux but evolving; others became sidetracked by events. The major event of the year for me was cancer, a life-altering, if not mind-altering, experience.

Overcoming Fear

Those first words over the telephone from the doctor caused time to stand still: "It's not good." The initial reaction was a chilling numbness, followed by confusion, then fear.

Fear is such a waste of emotional energy. Although it's natural enough, it's not very productive. Sure, it can motivate, but it does that negatively, so it's best to shed fear as soon as possible. Easier said than done, but fear does pass.

An hour after that dolorous phone call, my husband and I sat at the dining-room table to make our plans. Our first agreement was that we would keep life as normal as possible. The second was that we would eliminate the extraneous and unnecessary—whether it was thoughts, activities or people. We simply had enough to occupy us without saddling ourselves with junk.

Reprinted from Georgia Brown, "Seeing a Bigger Picture Through Prism of Cancer," *Insight*, Last Word column, January 5, 1998, by permission of *Insight*. Copyright ©1998 News World Communications, Inc.

Immediately, I found great comfort in routine. It was a pleasure to go to work every day. I enjoyed the calming monotony of unloading the dishwasher or folding laundry. Even cleaning the cat's litter box became a pleasant task because it was homey, familiar, routine.

The Learning Curve

The learning curve associated with cancer was, in my case, blessedly rapid. I already was in an excellent medical environment with superb physicians and other professionals. Their facilities are among the best in the country. In very rapid succession we scheduled and followed through on surgery and radiation therapy. There were no glitches, even in the sea of administrative details associated with medical insurance.

We quickly had good news: a clean pathology report. In the space of an afternoon, we spread the good news around the country, advising everyone who had surrounded us in a broad, strong circle of love. That circle was part of our action plan and we have no doubts that the prayers associated with it were our principal sustenance during the dark days and nights of uncertainty and fear. In my deep subconscious, I had culled images of the positive forces in my life, and I called them all. The message was, "I love you and it's time for you to love me back and keep loving me back until I tell you to stop." Now that I'm accustomed to all this love, I think I'll keep it. Love is strong currency.

Every day when I went for my radiation treatment, I looked around at the other patients and saw the support and love in their lives. We were a cheerful bunch waiting in the little room together. We became friends, even though we previously didn't know each other. We came to understand that none of us was unique. We all had this common bond of cancer. None of us felt we had been singled out. We all knew that cancer can and does strike anywhere. I never saw an ounce of self-pity. We were all confident and determined to make the best of our situations and get on with our lives. And each of us admitted the others into her own circle of love.

A Changed Perspective

Months have passed since the diagnosis, and life in many ways seems back to normal. But I know I'll never be the same. Cancer completely changes one's perspective. Priorities have become permanently rearranged. The big picture is what matters and it's fuller and richer for the experience. I could never say that it pleases me that I've had cancer, but I do cherish the learning and the growth that came out of it. And those will carry over into the new year and all the years to come.

Nutrition, rest and exercise now are prime concerns. Money, and the pursuit of it, is less important—as long as there's enough to go around. Abstract concepts such as kindness and honor mean more than ever. I don't sweat the small stuff—in fact, I can tell you that these days I hardly notice the small stuff.

This morning, my husband called out to me from the kitchen, "Honey, can you come in here? We've got a problem." I hurried in, found the sodden results of a leaky dishwasher, and said to my husband, "That's not a problem. It's just a detail."

When Treatments Fail

Stewart Massad

Some battles against cancer end in victory, but in other cases, despite all that medical science can do, a time comes when both patient and doctor must face the fact that the patient will soon die. In the following selection, Stewart Massad, a specialist in women's reproductive cancers at Cook County Hospital in Chicago, tells the story of the last days of one of his patients. He describes the choices she makes as her medical options narrow, as well as her courage in making a difficult journey to Taiwan to see her parents in spite of the pain caused by her advancing cancer. Massad also expresses his own frustration at being unable to help this patient and his feeling of humbleness in the face of her unavoidable death. Finally, he recounts her last days, in which, supported by her son, she meets death peacefully. Massad has also written *Doctors and Other Casualties*, a collection of short stories about physicians.

Mrs. Chang lay in the emergency ward, fighting. She was fighting terminal cancer, pain, and despair, and as her oncologist, I was called to see her. Just back from a farewell visit to her parents in Taiwan, she lay on her gurney behind a green curtain, her son beside her. Her knees were drawn up, her arms crossed, her eyes closed. When I said hello and touched her frail shoulder through the worn hospital gown, she turned, her body stiff beyond her years. She fought to sit up, to smile, to regain the politeness and grace that were second nature to her. But fighting took everything she had. She grimaced and fell back against her plastic pillow.

"I can't," was all she said. "I can't."

Many Struggles

Mrs. Chang had cervical cancer and it was killing her. She was not yet 50, and because of her cancer she never would be. Her life—as immigrant, wife, mother, waitress, daughter—had been full of struggles. She had survived them all, but now she was struggling with things

---

Reprinted from Stewart Massad, "Final Battles," *Discover*, March 1998, by permission of *Discover* magazine, ©1998.

she could not overcome. I could not cure her, only help her to be more comfortable.

Nearly two and a half years had passed since she first came to see me, the gynecologic oncologist at Chicago's Cook County Hospital. At the time of diagnosis, her cancer had spread beyond the cervix, the opening from the vagina into the uterus, and into surrounding tissue. Although the cancer was advanced, it was not yet hopeless. I had told her of the odds and outlined her options. And at first she did well. Radiation treatments shrank her tumor. Then a hysterectomy removed the residual growth. For two and a half years, she was healthy. On visits to the clinic every few months, I examined her. I was looking for signs that cancerous cells remained in her reproductive tract. I also asked her about new pain, weight loss, leg swelling, and cough—all signs that cancer has recurred.

During these visits she described to me her triumphs and travails. Her son finished college and began work as a graduate student in molecular biology. She kept working in a Chinese restaurant, serving meals, pouring tea. She nursed, buried, and mourned the elderly husband she had traveled with from Taiwan years before. She kept her Chinatown apartment in order. And she hoped.

An Ominous Sign

Then she slipped at work and hurt her back. She took pills from the drugstore, and infusions from a traditional Chinese herbalist, but her backache did not go away. Her son noticed the bulge in her neck she had tried to ignore, and he brought her to me. I felt the stony lump and ordered tests to confirm what I already knew: that her cancer had recurred. A week later I stood in the dim, air-conditioned radiology suite studying Mrs. Chang's CT scan as the radiologist pointed out malignant lymph nodes along her spine. A surgeon later put a needle into the tumor above Mrs. Chang's collarbone and aspirated fragments of tissue.

When the cells were inspected under a microscope, they were indistinguishable from the malignant cells that had been in her cervix. Mrs. Chang's cancer had metastasized: the cancerous cells had spread beyond the local structures of the vagina and pelvis, passing through the lymph system up along the spine, behind the heart, until they had finally reached the neck. Cancers are often detected there because they form visible tumors.

Diagnosis: Incurable

Back in the clinic, I told Mrs. Chang and her son of her diagnosis. She sat with her hands folded and her eyes downcast. He stood, his hand on her shoulder. I told them her cancer was incurable, having spread too far for radiation or surgery to contain. Still, we would work to slow its spread. I saw that she was not surprised: we had spoken before of my suspicion that the cancer had recurred, a suspicion that she shared. When I was finished, she stood up, barely five feet tall. "What shall we do?" she asked.

We began by talking. Caring for patients with incurable illnesses requires a lot of talking. Patients always wonder why their treatments fail, even if some never speak the words. I know about probabilities and prognoses, but never the answer to the mystery of why treatments fail some and cure others. We still know too little about the biology of cancer and the mechanisms of therapy. I could only hold Mrs. Chang's hand and tell her so. And I told her I was sorry.

Then we moved on to more pragmatic issues; we discussed how far she was willing to go to resist the disease. We talked in a way that was new to her. Before, I had been able to tell her what treatments gave her the best chance for cure. Now I only reviewed her options, asking her to choose what seemed best. Cancer treatment is like that. In cancer therapy, initial treatment involves fairly clear-cut algorithms developed from scientific studies. Treatment is often difficult, with painful surgery, debilitating chemotherapy, or radiation—sometimes combinations of these. But usually, at the start, survival is the goal. Doctors coach patients through the therapy, and patients endure.

Preserving Quality of Life

Once hope for cure is gone, though, there are no algorithms, and the burden of decision making shifts from doctor to patient. The focus moves from cure to quality of life, and what determines quality only the patient can decide. Some elect aggressive therapy, fighting their disease in a battle to the death, never surrendering, regardless of the costs in terms of sickness, weakness, and pain. Others elect to yield immediately, refusing to compromise themselves, resigning themselves to death when their strength fails and they can no longer maintain the dignity and physical integrity they value. Most, like Mrs. Chang, choose a middle path, using conventional anticancer treatments like chemotherapy and pain medication until the escalating physical and emotional costs become too high.

For five months Mrs. Chang took intravenous chemotherapy. While it could not eliminate her cancer, it could shrink the tumors that caused her suffering. The drugs used in chemotherapy are powerful: they work by killing rapidly dividing cells. But they have powerful side effects: nausea resulting from interactions in the brain and gastrointestinal tract, and anemia from the depletion of normal but rapidly dividing red blood cells. Mrs. Chang found the nausea tolerable and the weakness that resulted from the anemia worth the benefit. She received chemotherapy every three weeks. Within six weeks, the metastatic cancer in her neck shrank from the size of an egg to a hard little pearl, and her pain faded.

But after five months, the cancer cells that the chemotherapy could not destroy became resistant to its effects. The cancer-ridden lymph node in her neck grew back. The pain returned. I offered alternative chemotherapy: regimens less proven, regimens that required longer hospital stays, that would make her bald, that would sap her immunity. She declined.

Controlling Pain

"How long will I live?" she asked.

"Few women in your situation live more than a year," I answered with intentional vagueness. Though she did not understand my explanation in English, her biologist son explained in Mandarin how chemotherapy fails for different women at different times: it fails some women in a few weeks, some live with indolent cancers for a year or two or three, most die after six months or so.

"I can tell you what will happen to a hundred women," I told her, "how many will beat the odds and live longer, how many will die earlier. But I can never predict what will happen to any individual, to *you*."

Instead of her future, we focused on her present pain. Pain can be a constant companion of patients with terminal cancer, and its cause is not well understood. The growing tumor may press on nearby nerves, and it may also induce local inflammation, part of the body's reaction—and unsuccessful defense—against cancer. Narcotics are the key to relieving cancer pain. But they carry a stigma, and when I told Mrs. Chang I was prescribing morphine, I saw fear in her eyes.

"I will not be an addict," she said.

"No," I told her. "You will be free of pain. I ask patients to think of morphine as a tool. Some people abuse it, and it hurts them. We'll use it to help you."

We began with a mix of short- and long-acting morphine to dampen its side effects and minimize the number of pills. I added laxatives to combat the constipation the morphine induces. When I saw her shortly after that, she sat straighter and smiled when she saw me.

A Final Journey

"I am going back to Taiwan," she announced. "I must see my parents one time more. I do not expect you to understand, but it is my duty."

"Who will go with you?" I asked, frowning. "Who will take care of you?"

"I take care of myself. I always have. Even before my husband died."

I looked at her son, who always accompanied her. He only shrugged.

"I tried talking her out of it," he said. "I can't do anything with her. It's a Chinese thing, Confucius and all that. Everyone from the old country is that way."

She scowled at him. "I am going," she said. I wrote out prescriptions for a supply of medication and hoped the customs agents wouldn't trouble her.

While Mrs. Chang was away, I read about experimental treatments and alternative therapies, but I found nothing new that offered real hope for extending her life. I realized I had grown to like Mrs. Chang. And I realized she would soon die.

Caught up in the hustle of clinics, wards, and operating rooms, doctors rarely reflect on their cases. Especially difficult to contemplate are the terminal ones—cases that offer no promise of the emotional reward that comes from triumph over disease. And yet, as an oncologist, I've come to realize that caring for the dying is a central part of the physician's role, one that goes back centuries before the development of the modern technologies that made possible the conquest of some diseases.

Accepting that role is difficult, because it means accepting mortality—not only the patient's but one's own. As a gynecologic oncologist, I had trained first in obstetrics, spending night after night during residency delivering babies. Perhaps witnessing the cycle of birth and death, the continuity of life and the span of generations, made it easier for me to confront the fact that neither Mrs. Chang nor I would live forever. Thinking about Mrs. Chang's life made me think about the limits to my own ambitions and the transience of my achievements. When Mrs. Chang returned after two months, it was to a humbler doctor.

Last Days

She came back fighting, heading straight from the airport to the emergency ward. When I arrived, she was overwhelmed with pain. She had run out of medication, her son told me, a week before her flight home, and she had been unable to afford the price of any earlier plane or the cost of an oncologist's care. She had barely survived the flight, the cancer gnawing at her while the jet bumped through turbulence.

I put her in the hospital. One of my residents pushed liquid morphine into an IV line. Her face unclenched. Her body relaxed. She fell asleep.

But her body had grown tolerant to the narcotic. Controlling her pain required so much morphine that the drug made her dizzy. She saw visions: childhood friends, grandparents. I reduced the doses and added other drugs. I used an antidepressant, which changes the way the body interprets pain, reducing the sense of suffering and despair. I gave anti-inflammatory agents, which reduce the pain that results from the body's reaction to the invading cancer. I consulted radiation oncologists, who gave short courses of X-rays to metastases eating into the bones of her spine, shrinking the tumors and temporarily arresting their growth. I called in a team of anesthesiologists who specialize in the outpatient management of pain. They prescribed new drugs to block the nerves that transmit pain.

And I called on hospice nurses. Over the last few decades, the hospice movement has grown up to fill a void left by conventional medical therapies. Hospice care offers terminal patients the opportunity to face death at home, among loving family and friends. Once that was the norm, but now most patients die in hospitals, their deaths too often prolonged by technologies that eat away at the quality of whatever life remains. Hospice care is an alternative many choose.

But it seemed not to be an alternative available to Mrs. Chang. Though founded on compassion, hospice care—the counseling, the nursing visits, the commode and special bed, the drugs—costs money. Mrs. Chang had little money and, as a restaurant worker barely earning minimum wage, no health insurance. Though her son was a citizen, she was a legal alien, and the hospital's social worker found that since she had always worked off the books for cash, she was ineligible for Medicare. The county government had provided her clinic and hospital care, as it has for millions of immigrants over the decades. But in a time of shrinking budgets, there were few funds for hospice care for the indigent. The hospice team would visit once a week, but that would not be enough for Mrs. Chang, fragile as she was.

"It is not a problem," her son told me, after I outlined the obstacles to home care at Mrs. Chang's bedside one afternoon. "I will quit school."

"No," Mrs. Chang said. She tried to sit up, struggling to rise and to control her anger at the same time. "I am your mother, and I will never allow that. I would take my own life before I let you throw away your dreams." She fell back on her pillow. "After all," she asked him, "what do you think my life has been for?"

A Peaceful End

In the end, his sacrifice was not needed. The cancer grew rapidly, blocking the tubes that channel urine from the kidneys to the bladder. Obstructed, Mrs. Chang's kidneys failed.

"We could put in tubes," I offered. "That would relieve the obstruction and buy time."

"Time for what?" asked Mrs. Chang, ever the pragmatist. "My son is a scientist." She sighed. "I would like to see my grandchildren." She looked at her sheepish son. "But Mr. America says he hasn't found the right girl, so I will go."

She went into a coma and died with her son beside her. After he left to notify the aunts and uncles, the cousins and friends and the funeral home, I went in to see her. Her face was placid. She had finally risen above her struggles.

CHAPTER 5

THE OUTLOOK
FOR CANCER

Contemporary Issues
Companion

Managed Care, Cost Cutting, and Cancer

Susan Brink

In the following selection, *U.S. News & World Report* writer Susan Brink describes the difficulty some cancer patients have had in obtaining good treatment from health maintenance organizations (HMOs) and other managed-care organizations. Cancer treatment is costly, she points out, and certain managed-care organizations routinely refuse to approve treatments that they consider experimental. According to Brink, some patients have had to resort to lawsuits to gain coverage for treatments such as bone marrow transplants when their health care plans refused to pay for them. Such problems have led a number of experts to fear that in the future, treatment of diseases such as cancer will be governed more by economic factors than by principles of medical ethics, Brink concludes.

Doris Dunkleberger wasn't about to plunge her family into debt in a last-ditch effort to beat metastatic breast cancer. Never mind that her doctors at Memorial Sloan-Kettering Cancer Center in New York advised her to go ahead with a bone marrow transplant and high-dose chemotherapy and worry about the cost later. These were her stone-cold calculations: "Our house isn't paid for. We had about $80,000 in equity. We could probably get about $50,000 from retirement funds. Then we're down to selling furniture."

Calling in a Lawyer

The treatment would cost roughly $130,000, and, while it would increase her odds from nearly zero to about a 20 percent chance of perhaps five more years, she might die anyway. She decided to have this last-hope procedure only if her insurance company, a managed-care plan of Empire Blue Cross and Blue Shield, agreed to pay.

It initially refused, calling the clinical trial "experimental." Then Doris and Jay Dunkleberger hired a lawyer. Within a week, Empire agreed to pay. In 1996, three years after the treatment, Dunkleberger

---

Reprinted from Susan Brink, "The Cancer Wars at HMOs," *U.S. News & World Report*, February 5, 1996, with permission. Copyright, 1996, U.S. News & World Report.

is walking 2 miles a day and teaching kindergarten. The family still owns their home—and furniture.

Resorting to a lawsuit when insurers refuse coverage can prove effective, according to a 1994 study in the *New England Journal of Medicine*. Researchers at the Duke University Bone Marrow Transplant Program examined insurance company decisions on coverage of bone marrow transplants for the treatment of breast cancer and concluded the process is "arbitrary and capricious." They also found that of 39 women whose insurance companies had first refused and then agreed to cover the procedure, 19 had hired attorneys.

A Push to Save Money

The insurance world increasingly relies on managed-care companies to keep health costs down, and those organizations can both improve and stall cancer diagnosis and treatment. Such companies include health maintenance organizations (HMOs), which often hire their own doctors; independent practice associations (IPAs), which contract with doctors to care for plan members; and preferred provider organizations (PPOs), which steer patients to physicians with records of cost-efficient care.

The potential to improve cancer care comes largely from managed care's reliance on primary-care doctors who are charged not only with patients' basic care but also with making sure patients have access to preventive efforts like screening tests for, say, prostate or cervical cancer. HealthPartners in Minneapolis, for example, has improved its breast cancer early-detection rate from 85 percent to 92 percent, says George Halvorson, president of the firm. It used computer-generated postcards with data provided by primary-care doctors reminding women to make appointments for mammogram screening.

But reliance on managed-care organizations also causes concern that patients with expensive diseases could suffer from the caregivers' emphasis on the bottom line. "People with high-cost diseases like cancer were well known to the plans," says Linda Peeno, chair of the ethics committee at University Hospital in Louisville. Before permanently quitting her career as a physician executive medical reviewer, she had worked for three managed-care companies as part of their team of doctors whose job was to grant approval—or deny it—when gatekeeper doctors suggested hospitalizations or tests for their patients. The pressures to deny care, she says, resulted in decisions that still haunt her. "If there was any way at all to claim that something requested was experimental or nonstandard, we took it. We looked for ways *not* to cover treatment," says Peeno.

One insurer found a way to say "No" that stunned Larry White, director of education and research for radiation oncology at the Washington Hospital Center's cancer institute. Following a lumpectomy, a woman was referred to White for radiation treatment. A standard round consisted of 33 treatments over six weeks. But the insurer denied payment. "The managed-care company expected us to reverify treatment every three days. That would be like telling a surgeon he has to call the company every 10 minutes to see if he can keep doing the surgery," says White.

No Support for Clinical Trials

Until recent cost-tightening measures took hold, insurers were often partners with government and research institutions in funding clinical trials that tested innovative cancer treatments and compared the results with conventional treatments. That is the kind of experimental trial that Doris Dunkleberger chose. These trials are especially valued because they have been rigorously examined by the National Institutes of Health (NIH).

But while a few managed-care companies agree to pay for treatment in such clinical trials, many refuse to cover the treatments because their effectiveness is unproven. Those concerned about their coverage should check to see if a managed-care plan allows subscribers to participate in NIH- or Food and Drug Administration–approved clinical trials for procedures or chemotherapy drugs, recommends Ernest Borden, director of the University of Maryland Cancer Center. He notes that when all else has failed, those are the treatments that offer the last best hope.

A Need for Guidelines

To help allay the fear that accountants will decide how to treat cancer, 13 of the nation's top cancer centers have formed an alliance called the National Comprehensive Cancer Network. The network is developing treatment guidelines for the most common cancers.

Firmer guidelines on who should be eligible for treatment might have helped Harry Christie avoid a lengthy fight after his daughter, Carley, was diagnosed at age 9 with a rare kidney cancer called Wilms' tumor. Christie wanted his daughter treated by physicians who had extensive experience with her disease—a basic recommendation for those with life-threatening illnesses. When he found out the surgeon his HMO had suggested had never performed the required surgery on a child, Christie and his wife decided to go to a pediatric surgical oncologist experienced in treating Wilms' tumors. Now 12, Carley has no sign of cancer, but her parents' decision to bypass their HMO's recommendation led to a nearly yearlong battle that resulted in an arbitrator's ruling that the HMO pay all medical bills.

Christie and others fear that the new economics of medicine is creating a rift between doctors and patients that may never heal. "We are replacing medical ethical principles with contract medicine," he laments. "If it's not in the contract, you don't get it covered."

Arsenal of Hope: New Approaches to Cancer Treatment

Robert Langreth

> Robert Langreth, a staff reporter for the *Wall Street Journal*, takes a look at a variety of new approaches to cancer treatment in the following selection. Unlike current treatments, Langreth notes, these new approaches are based on recent discoveries about the changes in genes and cell chemistry that cause cancerous tumors to develop. According to Langreth, these treatments include attempts to prevent the growth of blood vessels in tumors, block the products of cancer-causing genes, and repair damaged genes that, when healthy, stop the formation of tumors. Some of these treatments have had highly promising results in animal or preliminary human tests, but they all still face years of testing before they will become available to patients, Langreth emphasizes. As has happened with other treatments in the past, he cautions, testing may eventually show that some of the new treatments do not work as well as they first appear to. If even a few of them succeed, however, they will offer a hopeful future for cancer research and treatment, Langreth concludes.

The war on cancer, fought for three decades marked by failure and frustration, suddenly is in overdrive. In April 1998, reports rocked the medical world about two drugs that show promise in preventing breast cancer. In early May, Wall Street and Main Street alike went wild over word of a bold experimental drug that wiped out tumors in mice.

These approaches are in very early stages of development and, even if all goes well, will require years of human testing before they can move into widespread usage. But they underscore a much bigger story: A quiet revolution in genetics has brought scientists closer than ever before to finding an actual cure for cancer.

The drugs that made headlines in May 1998 use the promising approach of blocking a tumor's blood vessels. Even farther along in development, however, is a whole new generation of gene-based drugs aimed at a strikingly broad range of cancers. Human testing is

Reprinted from Robert Langreth, "Arsenal of Hope: Revolution in Genetics Arms Cancer Fighters with Potent Weapons," *The Wall Street Journal*, May 6, 1998, by permission of the *Wall Street Journal*. Copyright ©1998 Dow Jones & Company, Inc. All rights reserved worldwide.

already underway for this new arsenal, which looks to be far more powerful and far less toxic than anything tried before.

Targeted Precisely

Some of the biggest pharmaceutical companies are pursuing the drugs, which attack cancer in a way entirely different from chemotherapy or radiation, the standard therapies. Where chemo and radiation assault all cells, cancerous and healthy alike, causing severe and even lethal side-effects, the new gene-based chemicals are precisely targeted. They take direct aim at the genetic machinery inside malignant cells to disable defective or mutated genes that provide the marching orders for unchecked growth.

Except for one far-along drug from Genentech Inc., it will still take several years to know whether these drugs can live up to their promise. But even guarded scientists are saying that the first new and highly effective therapy in decades is at hand, one likely to change forever the way cancer is treated.

"This is the dawn of the future of cancer therapy," says Richard Klausner, director of the National Cancer Institute. And J. Michael Bishop, a Nobel laureate in cancer research, says: "For the first time in my life, I believe we will eventually be able to conquer cancer."

War on Cancer

The target genes that hold this promise were discovered over the past 25 years, largely the result of a surge in federally funded research after President Richard Nixon declared war on cancer in 1971. But only in the past five years or so have scientists unraveled enough details of how genes operate to try to turn them off with drugs. Now genetic targeting has become the focus for developing most kinds of drugs, and the new anticancer compounds are leading the way. It adds up to nothing less than a new golden age of biology.

The war is being waged by corporate drug giants in a race for profits, their crack research teams working in secret and often unaware of the progress at rival labs. For years, many drug makers left most cancer research to university and government labs because it was a costly crap shoot. Now even some companies that never focused on cancer before are in hot pursuit, among them Merck & Co., Pfizer Inc. and Johnson & Johnson.

The first of the gene-based drugs could win federal approval by the end of 1998. It is Genentech's Herceptin, which attacks a virulent form of breast cancer.

Other companies are tackling a far broader range of cancers. Human testing of gene-based weapons against cancers of the lung, colon, pancreas and other organs has begun at Merck, Schering-Plough Corp. and J&J. Bristol-Myers Squibb Co. and Warner-Lambert Co. are close behind. Drugs targeting tumors in the prostate, breast, head and neck, based on a different gene, have entered human testing at Pfizer Inc. and Zeneca Group PLC.

Destroying Tumors

Originally, scientists just hoped gene-based cancer drugs would be strong enough to hinder or halt tumors' growth. In a great surprise, several of the drugs have surpassed all expectations and shown an ability to kill cancer cells outright. In animal tests, experimental drugs from Merck and Bristol-Myers can destroy tumors of the breast, lung or colon.

Now researchers must determine whether the drugs are both safe and effective in humans, enduring the three phases of testing where so many promises have been dashed. They "will undeniably be a major advance," predicts Robert Kramer, who heads oncology research at Bristol-Myers Squibb. "The only question is how major." Even though some drugs are bound to falter, researchers clearly have turned a corner in their unending battle against cancer, thanks to a profound change in how their weapons are developed.

New Insight

For decades scientists essentially wandered around in the dark, randomly testing thousands of natural chemicals for antitumor activity. Even when scientists found one that killed cancer cells, they often didn't know why.

In the past decade, researchers have flicked on a light illuminating the molecular processes by which cancer cells get the instructions needed for rampant growth. By identifying some of the defective genes at work, they have been able to spot vulnerabilities in the molecular mechanics. They try to disrupt these processes with newly designed drugs—tossing a chemical monkey wrench into the tumor-making machinery.

This keener insight has helped researchers with other new approaches as well, including blocking formation of the blood vessels that large tumors must have to thrive. Another method in very early stages of study involves "suicide genes" that are otherwise disabled in cancer cells, aiming to turn them back on so they can tell the cell it is time to die.

"Traditional anticancer agents have been discovered through chance. We are now going after the fundamental mechanisms of cancer," says Allen Oliff, the top cancer researcher at Merck.

Slow Progress

High hopes, however, have proved to be premature in the past. Cancer is a cunning foe, coming in more than a hundred different forms and traceable to as many different genetic defects. The list of disappointments and outright flops in the quest to cure cancer is long and storied: monoclonal antibodies in the late 1970s and again in the 1980s; tumor necrosis factor, a natural protein whose promise rose and fell in the mid-1980s; interferons, immune boosters that held out great hope a decade ago but have only limited uses; Interleukin-2, a natural cancer-fighting protein that made headlines in the late 1980s but proved to be violently toxic.

Tangible progress has been slow. Although survival rates for some childhood cancers have risen and leukemia, lymphoma and testicular cancer now can often be cured with radiation and chemo, for most other cancers the advances have been slight. Despite tens of billions spent on research, cancer remains the second leading cause of death after heart disease. Eight million Americans have cancer or have survived it. Each year it kills 560,000 people in the U.S., and 1.2 million more are diagnosed with it.

About 96% of those who get pancreatic cancer still die within five years. So do 94% of liver-cancer patients, 86% of lung-cancer patients and 79% of people who get stomach cancer.

The new gene-based drugs could change all that.

Genetic Formulas

To understand them, a quick primer: In each of the body's billions of cells is a nucleus holding a genetic formula, 23 pairs of chromosomes. The chromosomes—long strands of DNA—each carry thousands of smaller segments of DNA called genes. In different types of cells, different sets of genes are active or inactive, with each "on" gene holding an instruction telling the cell to produce a particular protein. The on genes in, say, a skin cell carry the code for producing the proteins needed to give it skin-like properties.

Only several hundred of the 50,000-plus genes hold instructions for producing proteins that regulate cell division. These are the ones involved in cancer. Scientists have identified at least 20 defective genes that sometimes tell cells to just grow and grow.

Their defects probably reflect a slow accumulation of genetic mutations over a lifetime. Molecular "typos" in just one or more of the thousands of genes in a cell can result from environmental toxins or exposure to radiation, or they can occur randomly during cell division as new copies are made. As more typos occur over many years, enough errors build up to overwhelm the body's defenses against unrestrained cell growth.

What to do? Researchers, for the most part, can't tinker directly with a flawed gene. Instead, they disable proteins that the genes order to be made.

To accomplish that, they copy the strategy of more conventional drugs. Their molecules maneuver into tiny keyholes, or "active sites," that a protein or enzyme needs to function. Plug up the keyhole and the troublesome protein can't do its job.

Identifying the First Cancer Genes

When researchers first responded to the 1971 call for a war on cancer, no one knew what caused the disease. Millions of dollars initially were spent studying the wrong suspect, cancer-causing viruses in animals. The virus theory failed for most human cancers.

Then in 1975 Dr. Bishop and another biologist at the University of California at San Francisco, Harold Varmus, astonished fellow researchers by identifying the cause of a chicken cancer: a defective gene. Although the gene turned out to be restricted mostly to animal cancers, the work triggered a frenzied search for genetic cancer causes in people.

The next breakthrough came three years later when an ambitious young researcher at the National Cancer Institute, Edward Scolnick, discovered a cancer gene in rats. He named it RAS, for rat sarcoma. Other scientists eventually showed it played a central role in as many as 30% of human cancers, including major killers. They found that half of all colon cancers, 90% of pancreatic tumors and 25% of lung cancers involve defective RAS genes.

Targeting the RAS Gene

RAS now is one of three main genes the drug scientists are targeting. About nine others are getting earlier-stage attention.

In 1982 Dr. Scolnick moved to Merck, hoping research on RAS by a giant drug company could lead to a new way to treat cancer. Now 57 and head of Merck's entire research operation, he vows to deliver a major new cancer drug by the time he retires. But in the early 1980s, for Merck and for others throwing money into the genetic approach, it was leap of faith.

The work proved far more difficult than expected. "We wasted a lot of time on things that were completely impossible," says Dr. Oliff, whom Dr. Scolnick hired to head Merck's cancer program. "The first five years were a total waste."

The problem was that they knew little about how the RAS gene actually worked. It was like trying to repair a car engine without knowing just what the parts did.

They know a lot more now. Normally the RAS gene carries instructions for making a protein that perches near the inner surface of all cells and acts as a central relay station for cell division. When growth hormones outside the cell send chemical messengers telling it to multiply, the RAS protein relays that directive to the cell's nucleus; otherwise, RAS stays quiet and the cell refrains from dividing.

In cancer cells, a single chemical bead among the thousands that make up the RAS gene is out of place; this turns the RAS protein into a monster. Stuck in the "on" position, it continuously conveys a phantom message telling the cell to divide and multiply.

Cancer researchers tried to create molecules that could interfere with the RAS protein and stop it from functioning, but they couldn't find the right spot for attack. In addition, RAS functions in all cells, so blocking it in cancer cells risked thwarting it in healthy cells where it was needed.

That has always been a major obstacle in creating cancer drugs. Bacterial, fungal and viral infections introduce a foreign intruder, posing a ready target for drug design, but in cancer the enemy comes from within. The differences between normal cells and cancerous ones are often so subtle that drugs can't distinguish them. This is why current cancer drugs cause such toxic side effects; they're hammering regular cells, too.

The new gene-based drugs, narrowly targeted at a cancer cell's innermost workings, may clear this hurdle.

Blocking a Killer's Helper

In 1990 two Nobel-laureate chemists at the University of Texas, Michael Brown and Joseph Goldstein, found a promising target: a helper protein that the RAS gene needs for forwarding messages. Called farnesyl transferase, or FT, it is an enzyme that triggers a chemical reaction. The search was on for a drug that could block FT.

Merck had been winding down its RAS research, but it decided to take one last shot. By 1993, it had compounds that blocked the RAS helper protein. But then for five long years, one after another turned out to be toxic. "It's very frustrating because we've had compounds that [blocked RAS] since 1993," Dr. Oliff says.

Early in 1998, Merck finally completed successful safety tests in animals of a powerful anti-RAS drug—so secret it won't even reveal the code name. In April 1998 it began human safety tests. If the drug is found safe, a small efficacy test will begin, the Phase II trial. If the drug clears that, the final, Phase III trial to test for efficacy in a large group of people could begin in a few years.

Other drug companies rushed into the fray, too, and Bristol-Myers Squibb found a chemical that could turn off the FT helper protein in test tubes. Animal tests showed it to be far more potent than anything the company had tested before against cancer. In one animal test of a colon-cancer strain that was resistant to existing drugs, the substance obliterated the tumors 100% of the time. Human trials could begin in a few months.

Unknown to these drug powerhouses, a neighbor also was hard at work. A mere three miles from Merck's main lab in West Point, Pa., a small group of scientists studied the RAS gene at Janssen Pharmaceutica, owned by Johnson & Johnson.

In 1990, a young scientist at Janssen, David End, had read a scientific article that led him to test for anti-RAS powers in a class of drugs that included J&J's toenail-fungus drug, Nizoral. It didn't work, so he tried related chemicals similar to J&J's cream for vaginal infections, Monistat. Bingo.

Janssen scientists in France later designed a compound 100,000 times more potent than the over-the-counter product. Safety tests in humans began more than a year ago, and the company hopes to begin efficacy tests soon.

EGF Receptors

RAS wasn't the whole story. Also becoming a key target at some drug companies was a gene called EGF receptor.

The EGF receptor plays a central role in division for all cells, acting as a chemical gatekeeper on their surface. In the early 1990s, scientists learned that the EGF receptor and the RAS protein are terminals on the same chemical relay system. The receptor gets signals from growth hormones secreted by other organs indicating it is time for cells to divide, then relays the message to RAS, which dispatches it to the cell nucleus.

Normal cells have 10,000 or so copies of the EGF receptor. But many lung, prostate and brain tumors have extra copies—as many as a hundred times as many. That means a normal growth message is amplified tremendously, causing the cell to reproduce madly and grow into a tumor.

Pfizer attacked this gene through a biotech partner, now called OSI Pharmaceuticals Inc. Vastly speeding its search for a chemical to jam the EGF receptor was new robotic testing of compounds. Pfizer and OSI screened nearly 300,000 compounds, Pfizer's entire chemical collection at the time, and in 1993 isolated a group of related molecules that did the job.

But the EGF receptor strategy has a big obstacle. The risk of terrible side effects is high because this receptor is very similar to other receptors involved in nourishing the nerves, processing messages from insulin and handling other critical functions. A drug that blocked the EGF receptor might also thwart those processes, causing diabetes or even brain damage.

After years of searching, Pfizer now has a drug that can block the EGF receptor selectively. In early human tests, it looks safe. Zeneca has a similar EGF drug that has already moved into Phase II, the initial efficacy test.

The EGF approach may fail to kill tumors outright. But scientists hope it will stop them from growing and spreading, thus turning some cancers into chronic, manageable diseases.

"The enthusiasm here is incredibly high but so is the pressure, because Pfizer has spent millions on cancer research and we still don't have a drug," says Michael Morin, who heads Pfizer's cancer research at a huge lab in Groton, Conn. "It takes a long time to test a drug when you have a totally novel mechanism."

A New Breast Cancer Drug

The third gene the drug companies are targeting heavily may be the first to yield a marketable drug. It is called HER2, and it is the one Genentech is aiming at. HER2 is a cousin of the EGF receptor: a growth-message relay switch that is hyperactive in many patients with severe cases of breast cancer.

Genentech has taken on HER2 using monoclonal antibodies, the once-promising approach that faded with the 1980s and now is making a comeback. They are clones of human antibodies that target a single protein.

A lot of the credit for Genentech's drug goes to a researcher at the University of California at Los Angeles, Dennis Slamon. Genentech scientists exploring new genetic-splicing techniques in the 1980s sent him a clone they had produced of the HER2 gene, not knowing what its function was. Dr. Slamon, who was looking for genes that might be involved in cancer, compared the cloned gene and the protein based on it with tumor samples from patients with breast cancer. He found abnormally large quantities of the HER2 protein in about 30% of breast-cancer tumors, including the most virulent.

He urged drug makers to attack this gene by designing a monoclonal antibody that would bind to the HER2 protein and block it. Most companies didn't bite. The monoclonal method had fallen from favor, and drug companies knew how easy it was to spend millions working on cancer drugs and get nothing.

Top officials at Genentech, too, were highly skeptical, but a handful of scientists there kept the research going for years. Finally, their work produced the genetically engineered drug that has now gone through all three phases of human testing. Herceptin has been given to about 400 women with a virulent form of breast cancer, and in combination with chemotherapy it helps at least some of the time. A few women on the drug remain alive and well several years after being told their breast cancer was terminal.

Detailed trial results will be released May 17, 1998. At the beginning of May 1998, Genentech applied to the Food and Drug Administration for approval to sell Herceptin, which the company's chief medical officer, Susan Hellmann, calls "a breakthrough by any criteria."

Hope for a Miracle

How much longer patients will live thanks to such gene-based drugs won't be clear for years. The new chemical weapons are so different that testing poses immense challenges in deciding what doses to use, for how long, and in which patients. Scientists may end up having to combine several types into a cocktail that blocks the products of several defective genes.

But even with all the caveats, legions of veteran cancer researchers have the palpable sense that a revolution in cancer treatment is at hand—that the notion of an outright cure, someday, has become an attainable goal.

"It's unpredictable what will happen," says Merck's Dr. Scolnick. As he and other scientists repeatedly point out, many prototype drugs, once so full of promise, ultimately failed. But even the always-cautious Dr. Scolnick is hopeful. It is possible, he says, that under the attack of the new gene-based drugs "the tumors will just melt away." If that happens, "it would be a miracle."

The Ordeal of Testing a New Treatment

Terence Monmaney

Terence Monmaney is a medical writer for the *Los Angeles Times*. In the following selection, he explores the process by which new cancer treatments are tested. Monmaney focuses on the personal experience of Valli Lopez-Lasker, a woman with advanced breast cancer who participated in clinical tests of a new drug called Herceptin. Through Lopez-Lasker's story, Monmaney illustrates the physical and emotional turmoil that can be involved in helping to shape the future of cancer treatment by testing the safety and effectiveness of a new medication. For instance, at one stage of the test Lopez-Lasker discovered to her dismay that she had been chosen to be part of a control group that would receive a standard anticancer drug rather than Herceptin. Although such procedures are necessary to determine whether a new treatment is more effective than existing ones, Monmaney writes, they can become an ordeal for the patients who undergo them.

She remembers the doctor opening his office door and not looking at her.

"You don't even have to say it," she told him. "It's bad, isn't it?"

"Yeah, it's pretty bad."

They agreed that he would perform exploratory surgery on her left breast, where the tumor was, and that he would decide whether to remove just the lump or take more tissue. When she awoke from the operation, she found layers of gauze where the breast had been.

That was the spring of 1992, and Valli Lopez-Lasker, then 42, figured the worst was over. But the cancer spread further into her lymph system, and also to her backbone and liver.

Over three years, she underwent a barrage of treatments, including radiation therapies, chemotherapies and a $150,000 bone marrow transplant that left her with a scorched lung, impaired hearing and arthritis, she says. "And it didn't work."

Then, while in such despair she sought out a spiritual healer, she

Reprinted from Terence Monmaney, "A Lottery of Life, Death—and Hope," *Los Angeles Times*, August 3, 1996, by permission. Copyright, 1996, Los Angeles Times.

heard about a new drug being tested by Dr. Dennis Slamon at the UCLA Medical School.

Immunotherapy: Picking the Lock

The study involved women with advanced breast or ovarian cancer of an especially aggressive type: The tumors are spurred by overproduction of the so-called HER2/neu receptor, a protein structure on the cancer cells that appears to regulate their growth.

Among the most innovative cancer medicines ever devised, the drug is a genetically engineered antibody that sticks to the HER2/neu receptor, interfering with the cancer cells' life cycle.

Cancer researchers view the HER2 antibody drug as a hint of cancer treatments to come, the advance guard of an approach called immunotherapy. The way proponents see it, if radiation, chemotherapy and surgery are like battering down cancer's door, immunotherapy is like picking the lock.

"We believe that's the paradigm that's going to be coming on board in the next few years in cancer therapy," Slamon said.

The drug is so specific for this form of cancer that it has much the same name: MAb HER2, "MAb" being short for "monoclonal antibody." It is suitable only for the 30% of women with breast or ovarian tumors abetted by an excess of the HER2/neu receptor, Slamon says.

As it happened, Lopez-Lasker was one of them. She started receiving the drug in December 1995.

An Abundance of Spirit

She lives on a steep Santa Barbara hillside in a stucco house with priceless views of the ocean. Avocado trees range across an adjacent hill. Swallows wheel in the rosemary-scented air. And four cats and 13 dogs make chaos of the sun-washed chaparral.

Yes, the dogs are excessive—she was once arrested for, in effect, running a kennel without a license—but perhaps it is not really so bizarre for someone clinging to life to immerse herself in a howling abundance of animal spirit. Many mornings, she said, she can hardly get out of bed, she feels so hopeless; but the dogs rouse her, and as she walks and feeds them she is grateful to be needed.

When the local pound and humane society chapter are about to put a mutt down, they call Lopez-Lasker, and often enough she has gone to the rescue. She has always been that way, she says, but allows that cancer has deepened her feel for the underdog.

In the summer of 1995, when Lopez-Lasker's health was bottoming out, her husband, Lawrence Lasker, a screenwriter, got her to call Dr. Mark Renneker, a physician in San Francisco almost as well known for his surfing exploits as for the care he provides. Besides being a founder of the Surfer's Medical Assn. and seeing patients at clinics in Oakland and San Francisco, he steers seriously ill people into experimental treatments that might help them.

Recalling his first impression of Lopez-Lasker, he said: "It was hard for her to even use the word 'cancer.' She was frightened."

Entering a Clinical Trial

He lobbied to get Lopez-Lasker into the UCLA study. It had been set up to test the HER2 antibody in combination with another drug, cisplatin, which often has serious side effects, including kidney damage and hair loss. Lopez had taken cisplatin before and wanted no more of it.

To help persuade UCLA to give her the antibody drug alone, Renneker invoked her in-laws' golden name. Perhaps no family in U.S. history has done more for medical research than the Laskers. Her husband's step-grandmother was Mary Lasker, a grand patroness of biomedical research. Each year the family foundation honors several medical researchers with the Lasker Awards, surpassed in prestige only by the Nobel.

But in the end, Slamon said, the family connection was not important. "Absolutely not," he said. Lopez-Lasker got into the study because she had the exact cancer being studied. All the legwork and paperwork done to enroll her was simply aimed at ensuring she would receive the antibody drug without cisplatin, he said.

An Extremely Important Drug

Slamon is more than an advocate of HER2 therapy—he helped invent it. A decade ago he established the role of the previously discovered HER2/neu gene in especially aggressive breast cancer tumors. And he laid the groundwork for using an antibody directed against the HER2/neu receptor to hinder the cancer cells' growth.

Along with UCLA, more than 100 hospitals in North America are cooperating in the HER2 antibody study, which is being funded largely by the South San Francisco biotechnology firm Genentech, producer of the HER2 antibody. The study will eventually involve 750 women with breast cancer—the third and final research phase before the drug is considered for Food and Drug Administration (FDA) approval.

"HER2 is extremely important," said Dr. Larry Norton, chief of breast cancer medicine at Memorial Sloan Kettering Institute in New York. His research team is also testing the drug and has had at least one spectacular result—complete remission of metastatic breast cancer in one woman for three years. He has also seen it have no effect on patients whatsoever.

"I don't think anyone is saying that this is a cure for cancer," he said. "The important thing is that at least in somebody it has been shown to work, and that is a proof of the principle."

An editorial in March 1996 in the *Journal of Clinical Oncology*, a leading publication for cancer specialists, said that many questions about

HER2 therapy remained to be answered. Still, it said, the therapy held enough promise that studies like the one Lopez-Lasker is involved in may someday be regarded as a "landmark" in cancer research.

Her friends congratulate her for venturing onto the frontier of research on cancer, long America's most dreaded disease. "They say, 'You're so brave!'" Lopez-Lasker recalled. "But it's no more brave than brushing your teeth or whatever: It's just something you've got to do."

Her progress since entering the UCLA study in December 1995 can be seen in the periodic CT scans made of her liver.

Arraying the films against a light box, Slamon pointed to scans done before the treatment started. In one image, numerous large blackish splotches—tumors—appear against the light gray of normal liver tissue. Two months later, the splotches were measurably smaller and fainter; at four months, smaller and fainter still. A few had vanished.

When Lopez-Lasker first heard that the tumors were shrinking, she was elated. She sent vases of flowers to her doctors and nurses. She spent thousands of dollars joining a swim club in Santa Barbara. She felt better than she had in memory.

And, wonderfully, the drug had no side effects except a mild fever the first time she received it. Going to the clinic once a week for treatment, she lounged on a daybed while the clear HER2 solution dripped from an IV sac into a vein in her hand.

Usually her daughter, Bianca Ryan, was there, and they joked and ate chocolates. Lopez-Lasker felt so upbeat she referred to herself as the treatment's "poster child."

Ryan, 29, born when Lopez-Lasker was a senior at Palisades High School, has been the person most often at her side. They are like sisters now, similarly dark-haired and brown-eyed, with siblings' easy, wisecracking ways. "You'll be able to take care of me when I get old," Lopez-Lasker once said.

"Mom," Ryan said, "when you're old, I'll be old."

Successes and Setbacks

In late April 1996, UCLA sent out a press release to help recruit more patients for HER2 studies. "We are extremely optimistic about these trials," Slamon said in the release. "Our early findings are very promising, with some outstanding results."

Of the six women that UCLA had tested by then, one had her tumors disappear completely, three (including Lopez-Lasker) had tumors shrink, one stayed the same, and one got sicker, with the tumors spreading to her brain.

To take part in a medical experiment is to enter "no man's land," as Slamon said in a recent interview, where even the most dramatic progress can suddenly give way to a setback.

After Lopez-Lasker had received HER2 antibody therapy for six months, a CT scan of her liver revealed several new blackish marks—

tiny blotches representing incipient tumors of less than half an inch across, Slamon said. He cannot explain why the therapy suddenly failed to hold the cancer in check. "I don't know what to make of it," he said. "We're in a no man's land. This is new ground in terms of therapy."

Early one June evening, Slamon called Lopez to tell her about the CT scans. "I'm concerned," he said.

Speeding Up the Approval Process

Although advances in diagnosis and care have lengthened and improved patients' lives, the overall breast cancer death rate—which researchers view as the ultimate measure of success against the disease—has barely budged in decades. In 1993, about 26 out of every 100,000 American women died of breast cancer, just as in the 1930s, according to the American Cancer Society.

Still, breast cancer research is booming. National Cancer Institute funding for the disease has increased tenfold since 1981, to $336.8 million in 1996. The number of cancer medicines in development at drug companies has nearly doubled in the last few years, to more than 200, according to Manufacturers of America.

Meanwhile, the FDA, reacting to complaints from drug companies and patient advocacy groups, has both speeded up the review process for new cancer drugs and, perhaps more important, eased the criteria for approval.

Previously, the agency required that a drug actually lengthen patients' lives before approving it; beginning in late March 1996, with a new initiative hailed by President Bill Clinton, a cancer drug may be approved if it "shows evidence of tumor shrinkage for patients who have no satisfactory alternative therapy," the agency said.

Some cancer researchers are troubled by the agency's shift. "I think this was a big step backward," said Dr. John Bailar, a noted cancer researcher at the University of Chicago. He said that the benefits of many highly touted experimental cancer drugs turn out to be overstated, while their often considerable side effects are understated. "I'm very much concerned about the hazards of cancer therapy, because those are immediate, real and big."

Researchers working on the HER2 antibody drug don't know if it will pass FDA review when the study is finished in two years or so. But the chances of its eventual approval appear quite good. In preliminary studies the drug has reduced tumors in 12% of those eligible patients who received it. And the FDA has already approved a cancer drug that is less effective than that.

Options

In the dusky stillness after Slamon had telephoned Lopez-Lasker with word of possible new tumors, her tears flowed and she started brooding again over who would take care of her dogs when she was gone.

But her condition wasn't hopeless, Slamon said. There were other options. She could start taking the HER2 antibody along with cisplatin. Or, if she still didn't want that, there is a separate study involving taxol, a newer drug used against ovarian cancer and breast cancer.

How she has grown to hate the word "options." To her, it makes her feel she has very few options indeed. It is another one of those white-coat euphemisms, like "quality of life," which gravely ill people realize is a signal that little quantity remains.

For days she thought it over, weighing the possible benefits of taxol and cisplatin against their side effects. Like cisplatin, taxol can cause nausea and hair loss, among other things. She settled on taxol, even though there was a catch: To test whether the HER2 antibody really boosts the effectiveness of taxol, half the women in Slamon's study receive taxol plus antibody, while the other half receive just taxol. And to avoid skewing the study results, neither the researchers nor the subjects determine which group each patient ends up in. Lopez-Lasker would be "randomized," as researchers call it.

A Hard Time

A week before the treatment was to start, she learned that she was a victim of chance after all. "I've randomized out, I'm in the control group," she said over the phone. She was crying. "I'm losing my mind over this."

But she went ahead anyway, and one afternoon in late June 1996, she sat in the day ward at UCLA's Jonsson Comprehensive Cancer Center, a taxol IV emptying into a vein in one hand.

By the time she got home, her stomach ached and her heart seemed to strain with every beat. "I had a very, very hard time," she said. "I felt like I was dying." It became so hard for her to breathe she went to the emergency room at a Santa Barbara hospital for treatment.

Slamon said it was a shame she wasn't getting the HER2 antibody, but taxol alone had a good chance of fighting the tumors, he told her. And if she took a turn for the worse, he went on, she could switch to cisplatin, and she would definitely get the HER2 antibody then.

He grapples every day with the dilemma of having to withhold a potentially useful experimental treatment from patients in need. "It's very frustrating," he said. "As a physician, it's extremely frustrating because patients say, 'I'm dying, why can't I get this?' There's just no counter-argument to that.

"But from the standpoint of a new drug, whether or not it works has to be proven. No one believes in HER2/neu more than I do, but I can't in good faith say unequivocally that it's effective. We have to actually prove that it's more effective than the best available therapy."

Lopez-Lasker wearies of the struggle, naturally. "There's something really monumentally unjust about the fact that doctors have developed all these techniques to tell you you have cancer and how long you can live, but then they can't do anything about it. It sort of makes me long for the old days, you know, when people put their hoe down on the north forty and went in for a nap and just died two weeks later."

Renneker cheered her up a bit the other night over dinner in Santa Barbara. "There are other things coming up"—other treatments, he meant. "They're a year or two away and we're going to keep you alive for that."

Who Knows How Long?

At the animal hospital a while ago, Lopez-Lasker came across a stray cat with skin cancer.

She said she would take it home. But before she could do so, it had to be returned to the pound for a while, in case its owner turned up.

After a few days, she called the pound to arrange to pick the cat up. An attendant said the cat had been put down. "It had cancer," he explained. "It wasn't going to live."

"How did he know what that animal wanted?" Lopez-Lasker said, fuming. "How did he know how long it had to live?"

A Turnaround in Cancer Statistics

Sheryl Gay Stolberg

In the following selection, Sheryl Gay Stolberg, a writer for the *New York Times*, presents the hopeful news announced in early 1998 that, for the first time since the 1930s, both the number of new cancer cases and the number of cancer deaths in the United States are declining. Authorities believe that these reductions are due to a combination of changes in behavior such as a decrease in smoking, an increase in the use of cancer screening tests, and improvements in treatment, Stolberg explains. Nonetheless, she says, problems still remain; for instance, the incidence of certain types of cancer actually rose among some groups of women and minorities. These and other puzzling facts reveal that researchers need to explore further before they truly understand the future of cancer, Stolberg reports, but the general trend is encouraging.

For the first time since the 1930s, the number of new cancer cases in the United States is declining, federal officials said on March 12, 1998, in announcing a sharp reversal in the incidence of diseases that kill more than 1,500 Americans each day.

Deaths from cancer are also dropping, continuing a trend that was first reported in November 1996. Together, the two developments offer experts new hope that 27 years after president Richard M. Nixon declared "war on cancer," the nation may have reached a turning point.

"The burden of fear the public has been feeling should begin to lift," Dr. James S. Marks of the Centers for Disease Control and Prevention said in releasing a national report card on cancer at a news conference in Washington, D.C. "Cancer is conquerable and progress is being made."

Minorities Are at Greater Risk

Experts attribute the decline in new cases to changes in behavior, most notably a drop in smoking, and the decline in deaths to increased screening and better therapies. But the positive trends are

Reprinted from Sheryl Gay Stolberg, "New Cancer Cases Decreasing in U.S. as Deaths Do, Too," *The New York Times*, March 13, 1998, by permission. Copyright ©1998 by The New York Times.

not benefiting all Americans; minorities and women remain particularly at risk.

From 1990 to 1995, the study found, cancer rates for men and women of every race dropped, with one notable exception: black men. They have the highest cancer rates of any group in the nation, mainly because of a sharp rise in new cases of prostate cancer.

In the same period, new cases of breast cancer increased for black women. And new cases of lung cancer, while dropping sharply among men, rose among women who were white, Asian and Pacific Islander.

"The gaps between what we know and what we do are greater for racial and ethnic minorities," said Dr. Marks, director of the National Center for Chronic Disease Prevention and Health Promotion.

Minorities, he added, are "less likely to be screened, less likely to have cancer detected early and less likely to get the best therapy."

Statistics of Hope

The incidence of cancer in the United States has been rising since the 1930s, although the government has been keeping detailed annual statistics only since 1973. The rate of all new cancers combined dropped an average of 0.7 percent per year from 1990 to 1995, according to the report, which was jointly released by the disease control centers in Atlanta, the National Cancer Institute in Bethesda, Md., and the American Cancer Society in New York.

That drop is in contrast to a steady climb from 1973 to 1990, when incidence increased an average of 1.2 percent annually. The sharpest drop occurred after 1992, when new cases of cancer appeared to have peaked. That year, cancer was diagnosed in 426 of every 100,000 Americans; by 1995, the figure had dropped to 392.

Death rates, meanwhile, declined one-half of 1 percent per year from 1990 to 1995; from 1973 to 1990, death rates increased 0.4 percent each year. Preliminary data from 1996 indicate that the recent downward trend is continuing. But men benefited more from the recent declines than did women. And among Asian and Pacific Islander women, death rates are up.

According to the cancer society, cancer accounts for 1 of every 4 deaths in this country; an estimated 564,800 Americans are expected to die of cancer in 1998. In the United States, men have a risk of 1 in 2 for developing cancer in their lifetime; for women, it is 1 in 3.

At the same time, there are more cancer survivors than ever before. Dr. Richard D. Klausner, director of the National Cancer Institute, said that today 8.5 million Americans were living with a history of cancer, but not all are considered cured.

Winning the War?

Since 1971, when President Nixon announced a national crusade to cure cancer, to be fashioned in the mold of efforts that "split the atom

The Outlook for Cancer

Top Four Types of Cancer

More than half of the diagnosed cases of cancer are prostate, breast, lung and colon/rectum. The graphs show the rates of diagnosis per 100,000 among various groups.

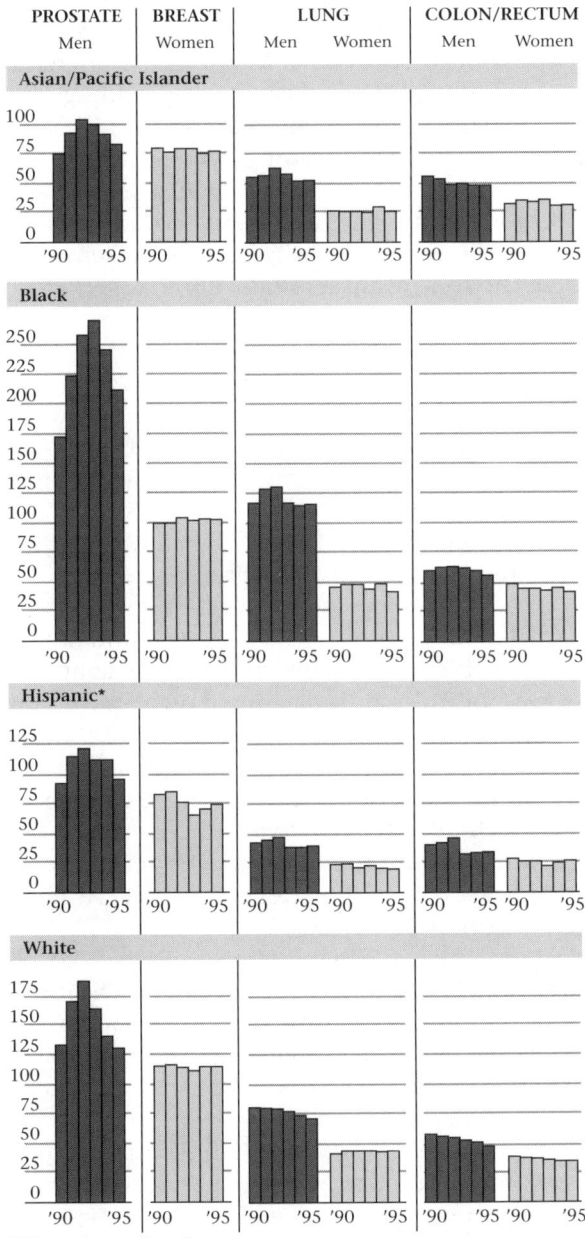

*Hispanic may be of any race.

Source: American Cancer Society; National Cancer Institute; Centers for Disease Control and Prevention.

and took man to the moon," the United States has spent more than $30 billion on cancer research. Dr. John R. Seffrin, chief executive of the cancer society, said the report card proved that investment had paid off.

"This is about results," Dr. Seffrin told reporters, "very positive results. It is about transforming hope into progress through science."

But because cancer is really a variety of different diseases lumped together under one umbrella, there are many subplots to the overall story, some of them more dismaying than hopeful.

The numbers "are just a snapshot of where we are and where we have been," said Dr. Klausner, the cancer institute director. Beneath them, he said, "are complexities and many questions."

Lung cancer, prostate cancer, breast cancer and cancer of the colon and rectum are the four most common types; together they account for about 54 percent of all newly diagnosed cancers. With the exception of breast cancer, the study found, African-Americans had higher rates of each of these diseases than Americans who are white, Asian, Pacific Islander and Hispanic, who can be of any race.

The research, being published in the March 15, 1998, issue of the journal *Cancer*, analyzed death statistics kept by the disease control centers, as well as figures from the Surveillance, Epidemiology and End Results program, a national registry of 23 cancers. The registry has been maintained by the cancer institute since 1973.

Puzzling Trends

Some of the trends identified by the study are difficult to explain. For instance, regions of the country that have reported the greatest decline in deaths from prostate cancer are those where men are screened less frequently. And while recent studies have shown that black women are catching up to white women in their use of mammography screening, death rates from breast cancer remain much higher among black women than among whites.

"For many diseases, including cancer," Dr. Klausner said, "incidence changes are often mysterious."

Experts do not fully understand, for example, why new cases of prostate cancer and breast cancer are dropping. One theory, offered by Dr. Marks of the disease control centers, is that the numbers rose sharply as more people were screened in the late 1980s and early 1990s. With so many new cases diagnosed, he said, the incidence is now dropping.

The trends in lung cancer are directly linked to cigarette smoking. The percentage of Americans who smoke has been cut roughly in half since 1964, when the Surgeon General's office issued its first report warning of the dangers of smoking. That accounts for the overall declines in new cases and deaths due to lung cancer.

But the patterns for men and women "are absolutely the opposite from each other," said Dr. Phyllis A. Wingo, director of surveillance research for the cancer society and lead author of the study. Declines in smoking among women have lagged behind those of men; so rates continue to climb among women while they are dropping among men.

Experts caution, moreover, that the overall downturn in lung cancer may easily be reversed if the recent rise in smoking among teenagers continues.

"We must protect our children," said Dr. Seffrin of the cancer society, which is pressing Congress to act on the accord that was reached in June 1997 between the tobacco industry and 40 state attorneys general. "If we and Congress allow this reversal to happen, shame on us."

Glossary

adduct A chemical bond between a possible carcinogen and **DNA**.

adjuvant Treatment added before or after a different type of treatment in order to enhance the main treatment's effectiveness.

aflatoxin A substance produced by mold that grows on grain; it is a powerful carcinogen for liver cancer.

angiogenesis The formation of blood vessels, especially inside cancerous tumors.

antibody A protein, usually made by certain cells of the immune system, that stimulates other immune system cells to attack foreign substances in the body, such as bacteria or cancer cells.

apoptosis Natural cell death, caused by a program in the cell that is activated by aging or genetic damage.

biologic response modifiers Substances that treat disease by affecting the immune system, such as **monoclonal antibodies**.

biomarker A chemical product that reveals interaction between a suspected carcinogen and human cells.

complementary care Treatments intended primarily to make a patient feel better; used along with other treatments designed to affect disease directly.

control group A group of people or animals in a test who are not exposed to the factor (drug, possible carcinogen, etc.) being tested but are otherwise similar to those subjects who are exposed to the factor.

DDE Dichloro-diphenyl-ethane; a toxic breakdown product of **DDT**.

DDT Dichloro-diphenyl-trichloroethane; an **organochlorine** pesticide that has been proven to disrupt the action of human hormones and may play a role in some human cancers; it was banned in the United States in the 1970s, but traces still remain in the environment.

dioxin An **organochlorine**, produced as waste in several industrial processes, that is associated with hormone disruption and possibly with several kinds of diseases or defects, including cancer.

DNA Deoxyribonucleic acid; the substance of which **genes** are made.

dose-response curve A graph used in testing that shows the relationship between different doses of a substance and the subject's response to those doses.

EGF (Epidermal Growth Factor) receptor A chemical on the surface of a cell that relays signals from certain hormones that tell the cell to divide.

endocrine disrupters Substances that can disrupt the body's endocrine (hormone) system by mimicking or blocking the action of particular hormones.

gene The part of a **DNA** molecule that contains instructions for making a protein or part of one; the unit of a cell's inherited information.

genome A cell's complete collection of **genes**.

lumpectomy A surgical treatment for breast cancer in which only the cancerous lump and a small amount of surrounding tissue is removed; it is an alternative to mastectomy, or removal of the whole breast.

maximum-tolerated dose The largest estimated dose of a substance that an organism can tolerate without experiencing considerable weight loss.

metastasis The transfer of cancerous cells from one part of the body to another; a secondary cancerous tumor that arises in a location different from that of the primary or original tumor.

molecular epidemiology A research field that studies interactions of natural and foreign chemicals within cells in order to determine how disease spreads through a human community and how it can be controlled.

monoclonal antibodies Identical **antibodies**, all reacting to the same substance, produced by cloned cells in the laboratory.

nucleus The central body of a cell, which contains the cell's chromosomes and **genes**.

oncogene A gene found in normal cells that has the potential to make the cell cancerous if the gene is mutated or moved.

organochlorines Complex compounds containing the elements carbon and chlorine that are used in many industrial processes and products; they can disrupt the action of hormones and are suspected of increasing cancer risk.

pathogen Something that causes disease, such as a bacterium or virus.

PCBs Polychlorinated biphenyls; **organochlorines** formerly used in industry that disrupt human hormones and may play a role in some human cancers; their use has been restricted internationally since 1973, but traces still remain in the environment.

petrochemical A chemical made from oil (petroleum).

RFLP markers (RFLPs) Restriction fragment length polymorphisms; stretches of **DNA** that exist in several different normal forms and therefore can be used as markers to help scientists locate unknown genes in a molecule of DNA.

RNA Ribonucleic acid; a substance related to **DNA** that helps cells form proteins based on the information in genes.

tumor suppressor gene A gene that prevents cancerous growth.

VEGF Vasculo-endothelial growth factor; a protein secreted by tumors that stimulates the growth of blood vessels in the tumors.

Organizations to Contact

The editors have compiled the following list of organizations concerned with the issues presented in this book. The descriptions are derived from materials provided by the organizations. All have publications or information available for interested readers. The list was compiled on the date of publication of the present volume; the information provided here may change. Be aware that many organizations take several weeks or longer to respond to inquiries, so allow as much time as possible.

American Brain Tumor Association
2720 River Rd., Suite 146, Des Plaines, IL 60018-4110
(800) 886-2282 • fax: (847) 827-9918
e-mail: info@abta.org • website: http://www.abta.org

The American Brain Tumor Association assists people with brain tumors and their families. It offers information and support, including telephone consultations concerning social services, referral to support services, and a pen-pal program. The association's publications include the pamphlets *A Primer of Brain Tumors: A Patient's Reference Manual* and *Alex's Journey: The Story of a Child with a Brain Tumor*.

American Cancer Society
1599 Clifton Rd. NE, Atlanta, GA 30329
(800) 227-2345
website: http://www.cancer.org

The American Cancer Society is one of the primary organizations in the United States devoted to educating the public about cancer (including prevention and early detection) and to funding cancer research. It also provides patient services such as transportation and support groups. The society publishes hundreds of publications, from reports and surveys to position papers.

Canadian Cancer Society
10 Alcorn Ave., Suite 200, Toronto, Ontario, CANADA M4V 3B1
(416) 961-7223 • fax: (416) 961-4189
website: http://www.cancer.ca

The Canadian Cancer Society is a national community-based organization of volunteers. Its mission is the eradication of cancer and the enhancement of the quality of life of people living with cancer. Its priorities include reduction of tobacco use, promotion of a healthy diet, and increased screening for breast and cervical cancer. In partnership with the National Cancer Institute of Canada, the society works to further research, education, patient services, and advocacy for what it sees as healthy public policy. It publishes the *Canadian Cancer Encyclopedia*.

Cancer Care
1180 Avenue of the Americas, New York, NY 10036
(212) 221-3300 • fax: (212) 719-0263
e-mail: info@cancercareinc.org • website: http://www.cancercareinc.org

Cancer Care provides free professional assistance to people with any type or stage of cancer. Its services include counseling, referrals, and financial assistance. Cancer Care publishes *Cancer Care News* and pamphlets such as *A Helping Hand: The Resource Guide for People with Cancer*.

Cancer Federation
PO Box 1298, Banning, CA 92220-0009
(909) 849-4325 • fax: (909) 849-0156

The Cancer Federation provides counseling, educational materials, and meetings for cancer patients, their families, and their friends. It maintains a counseling and referral service. It also funds high school and college scholarships in the natural sciences. The federation publishes a quarterly magazine, *The Challenge*, as well as books, pamphlets, monographs, and leaflets, including *Cancer—Symptoms and Treatments*.

The Candlelighters Childhood Cancer Foundation (CCCF)
7910 Woodmont Ave., Suite 460, Bethesda, MD 20814-3015
(800) 366-2223 • fax: (301) 718-2686
e-mail: info@candlelighters.org • website: http://www.candlelighters.org

CCCF is an international network that offers information and support to children with cancer and their families. Its publications include three newsletters (the *CCCF Quarterly Newsletter*, the *CCCF Youth Newsletter*, and *CCCF Progress Reports*), a resource list of publications, and books and pamphlets about childhood cancer.

The Chemotherapy Foundation
183 Madison Ave., Suite 403, New York, NY 10016
(212) 213-9292 • fax: (212) 689-5164

The Chemotherapy Foundation is dedicated to the control, cure, and prevention of cancer through innovative medical therapies, especially drug treatments. It provides grants for teaching at medical schools and for research into new treatments, continuing education programs for doctors who treat cancer, and information that educates patients and the public about the progress and promise of chemotherapy. The foundation's publications include the booklets *Chemotherapy: Your Weapon Against Cancer* and *The Breast Cancer Epidemic in the United States*.

Foundation for Advancement in Cancer Therapy (FACT)
PO Box 1242, Old Chelsea Station, New York, NY 10113
(212) 741-2790

FACT distributes information about alternative treatments for cancer that it considers safe and nontoxic. It believes that tumors are symptoms of a gradual breakdown in the balance of body chemistry and that treatments should focus on correcting this imbalance and building up the body's resistance to cancer rather than on destroying the tumors themselves. The foundation publishes the bimonthly newsletter *Cancer Forum*, a book list, and pamphlets such as *What Is F.A.C.T.?*

Leukemia Society of America
600 Third Ave., New York, NY 10016
(212) 573-8484 • fax: (212) 856-9686
website: http://www.leukemia.org

The Leukemia Society of America is a national health agency dedicated to curing leukemia, lymphoma, Hodgkin's disease, and myeloma and to improving the quality of life for people with these diseases and their families. It supports research on these cancers and sponsors several patient services programs, including a patient aid program and a family support group. Its fact sheets, educational brochures, pamphlets, and educational videos include "Facts You Should Know About the Leukemia Society of America" and *What Everyone Should Know About Leukemia*. The society also offers some of its publications in Spanish.

National Alliance of Breast Cancer Organizations (NABCO)
9 E. 37th St., 10th Fl., New York, NY 10016
(888) 806-2226 • fax: (212) 689-1213
e-mail: NABCOinfo@aol.com • website: http://www.nabco.org

NABCO, a network of more than 375 breast cancer organizations, coordinates resources and information related to breast cancer. It cooperates with private corporations and such organizations as the National Cancer Institute to provide breast cancer patients and their families with lists of clinical trials, support groups, workshops, and other resources. NABCO also acts as a political voice for the interests and concerns of breast cancer survivors and women at risk, providing information to the media, medical organizations, and professionals as well as the public. It publishes the monthly *NABCO News*, fact sheets, and a resource list of publications about breast cancer.

National Cancer Institute (NCI)
PO Box 24128, Baltimore, MD 21227
(800) 422-6237
websites: http://rex.nci.nih.gov • http://cancernet.nci.nih.gov

Part of the government-sponsored National Institutes of Health, the NCI sponsors research on cancer. It also offers a wide variety of educational material about cancer for cancer patients and their families, health professionals, educators, and the interested public, including the pamphlets *Facing Forward: A Guide for Cancer Survivors* and *What Are Clinical Trials All About?*

National Cancer Institute of Canada (NCIC)
10 Alcorn Ave., Suite 200, Toronto, Ontario, CANADA M4V 3B1
(416) 961-7223 • fax: (416) 961-4189
e-mail: ncic@cancer.ca
website: http://www.cancer.ca/englishp/research.htm

Formed in 1947 on the joint initiative of the Department of National Health and the Canadian Cancer Society, the NCIC coordinates and correlates the efforts of individuals and organizations with the aim of reducing cancer cases and deaths. It provides grants and other funding to support clinical and laboratory-based research, sponsors workshops, and facilitates cancer control planning. The NCIC publishes a manual of support for research and training, as well as an annual list of Canadian cancer statistics.

Patient Advocates for Advanced Cancer Treatments (PAACT)
1143 Parmelee NW, Grand Rapids, MI 49504-3844
(616) 453-1477 • fax: (616) 453-1846
e-mail: paact@osz.com • website: http://www.osz.com/paact

PAACT offers information about the most advanced methods of detection, evaluation, and treatment of prostate cancer. It recommends treatment with a combination of drugs. Its publications include the quarterly newsletter *Cancer Communication* and the pamphlet *Detection, Diagnosis, Evaluation, and Treatment of Prostate Cancer*.

People Against Cancer
604 East St., PO Box 10, Otho, IA 50569
(515) 972-4444 • fax: (515) 972-4415
e-mail: nocancer@ix.netcom.com
website: http://www.dodgenet.com/nocancer

People Against Cancer is a grassroots organization dedicated to finding new, nontoxic treatments for cancer and changing government policy to support prevention and innovative treatments. It promotes the use of alternative therapies for cancer and increasing government efforts to prevent cancer by removing carcinogens from the environment. People Against Cancer publishes the quarterly newsletter *Options* and booklets such as *The Alternative Therapy Program for People with Cancer.*

The Skin Cancer Foundation
245 Fifth Ave., Suite 1403, New York, NY 10016
(212) 725-5176 • fax: (212) 725-5751
e-mail: info@skincancer.org

The Skin Cancer Foundation conducts numerous public and medical education programs, including the Melanoma Campaign, the Children's Sun Protection Program, and Sun Alert America. It also provides grants and fellowships for training and research related to skin cancer. The foundation publishes brochures, newsletters, books, manuals, audiovisuals, posters, and other materials about skin cancer. Its publications include the pamphlets *What You Need to Know About Skin Cancer* and *The Many Faces of Malignant Melanoma.*

The Susan G. Komen Breast Cancer Foundation
5005 LBJ Freeway, Suite 370, Dallas, TX 75244
(972) 855-1600 • fax: (972) 855-1605
e-mail: education@komen.org
websites: http://www.breastcancerinfo.com • http://www.komen.org

This foundation works to eradicate breast cancer through research, education, screening, and treatment. It sponsors fund-raising activities such as Race for the Cure, a series of five-kilometer and one-mile runs and fitness walks. Proceeds provided by individual entrance fees and company sponsorships fund educational programs, mammography screening and treatment programs for minority women, and grants for breast cancer research. Volunteers in local chapters of the organization establish community breast health services where needed. The foundation publishes pamphlets and fact sheets about breast cancer, including "Questions to Ask the Doctor About Breast Cancer" and "Breast Health: Learn the Facts."

Y-Me National Breast Cancer Organization
c/o Susan Nathanson
212 W. Van Buren, Chicago, IL 60607-3908
(800) 221-2141 • fax: (312) 294-8597
e-mail: help@y-me.org • website: http://www.y-me.org

Founded by two breast cancer patients in 1978, the Y-Me National Breast Cancer Organization offers information and support to women with breast cancer. The organization helps those with breast cancer and their families meet others who have survived similar experiences. The group's services include a 24-hour, toll-free national hotline, open door groups, early detection workshops, and peer support groups. The organization publishes educational material about breast cancer in English and Spanish, including *Just for Teens!* and *Spanish Video for Breast Care Early Detection.*

Bibliography

Books

Malin Dollinger, Ernest H. Rosenbaum, and Greg Cable	*Cancer Therapy.* Kansas City, MO: Andrews and McMeel, 1994.
Dean King, Jessica King, and Jonathan Perlroth, eds.	*Cancer Combat: Cancer Survivors Share Their Guerrilla Tactics to Help You Win the Fight of Your Life.* New York: Bantam Books, 1998.
Michael Lerner	*Choices in Healing: Integrating the Best of Conventional and Complementary Approaches to Cancer.* Cambridge, MA: MIT Press, 1994.
Brent Ryder	*The Alpha Book on Cancer and Living.* Alameda, CA: The Alpha Institute, 1994.
Karen Stabiner	*To Dance with the Devil.* New York: Delacorte Press, 1997.
Sandra Steingraber	*Living Downstream: An Ecologist Looks at Cancer and the Environment.* Reading, MA: Addison-Wesley, 1997.
Midge Stocker, ed.	*Confronting Cancer, Constructing Change: New Perspectives on Women and Cancer.* Chicago: Third Side Press, 1993.
Harold Varmus and Robert A. Weinberg	*Genes and the Biology of Cancer.* New York: Scientific American Library, 1993.
Robert A. Weinberg	*One Renegade Cell: How Cancer Begins.* New York: Basic Books, 1998.
Beverly Zakarian	*The Activist Cancer Patient: How to Take Charge of Your Treatment.* New York: John Wiley & Sons, 1996.

Periodicals

Marcia Barinaga	"From Bench Top to Bedside," *Science*, November 7, 1997.
Sharon Begley and Claudia Kalb	"One Man's Quest to Cure Cancer," *Newsweek*, May 18, 1998.
Shannon Brownlee and Nancy Shute	"Killing Cancer," *U.S. News & World Report*, May 18, 1998.
Geoffrey Cowley	"Cancer and Diet," *Newsweek*, November 30, 1998.
Henry Dreher	"Cancer and the Politics of Meaning," *Tikkun*, January/February 1998.
Tamara Eberlein	"Cancer Genes," *Redbook*, May 1995.
Samuel Epstein	"Winning the War Against Cancer? . . . Are They Even Fighting It?" *Ecologist*, March/April 1998.
Kathleen Fackelman	"Variations on a Theme," *Science News*, May 6, 1995.

Gayle Feldman — "When Women Know Too Much," *New York Times*, October 12, 1994.

Kristen Lidke Finn — "Breast Cancer: Alternatives to Mastectomy," *USA Today*, May 1995.

Christine Gorman — "The Hope and the Hype," *Time*, May 18, 1998.

Jerome Groopman — "Too-High Hopes," *New York Times*, May 6, 1998.

Stephen S. Hall — "Monoclonal Antibodies at Age 20: Promise at Last?" *Science*, November 10, 1995.

Patricia Hittner — "Seven Cancer Fighters That Really Work," *Better Homes and Gardens*, July 1995.

Maggy Howe — "Unconventional Cures," *Country Living*, May 1997. Available from 224 W. 57th St., New York, NY 10019.

Gina Kolata — "A Cautious Awe Greets Drugs That Eradicate Tumors in Mice," *New York Times*, May 3, 1998.

Gina Kolata — "Mammogram Talks Prove Indefinite," *New York Times*, January 24, 1997.

Walter Last — "The Diversity and Effectiveness of Natural Cancer Cures," *Ecologist*, March/April 1998.

Warren E. Leary — "Scientists See No Risk in EMFs," *New York Times*, November 1, 1996.

S. Robert Lichter — "Why Cancer News Is a Health Hazard," *Wall Street Journal,* November 12, 1993.

Robert Lipsyte — "Fighting Cancer, and the Bean-Counters," *New York Times*, March 2, 1997.

Jean Marx — "Oncogenes Reach a Milestone," *Science*, December 23, 1994.

J. Madeleine Nash — "The Enemy Within," *Time*, Fall 1996.

J. Madeleine Nash — "Stopping Cancer in Its Tracks," *Time*, April 25, 1994.

Janet Raloff — "EMFs' Biological Influences," *Science News*, January 10, 1998.

Andrea Rock — "Cause vs. Cure," *Working Woman*, October 1994.

Rita Rubin — "Do You Have a Cancer Gene?" *U.S. News & World Report*, May 13, 1996.

Rita Rubin — "The War on Cancer," *U.S. News & World Report*, February 5, 1996.

Gary Taubes — "Fields of Fear," *Atlantic Monthly*, November 1994.

INDEX

acupressure, 125
acupuncture, 133
adducts, 75–77
adenomas, noncancerous, 26
adjunctive treatments. *See* complementary treatments
African Americans, 48, 172
   men, 170, 171
   women, 51, 95, 170, 171
agricultural industry, 61, 85
AIDS, 91
air contaminants, 45–46, 72
   in Poland, 76–77
   from secondhand smoke, 40–44
alcohol, 72, 89, 90, 91
Allen, Paul, 136
alternative treatments, 124–26
   in hospitals, 124–25
Alzheimer's disease, 100
American Cancer Society, 36, 81
   on breast cancer, 53, 54, 56, 166
   on cancer deaths, 38, 81
   on cancer rates, 170, 171
   on chemical exposure, 48, 51
   on mammograms, 94, 95
American Council on Science and Health, 49, 68
American Hospital Association, 48
American Medical Association, 86
Ames, Bruce, 49–50, 67, 73, 74
animal testing, 49–50, 58, 73, 157
   across species, 69–70
   bans useful chemicals, 66, 68–69
   for carcinogenicity, 66, 67, 69
   cost of, 67
   is not valid, 67, 69–70, 73, 74
   maximum-tolerated dose in, 67, 69
   "mouse terrorism" as, 65–66, 68–69
   on new drugs, 130, 153, 155, 157, 158
   regulations based on, 65–66, 67, 69, 70–71
Archives of General Psychiatry, 125
asbestos, 9, 69, 72, 81
Asian Americans, 51, 170, 171, 172
Associated Press, 99

Bailar, John C., III, 11, 47–48, 81, 166
Baker, Ben, 24
Barela, Mike, 137

Beil, Kathleen, 124
Belman, Orli, 53
Berke, Jerry, 62–63
biofeedback, 125
biologic response modifiers (BRMs), 121
biomarkers, 75–76, 77
Bishop, J. Michael, 11, 154, 157
blacks. *See* African Americans
bladder cancer, 37, 58–59, 61
   and dry cleaning fluids, 60
   and the tuberculosis vaccine, 130
Blair, Aaron, 49, 51
Bliss, Garrison, 136
blood vessels, 33, 34, 153, 155
Blue Cross and Blue Shield, 150
bone marrow transplants, 121–22
   insurance coverage for, 122, 151
   side effects of, 119, 162
Borden, Ernest, 152
Borlaug, Norman, 47
Bowen, John, III, 114
Bowen, Mimi, 114
brain cancer, 47, 48, 51, 159
BRCA-1 gene, 60, 72
breast cancer, 47, 53–56, 171, 172
   in black women, 51, 95, 170, 172
   and bone marrow transplants, 121–22, 150–51
   death rates on, 53, 113, 166
   drugs for, 115, 153, 154–55, 160
   and estrogen levels, 50, 53–56, 92, 112
   genetic testing for, 60, 72, 99–101
   and the Halsted radical operation, 113
   and HER2/neu receptors, 116, 160, 163, 164, 167
   and the intercostobrachial nerve, 112
   in Japanese women, 9
   on Long Island, New York, 54–55
   making informed decisions about, 111–16
   and mammograms, 94–98
   and reconstruction issues, 113–14
   research on, 50–51, 54–56, 60, 116, 121–22
   risk factors for, 23, 61, 89, 94
   survival rates for, 36, 81

INDEX

Breast Cancer Research Foundation, 116
Brink, Susan, 150
Brinker, Nancy, 114
Bristol-Myers Squibb Co., 154, 155, 158
Brody, Jane E., 36
Brown, Georgia, 140
Brown, Michael, 158
Buckman, Robert, 13, 102
Burzynski, Stanislaw, 126

Caldwell, Mark, 72
Canada, 85, 95
cancer, 9–11, 13–14
  as DNA disease, 28, 31
  false beliefs about, 13–16
  fear of, 13–16, 72, 103, 104, 108–10, 140, 169
  rates of, 9, 48, 58, 169–73
  stages of, 30–31, 33
  warning signs of, 92
  see also death rates; drugs; prevention; research; treatments; *specific type of cancer*
Cancer (journal), 172
cancer cells, 14, 15, 18–19, 60
  blood supply to, 33, 34
  EGF receptors in, 159
  and experimental drugs, 155
  growth regulators in, 27–33
  HER2/neu receptor in, 116, 163, 164
  natural selection in, 31–32, 33
  and RAS protein, 157–58
  S-phase fraction, 112
  viral cause of, 22, 29–30, 82, 157
cancer genes, 60–61, 62, 156
  and breast cancer, 60, 72, 100, 101
  and experimental drugs, 153–61, 163, 164–67
  oncogenes as, 10, 32, 74, 75, 77
  research on, 21, 23–27, 31–34
  as tumor suppressors, 10, 26, 27, 32, 34
  and tumor viruses, 29–30
cancer registries, 58, 62, 172
carcinogens, 66, 72–73, 74
  and adducts, 76–77
  in food, 46–47, 67, 72
  future research on, 74–76, 77–78
  non-toxic alternatives for, 63–64
  not linked to human cancer, 69
  perchloroethylene as, 63–64
  and public relations campaigns, 84
  research on, 49, 58, 68, 69–70, 82
  in tobacco, 37, 40, 41, 42
  U.S. export of, 86
  see also chemicals
carcinomas, 25, 26
Cardin, Ilene, 22
cardiovascular disease, 37–38, 39
  from secondhand smoke, 41, 43–44
Carson, Rachel, 10
Cassileth, Barrie R., 127
cells, 72, 156
  affected by secondhand smoke, 43–44
  aging of, 33
  apoptosis of, 32
  chemotherapy effects on, 120, 154
  divide when injured, 74
  growth regulator in, 18, 159
  p53 protein in, 32
  see also cancer cells; cancer genes
cellular detoxification/restoration, 130–31
Centers for Disease Control and Prevention, 170, 171
cervical cancer, 37, 89, 143–48
Chang, Mrs., 143–48
Chassin, Mark, 51
Chemical Manufacturers Association, 47
chemicals, 32, 45–52
  aflatoxin, 69, 70
  Alar, 65, 68
  and animal carcinogenicity, 49, 66, 67
  banned by animal testing, 66, 68–69
  DES (diethylstilbesterol), 68, 69–70
  dioxin as, 46, 49, 50, 52, 56, 61
  in dry cleaning fluids, 60, 63–64
  EPA standards for, 41, 46, 55
  in foods, 45, 65
  hormone-disrupting, 53–54, 55–56
  need government regulation, 64, 70
  non-toxic substitutes for, 63–64
  perc (perchloroethylene), 63–64
  safrole, 68
  in tobacco, 40, 43
  toxicity data on, 46
chemotherapy, 120–21, 127, 154
  for breast cancer, 115
  failure of, 145–46
  for Hodgkin's disease, 136–37
  research funding for, 82
  side effects of, 118, 119, 122,

136–37, 138–39
children, 38, 118
    cancer in, 48, 58, 156
Christie, Harry, 152
chromosomes, 31, 156
    and pesticides, 62
    research on, 23–24, 25–26, 31, 32
Cigarette Controversy, The (Tobacco Institute), 84
cigarettes. *See* smoking
Clinton, Bill, 54, 55, 86, 166
Coffey, Donald, 22
Collins, Francis, 21, 100
colon cancer, 171, 172
    drugs for, 130, 154, 155, 158
    hereditary nonpolyposis syndrome, 32–33
    is increasing, 47
    research on, 10, 24–27, 60, 100, 157
    risk factors for, 43, 61, 89
    survival rates for, 81
colorectal cancer, 89
Colvin, O. Michael, 124–25
communication techniques, 102–10
complementary treatments, 125, 129
    information resources for, 133
    standards for, 132
cyclamates, 65, 68

D'Amato, Alfonse, 54, 55
Darwinian theories, 28–29, 33–34
Davis, Devra Lee, 51
DDE, 46
    and breast cancer, 50–51, 55
DDT, 46, 50–51, 55, 69
    as cancer risk factor, 54, 55–56, 88–89, 90
death rates, 45, 47–48, 72, 156
    for African Americans, 48
    are dropping, 169
    are increasing, 80–81
    from breast cancer, 53, 113, 166
    for children, 48
    from lung cancer, 36, 37, 38, 48
    for minority groups, 170
    root causes of, 90–91
    from secondhand smoke, 42, 43
    for women, 88
Delaney Clause, 67–68, 70
Dennett, Daniel, 28
depression, 104
Des Moines Register, The (newspaper), 45
Dickey, Nancy W., 97

diet, 131
    as risk factor, 10, 48, 50, 61, 72, 89, 90, 91–92
dioxins, 52
    as anti-estrogens, 56
    in our bodies, 46, 50, 61
DNA, 23, 156
    and adducts, 76–77
    and carcinogenic substances, 50
    discoverer of, 81
    flow cytometry of, 112
    mutations in, 23–27, 30–31, 32–33, 75
    p53 protein levels in, 32
    radiation effects on, 121
    repair genes in, 32–33
    tumor viruses, 29–30
Dockery, Douglas, 41
Dresler, Carolyn M., 37, 38–39
drug companies. *See* pharmaceutical companies
drugs, 120
    Adriamycin, 137
    animal testing of, 130, 153, 155, 157, 158
    for breast cancer, 115, 153, 154–55, 160, 164, 166
    cisplatin, 164, 167
    CMF treatment, 115
    for colon cancer, 130, 154, 155, 158
    colony-stimulating factors (CSFs), 121
    experimental, 153–61, 164–67
    GCSF (granulocyte colony stimulating factor), 138
    HER2, 160, 163, 164–67
    Herceptin, 154, 160
    interferons, 121, 156
    interleukin-2, 121, 156
    Levamisole, 130
    for lung cancer, 154, 155
    MAb HER2, 163
    morphine, 146, 147
    side effects of, 121, 158
    tamoxifen, 112, 115
    taxol, 167
    Zofran, 138
    Zoladex, 115
dry cleaning industry, 60, 63–64
Dunkleberger, Doris, 150–51, 152

EGF receptors, 159
emotional support, 102–10, 129, 141
End, David, 158

INDEX

endocrine disrupters, 53–54, 55–56
energy field manipulation, 124, 125–26
England, 31, 32
environmental contaminants, 10, 45–52, 66, 72–73
   and bladder cancer, 59
   driven by economic system, 84–85
   effects on human body, 40–44, 46–47, 58
   endocrine disrupters as, 53–56
   need government regulations, 86
   in Poland, 76–77
   and right-to-know laws, 60
   and the Toxic Release Inventory, 62
   see also carcinogens
environmentalists, 47, 63, 66
EPA (Environmental Protection Agency), 52
   and chemical estrogenicity, 55
   on dioxin compounds, 46
   on secondhand smoke, 41, 42
epidemiological studies, 48–49, 66, 69
   see also molecular epidemiology
Epstein, Samuel, 47, 48, 50, 51–52
   and *The Politics of Cancer*, 57, 83
esophagus, 37
Estabrook, Alison, 116
estrogen, 50, 53–56, 112
   replacement therapy, 92
exercise, 89, 90, 91, 92
experimental drugs, 153–61, 163, 164–67
   and blood vessels, 153, 155
   for breast cancer, 115, 153, 154, 160
   and EGF receptors, 159
   and protein production, 153–56, 157–58, 160
experimental treatments, 121–22
eye cancer, 23–24
Eyre, Harmon, 96

farmers, 51, 61, 85
FDA (Food and Drug Administration)
   on breast cancer drugs, 160, 164, 166
   on food safety, 46–47, 65, 70
   and genetic testing, 101
   and mammogram facilities, 98
   review process of, 166
   on silicone implants, 114
Fearon, Eric, 25–26
Feldman, Jay, 47

Finland, 77
First, You Cry (Rollin), 113
Fleishman, Glenn, 135
food contaminants, 46–47, 50, 61
   overreaction to, 65, 68, 70
Food Quality Protection Act, 55
Ford, Betty, 113
Foulds, Leslie, 31, 33
France, 25, 159
Freedom of Information Act, 60
FT (farnesyl transferase), 158

Gammon, Marilie, 54
Garbage magazine, 50
Garry, Vincent, 62
Genentech Inc., 154, 160, 164
genes, 10, 31, 156
   p53 protein in, 32
   see also cancer genes
gene therapy, 34, 122
golden nematode, 55
Goldstein, Joseph, 158
Good Housekeeping magazine, 43
Greenpeace, 46, 51, 52
Gross, Ludwik, 29
Guthrie, Woody, 100

hair dye, 89, 90
Halsted radical operation, 113
Halvorson, George, 151
Hamilton, Stanley, 24, 25
Harkin, Tom, 54
Harris, Henry, 32
healing touch therapy, 124
HealthPartners, 151
Healy, Bernadine, 97
heart disease, 37–38, 39
   from secondhand smoke, 41, 43–44
Heath, Clark, 48, 51
Hellmann, Susan, 160
hepatitis B virus, 88–89, 92
herbal remedies, 126, 131
HER2/neu receptors, 116, 160, 163, 164, 167
Hilts, Philip J., 40
Hispanics, 171, 172
HIV/AIDS, 91
HMOs (health maintenance organizations), 151, 152
Hodgkin's disease, 120, 136–39
   mailing list for, 137, 139
homeopathy, 133
hormones, 53–56
hospice care, 148
humor, 108–109

Huntington's disease, 100
hypnosis, 125

imagery, 125, 129, 130, 131
immune missiles, 34
immune system, 29–30, 33
   in cancer theories, 22
   and metastatic disease, 130
   therapy for, 129–30
immunotherapy, 121, 163
informed consent, 122
insurance companies, 118–19, 125, 150–52
   and bone marrow transplants, 122, 151
   and genetic testing, 101
   lawsuits against, 151
Internet, 136, 137, 138
IPAs (independent practice associations), 151

Janssen Pharmaceutica, 158–59
Japanese tea ceremony, 125
Japanese women, 9
Jarvis, William, 125, 126
Johnson & Johnson, 154, 158
Journal of Clinical Oncology, 164–65
Journal of the American Medical Association, 126
Journal of the National Cancer Institute, 55

Kennedy, Donald, 81, 83
Kennedy, Edward M., 85
kidney cancer, 37, 43, 47
King, Mary-Claire, 101
Kinzler, Kenneth, 20–21, 26
Klausner, Richard D., 154, 170, 172
Klein, George, 28
Knudsen, Alfred, 23
Koch, Robert, 82
Koop, C. Everett, 86
Kramer, Robert, 155
Kushner, Rose, 113, 116

Lange, Dianne, 117
Langer, Amy, 98
Langreth, Robert, 153
larynx, 37
Lasker, Lawrence, 163
Lasker Awards, 164
Lauder, Evelyn, 116
Laurence, Leslie, 111
leukemia, 29, 48, 121, 156
Lewontin, Richard, 84, 85

LiFraumeni syndrome, 32
lip cancer, 51
Lippman, Marc, 112
listening skills, 102–10
   S-C-A-N-S mnemonic for, 105
liver cancer, 47, 89, 156
Living Downstream: An Ecologist Looks at Cancer and the Environment (Steingraber), 57, 58, 59
   reviews of, 62–63
Locke, Rosemary, 113, 116
Long Island Breast Cancer Study Project, 54
Lopez-Lasker, Valli, 162–64, 165–68
Love, Susan M., 96–97, 116
lumpectomies, 112, 113–14, 115
lung cancer, 36–39, 49, 171, 172
   death rates for, 36, 37, 38, 48
   downturn in, 170, 173
   increase in, 36–39, 170, 173
   new drugs for, 154, 155
   research on, 77, 157, 159
   risk factors for, 41, 42, 89, 90
   survival rates for, 81, 156
lymphoma, 89, 121, 156
   non-Hodgkin's, 47, 51, 61–62
lymph system, 144, 162

macrobiotic diet, 131
mammograms, 94–98
   and biopsy scars, 95
   false-negative rates for, 95, 96
   medical opinions on, 96–98
   research on, 95
   for women under fifty, 94–97
managed care, 150–52
Manufacturers of America, 166
Marblestone, Laura, 115
Marks, James S., 169, 170, 172
Marshall, Delia, 94
Massad, Stewart, 143
mastectomies, 112, 113–14
medications. *See* drugs
meditation, 125, 131, 133
melanoma, 47, 125
men, 51, 170, 171, 172–73
   lung cancer in, 36–39, 170
   semen of, 46
Merck & Co., 154, 155, 157, 158
metabolic treatments, 130–31
metastasized cancer, 18–19, 130, 144
Mike's Lymphoma Resource Pages, 137
mind-body therapies, 125–26, 131, 133

minority groups, 170–72
molecular biology, 21, 22, 58
molecular epidemiology, 74–78
  and adducts, 75–77
  and biomarkers, 75–76
  human samples in, 75, 76
  and PAHs, 76–77
Monmaney, Terence, 162
monoclonal antibodies, 121, 155–56, 160, 163
Morin, Michael, 159
Morris, Lois B., 117
"mouse terrorism," 65–66, 68–69
Multinational Monitor (magazine), 57
Murphy, Gerald P., 117
Murray, F. Jay, 49
Mushlin, Alvin, 95
mustard gas, 136
My Breast (Wadler), 113
myeloma, multiple, 47, 51

National Academy of Sciences, 101
National Breast Cancer Coalition, 54, 113, 116
National Cancer Act, 47
National Cancer Institute (NCI), 47, 80, 121, 137
  on breast cancer, 53, 54, 166
  on cancer deaths, 45
  on cancer rates, 48, 170, 171
  on farmers, 51
  on immune system stimulants, 130
  on mammograms, 94, 95, 96
  on toxic chemicals, 48, 51–52
National Center for Human Genome Research, 100
National Coalition Against the Misuse of Pesticides (NCAMP), 47
National Comprehensive Cancer Network, 152
National Institute of Environmental Health Sciences, 52
National Institutes of Health (NIH), 125, 133, 152
National Research Council, 46
National Toxics Campaign, 47
Natural Resources Defense Council, 65
Neely, Matthew, 80
nervous system cancers, 48
New England Journal of Medicine, 27, 56, 62–63, 81, 151
Newsday newspaper, 55
New York State Department of Health, 51, 54

nicotine, 41–42
  see also smoking; tobacco
Nixon, Richard, 47, 82, 170, 172
non-Hodgkin's lymphoma, 47, 51, 61–62
Norton, Larry, 164
Nowell, Peter, 27
nutritional therapy, 129, 131

obesity, 10, 89, 90
occupational hazards, 9, 49, 51
O'Connor, John, 47
Office of Alternative Medicine, 133
Olden, Kenneth, 52
Oliff, Allen, 155, 157, 158
Onassis, Jackie Kennedy, 61
oncogenes, 10, 32, 74, 75, 77
Onco Link, 136, 137
One-in-Nine: The Long Island Breast Cancer Action Coalition, 54
oropharyngeal cancer, 89
OSI Pharmaceuticals Inc., 159
Osuch, Janet Rose, 94–96, 97, 113
Ottoboni, M. Alice, 50
ovarian cancer, 43, 163, 167
oxygenation systems, 130–31

Pacific Islanders, 170, 171, 172
PAHs (polycyclic aromatic hydrocarbons), 76–77
pancreatic cancer, 37, 43, 154
  and RAS genes, 157
  survival rates for, 156
Park, Roswell, 81
PCBs, 46, 50, 55–56
Pearson, Cynthia, 97
Peeno, Linda, 151
People Against Cancer, 45
Perera, Frederica, 75–77, 78
pesticides, 45, 55
  DDE as, 46, 50–51, 55
  in food, 46–47, 61
  legislation on, 55
  and non-Hodgkin's lymphoma, 61–62
  see also DDT
Pfizer Inc., 154–55, 159
pharmaceutical companies, 154–55, 157–61, 166
Podolsky, Doug, 124
Poland, 76–77
Politics of Cancer, The (Epstein), 57, 83
polyps, 25–26
PPOs (preferred provider organizations), 151

prayer, 125, 126
pregnancy, 38
prevention, 11, 82–86
　and lifestyle changes, 88–93
　low prestige of, 83
　needs government regulations, 85–86
　requires societal change, 84–85
　ten steps to, 91–92
　see also risk factors
Proctor, Robert N., 80
prostate cancer, 51, 53, 154–55, 171, 172
　and EGF receptors, 159
　is increasing, 47, 170
　risk factors for, 89, 170
proteins, 156, 157–58
　p53, 32

radiation, 23, 32, 72, 81, 96
radiation therapy, 120, 121, 127, 154
　and breast cancer, 115
　research funding for, 82
　side effects of, 118, 119, 122
RAS genes, 157–58
reflexology, 125
relaxation techniques, 125, 129
Renneker, Mark, 163–64, 168
Repace, Jim, 42
research, 29, 33–34
　on breast cancer, 50–51, 54–56, 60, 116, 121–22
　on cancer genes, 20, 21–27, 31–34
　on cancer treatments, 82, 121, 141
　on carcinogens, 49, 58, 68, 69–70, 82
　on chromosomes, 22, 23–24, 25–26, 31, 32
　on colon cancer, 10, 24–27, 60, 100, 157
　and the dose-response curve, 49
　epidemiological studies in, 48–49, 66, 69
　on eye cancer, 23–24
　funding for, 22, 36, 54, 170, 172
　on HER2 gene, 160
　on HER2/neu receptors, 116, 163, 164, 167
　on immune-stimulating agents, 130
　lacks prevention focus, 83–84
　on listening techniques, 104
　on lung cancer, 77, 157, 159
　on mammograms, 95
　and miracle cures, 128–29, 132

　nested case control studies in, 76
　on non-Hodgkin's lymphoma, 61
　at pharmaceutical companies, 154–55, 157–61
　previous cancer theories in, 22, 27, 29–30, 81–82
　on radiation, 23
　on RAS genes, 157–58
　RFLP genetic markers in, 24, 25, 26
　on secondhand smoke, 41, 43–44
　toxicology tests in, 48–50
　zero-exposure control groups in, 66
　see also animal testing
retinoblastoma, 23–24
RFLP genetic markers, 24, 25, 26
right-to-know laws, 60
risk factors
　for breast cancer, 23, 61, 89, 94
　for colon cancer, 43, 61, 89
　DDT as, 54, 55–56, 88–89, 90
　diet as, 10, 48, 50, 61, 72, 89, 90, 91–92
　for lung cancer, 41, 42, 89, 90
　for prostate cancer, 89, 170
　smoking as, 10, 37–38, 48, 89, 91
R.J. Reynolds, 41
RNA tumor viruses, 29–30
Rockefeller, Happy, 113
Rollin, Betty, 113
Rous, Peyton, 29, 30, 31
Ryan, Bianca, 165

saccharin, 65, 68, 69, 70
Safe, Steve, 56
Saltzman, Dave, 136
Samet, Jonathan, 44
Santella, Regina, 76
S-C-A-N-S mnemonic, 105
Schering-Plough Corp., 154
Schlessinger, Joseph, 11
Science Watch (newsletter), 20–21
Scolnick, Edward, 157, 161
secondhand smoke, 40–44, 89
Seffrin, John R., 172, 173
Seskevich, Jon, 124
shame, 104
shark cartilage, 131, 132
Sharkey, Janine Jacinto, 111–12, 115
Sharks Don't Get Cancer, 132
Shaw, William, 114
side effects
　of bone marrow transplants, 119, 162
　of chemotherapy, 118, 119, 120, 122, 136–37, 138–39

of drugs, 121, 158
of radiation therapy, 118, 119, 122
Siegel, Michael, 43
Silent Spring (Carson), 10
60 Minutes (television show), 65
skin cancer, 14, 23, 48, 51
Slamon, Dennis, 116, 160, 163, 164, 165–67
Smith, Elaine M., 81
smoking, 36–39, 48, 66
 bans on, 42, 85–86
 drop in rate of, 169, 172
 effects on nonsmokers, 40–44
 pack-year history of, 39
 and PAH-DNA adduct levels, 77
 as risk factor, 10, 37–38, 48, 89, 91
 teenagers and, 37, 173
 women and, 36–39, 173
Snow, John, 82
soil contaminants, 45, 46–47, 52, 55
Sondik, Edward, 96
Soper, John, 124
Steen, R. Grant, 88, 89
Steingraber, Sandra, 57
Stolberg, Sheryl Gay, 169
stomach cancer, 37, 81, 89, 156
Streep, Meryl, 68
stress, 89, 90, 125
sudden infant death, 38
Superfund sites, 49
support, emotional, 102–10
Surgeon General, 36, 41, 86, 172
surgery, 82, 120, 127
Surveillance, Epidemiology and End Results program, 172
Sweden, 85

teenagers, 37, 118, 173
terminal cancer, 143–48
testicular cancer, 47, 58, 156
therapeutic massage, 125–26
Thornton, Joe, 10, 51
tobacco, 72, 85, 90, 91
tobacco industry, 41–42, 85–86, 173
 public relations campaigns of, 84
Tobacco Institute, 84
toxicology tests, 48–50
Toxic Release Inventory, 62
treatments, 117–23, 153–61
 alternative, 124–26
 antineoplaston, 126
 for breast cancer, 113–14, 115
 CAF, 115
 chemotherapy as, 120–21, 127, 154
 choosing, 118–19

combined approach with, 120
complementary, 125, 129, 132, 133
cost of, 49, 118–19
emotional support during, 102–10
experimental, 121–22
failure of, 143–48
have not progressed, 81
for Hodgkin's disease, 136–37
immune-enhancing, 129–30
informed decisions about, 111–16
medical insurance for, 150–52
metabolic, 130–31
miracle cures as, 127–29
radiation therapy as, 120, 121, 127, 154
research on, 82, 121, 144
right to choose, 122–23
standards of, 117, 119, 132
surgery as, 82, 120, 127
testing new, 162–68
see also side effects
tuberculosis vaccine (BCG), 130
tumor necrosis factor, 126, 156
tumors. *See* cancer cells
tumor suppressors, 21, 26, 27, 32
tumor viruses, 29–30

urinary system, 43
U.S. Department of Agriculture (USDA), 55
U.S. government, 40–42, 55
 and breast cancer research, 54
 and cancer prevention, 85–86
 and cancer research funds, 36, 172
 and the Office of Alternative Medicine, 133
 on saccharin ban, 70
 and the tobacco industry, 85, 86, 173
see also war on cancer

Varmus, Harold, 157
viruses, 91
 in cancer theories, 22, 29–30, 82, 157
 hepatitis B, 88–89, 92
Visco, Fran, 97–98, 113, 115
Vogelstein, Bert, 10, 20–27

Wadler, Joyce, 113, 114–15
Waldholz, Michael, 20
Waldman, Todd, 21
Wall, Carol, 115–16
Wall, Terry, 116
Warner, Lynn, 135, 136, 137

Warner-Lambert Co., 154
war on cancer, 22, 50, 83
   is being lost, 47–48, 81–82
   is making progress, 153, 154, 157, 169
   lacks focus on prevention, 82, 86–87
water contaminants, 59, 60, 63–64
Watson, James D., 81
Waxman, Henry, 55, 85
web sites, 136, 137
Weilbacher, Mike, 45
Weinberg, Robert A., 17, 27
Whelan, Elizabeth M., 49, 65
White, David, 136, 137
White, Larry, 151–52
White, Ray, 24
white people, 170, 171, 172
Wiewel, Frank, 45–46, 52
wildlife studies, 58
Wilms' tumor, 152
Wingo, Phyllis A., 173
Wolff, Mary, 50–51, 55–56
women, 51, 88, 169–70
   as activists, 113–14
   Asian, 170, 171
   black, 51, 95, 170, 171, 172
   breast density of, 94, 96
   breast milk of, 46
   and cardiovascular disease, 37–38, 39
   Hispanic, 171
   involved in treatment decisions, 111–16
   Japanese, 9
   on Long Island, NY, 51
   lung cancer in, 36–39, 170, 173
   Pacific Islanders, 170, 171
   see also breast cancer; mammograms
Women's Health in Primary Care (journal), 37
Wood, William, 115
W.R. Grace chemical company, 63

x-ray materials, 23

Y-Me National Breast Cancer Organization, 113
yoga, 125, 129

Zeneca Group PLC, 155, 159
Zinninger, Marie, 98